GUARDIANS OF THE GALAXY

NO GUTS, NO GLORY

MARVEL

GUARDIANS OF THE GALAXY

NO GUTS, NO GLORY

M. K. ENGLAND

TITAN BOOKS

MARVEL'S GUARDIANS OF THE GALAXY: NO GUTS, NO GLORY
Print edition ISBN: 9781789098310
E-book edition ISBN: 9781789098327

Published by Titan Books
A division of Titan Publishing Group Ltd
144 Southwark Street, London SE1 0UP
www.titanbooks.com

First edition: November 2021
10 9 8 7 6 5 4 3 2 1

FOR MARVEL PUBLISHING
Jeff Youngquist, VP Production and Special Projects
Caitlin O'Connell, Associate Editor, Special Projects
Sven Larsen, VP Licensed Publishing
David Gabriel, SVP of Sales & Marketing, Publishing
C.B. Cebulski, Editor in Chief

FOR MARVEL GAMES
Amanda Avila, Associate Manager, Integrated Planning
Loni Clark, Associate Product Development Manager & Project Lead
Tim Hernandez, Vice President, Product Development
Haluk Mentes, Vice President, Business Development & Product Strategy
Eric Monacelli, Senior Director of Product Development & Project Lead
Jay Ong, Executive Vice President
Bill Rosemann, Vice President, Creative
Tim Tsang, Creative Director

Cover art designed by Frederic Bennett and Bruno Gauthier-Leblanc,
and developed by Oxan Studio

Marvel's Guardians of the Galaxy developed by Eidos-Montréal

This is a work of fiction. Names, characters, places, and incidents either are the product of the author's imagination or are used fictitiously, and any resemblance to actual persons, living or dead, business establishments, events, or locales is entirely coincidental. The publisher does not have any control over and does not assume any responsibility for author or third-party websites or their content.

A CIP catalogue record for this title is available from the British Library.
Printed and bound by CPI Group (UK) Ltd, Croydon, CR0 4YY

For my Gamefest brothers.

PRESENT DAY

OBLITUS – 7801

PETER QUILL really needed to pay better attention to details. Details were the critical difference between, say, a deadbeat absentee dad and Darth-freaking-Vader. Or, between a cute-but-gross trash-eating Earth mammal and a genetically altered raccoon soldier with a very large gun.

Or, the difference between getting paid 100,000 units of actual spendable money... and ending up with 100,000 units of useless protein paste in your ship's hold. Plus, bonus: a crew ready to put your head on a spike.

Peter's steps sped up as the *Milano* came into view, hands shoved deep into the pockets of his rust-red armored jacket. His ship waited patiently for him in the exorbitantly priced berthing they'd rented, the first of many ill-advised dealings in this gods-forsaken place.

Mentally, emotionally, and spiritually, he had already teleported into the pilot's seat and left the cobbled together junk heap of a space station that was Oblitus in the rear view. Physically, it was all he could do to keep himself from sprinting for the ship's boarding ramp. You can't outrun shame.

This was just the latest in a string of failed missions that was starting to look less like "scrappy team of misfits struggling to get their business off the ground" and more like "hopeless group of idiots barely surviving basic tasks." The worst part about this particular mission was the fact that they'd actually nailed it, for once. Thing that needed guarding? Totally guarded! People who needed protecting? One hundred percent alive and well! A job well done, deserving of many pats on the back and satisfied handshakes for all members of the Guardians of the Galaxy: Drax (definitely not a serial murderer), Gamora (daughter of Thanos, former assassin), Groot (sole surviving member of the *Flora colossus* people), Rocket (genetically tinkered mammal of indeterminate species, but definitely not raccoon)… and Peter.

Yes, the failing on this particular occasion was completely down to Peter Jason Quill—Star-Lord, if you're nasty— bombing on the basic details of getting paid.

"I will kill you, Peter Quill," Drax said matter-of-factly, his heavy footfalls rattling the deck at their feet ominously. "But first, I will gut that miserable excuse of a flesh bag who hired us. I will rip his limbs from their sockets. I will tear this station apart with my bare hands. I will—"

Peter tuned out the tirade. It was all too easy to imagine

Drax, muscles bulging under teal skin and red markings, ripping the hastily welded together ship scrap that comprised Oblitus apart at the seams, cackling with glee all the while. A shiver ran down Peter's spine, and he gave in to the urge to jog up the ramp and straight for the flight deck.

"They said they were paying hard currency!" he called back in self-defense as he strapped himself into the pilot's seat and got the engines warming. "It sounded like a perfect deal!"

"But you didn't ask what currency, did you, Quill?" Rocket spat, his braided beard swinging as he whipped his head around to glare at Peter on his way past. The four crew stations were arranged in a square in front of the pilot, and Rocket climbed into his seat on the front right side. "Anything is currency if you call it that. For instance, I'd love to pay you for your stupidity in live grenades right now."

"Nah, the exchange rate is garbage," Peter said, half-braced for an actual grenade to come flying into his lap. You just never knew with Rocket. When he found himself still alive a beat later, he kicked in the lifts and smoothly took the *Milano* out into open space while the others wandered in to take their seats. Groot grumbled something unintelligible, likely consisting of the words "I" and "am" and "Groot." He towered like the tree he was over the back of Rocket's seat, one wooden finger poking him in the back of the head in admonishment before taking his own seat in the front left. Rocket spat a "Tch!" as he finished up his checks of the tactical and weapons systems he oversaw from his station.

"Well then, if we ain't going back, we should be blowing

that scumbag's fancy yacht into teeny tiny pieces. I could go either way," he said. "Someone is owed an explosion for this."

"Sorry to interrupt this amusing bit of flexing, but could we maybe talk about the Nova Corps ship that just pulled out right behind us?" Gamora cut in, bringing up a view of the ship on the main display, then turning to glare back at Peter. Or… was it a glare? It was hard to tell sometimes. With the black tattoos that filled the hollows of her eyes and ran down each green-skinned cheek, Peter sort of felt like her gaze was a black hole that sucked the life force right out of you. Couple it with the fire-red tips on her black hair and the sharp asymmetry of its cut, and Gamora presented an intimidating front.

Groot reached across to poke Rocket again and nodded at Gamora's words.

"I am Groot," he added.

"You're being paranoid," Rocket said, waving Groot's comment away. "They are not following us."

"Oh, they're definitely following us," Gamora said. Another few commands on the display, and a highlighted path illuminated in the wakes of both the Nova Corps ship and the *Milano*. Everyone fell silent and watched the two glowing stripes as the *Milano* moved farther from Oblitus, putting on speed. Perfect overlap.

"Shouldn't we stop and see what they want?" Gamora asked.

"Nooo, uh-uh, nope," Peter said, eyeing the ship warily. "I'm not stopping unless they tell me I have to."

Gamora sighed. "What was the point of registering with Nova Corps if we're going to keep running from them? It doesn't really help our image as a legitimate business to flee every time we see one of their ships."

"Maybe they haven't gotten one of our business cards," Rocket sneered. "How will they know we're legitimate? Quick, Drax, go throw one out the airlock at them."

Drax turned to go to the aft airlock, but Gamora reached across the aisle to catch Drax on the way out of his seat and silently shook her head. Drax sat back down.

"Yeah, okay, look, I'd rather not take my chances," Peter said. "Why are they following us if we haven't done anything wrong? Maybe we jaywalked while we were on Oblitus or something. Do you know their laws? I don't."

"I do," Rocket said. "Because they don't have any. And if they did, it definitely wouldn't be the flarkin' Nova Corps enforcing them."

Peter absolutely hated when Rocket made logic noises with his furry little mouth.

The comm alert light blinked over and over as the Nova Corps ship repeatedly hailed the *Milano*. The last time Peter had an unfriendly run-in with the Nova Corps had been during his pre-Guardians of the Galaxy days, before he'd ever met Rocket and Groot. He'd barely talked his way out of it, and only then because the officer in command, Centurion Ko-Rel, was an old fling. They'd left things on okay terms, but he still hadn't exactly reformed himself into the squeaky clean, responsible, upstanding citizen of the galaxy she'd hoped he would become. If they could just get this "heroes for hire" business off the ground for real…

"Look, we are not stopping. Any brilliant ideas for our next destination other than back to Knowhere?"

"Yeah, I've got one," Rocket said. "Turn this boat around and take us back to Oblitus so I can plant a little parting gift. Teach that piece of scut to pay in protein paste when he's got more units to burn than the whole of Xandar."

"I concur. He was a dishonorable dung pile of a being and his betrayal warrants a proportional response. We should go back," Drax said. "Also, there is no food aboard this contemptible vessel."

"There's protein paste," Rocket said with a smirk.

Drax turned his head and spat on the deck. "I will not lower myself to consume such vile sustenance."

"Can we please focus?" Gamora snapped. "If they're here to arrest us, they're being awfully polite about it."

"I would sooner eat the grotesque talking rodent," Drax continued, ignoring her.

Gamora rolled her eyes and pressed on. "No warning shots? No aggressive maneuvers? If they were out to arrest us—"

Rocket whipped his head around. "Is he talking about me? Because if he wants to eat that badly I'd love to feed him the barrel of my gun."

"I am Groot," Groot said soothingly.

"Can we please stop talking about food?" Gamora shouted.

An audible stomach rumble filled the momentary silence that followed. Gamora hissed. "Say something, I dare you."

"Deadliest woman in the galaxy, team. I would keep my mouth shut," Peter called back.

"Team? Ha!" Rocket barked. "This ain't no team. This here is a bunch of losers following another loser failing to make enough money to even keep their loser asses fed. If you ask me—"

"No one asked you," Peter and Gamora said in unison.

"And maybe that's the problem around here!" Rocket said. "No one ever asks what I—"

Gamora, in a fit of wisdom born of self-preservation, launched herself out of her seat and dove for the comm controls at Groot's station. A few quick taps on the control screen and the ceaselessly blinking comm light burned steady as the head and shoulders of a woman in a Denarian's uniform appeared on the main display. Peter looked back at Gamora with a *what the hell?* expression, then turned back to the screen.

"Heeey, sorry, didn't see you back there. What can I do for you, Denarian?" Peter said, all smooth casual charm.

"Are you willing to purchase from us one hundred thousand units of protein paste?" Drax asked.

The woman on the screen blinked. "Dear god, no."

"Are you here to arrest us?" Rocket asked.

She raised an eyebrow. "Should I be?"

Gamora covered her eyes with one hand and shook her head. "Are you here to put me out of my misery?"

"I am Groot," Groot echoed.

The Denarian opened her mouth as if to ask, then shook her head and met Peter's eyes through the screen.

"My name is Mox. You remember me, right, Peter?"

Peter mentally flailed in the practiced panic of one who often finds himself on the wrong end of that question.

"Uh, yeah, totally! Mox! Good to... see you?"

"Better than the last time we saw each other," she said ruefully. At Peter's awkward silence, she added: "On Mercury. During the war."

Peter snapped his fingers as if her words had prompted anything more than a vague sense of familiarity. The Galactic War against the Chitauri had ended almost twelve years ago, after all. Surely he could be excused for not remembering every person he'd crossed paths with. Especially when she was wearing the shiny gold helmet of the Nova Corps, obscuring all but her nose and mouth.

"Yeah. Dark times. Nasty stuff," Peter agreed.

Understatement. The war had significantly messed up everyone aboard the *Milano* in one way or another, though Peter knew only the very edges of the trauma that had shaped them all. Not exactly a topic any of them were eager to rehash.

"So, uh, if you aren't here to arrest us—not that you should be, we haven't done anything illegal in a while—"

"A while?" Mox said, her eyes narrowing.

"On the contrary," Drax said. "Just this morning the foul rat beast stole a rather large gun from a—"

"Hey, hey, hey, we were on Oblitus at the time, ain't no laws against nothin' there. If you leave your stuff just lying out in the open in a place like that, then you're asking for it."

"Is this really the smartest line of conversation to be having right now?" Gamora said to no one in particular.

"I am Groot."

Rocket stood up in his seat to look back at Groot.

"Aw, not you too, Groot. It was no big—"

"Will you shut up already?" Mox shouted over the line. The Guardians fell silent, turning as one to stare down the Denarian, who looked as frazzled as one can look in a big gold helmet.

"I'm here to hire you," she said. "Unless you don't like units?"

A beat of silence.

Someone snorted, trying not to laugh.

A packet of protein paste hit Peter in the face, dropped to the deck, and promptly exploded with gray goo.

Peter stared down at it for a long moment, then looked back to Mox.

"Units of what?" he asked.

PRESENT DAY

THE SPACE AROUND OBLITUS – 7801

MOX blinked, and the silence over the line stretched into deep, powerful awkwardness.

Peter held firm. He wouldn't make the same mistake twice.

"Units. Of… money? What else would it be? Why do you ask?" Mox said, her mouth turned down in a puzzled frown. Peter relaxed, his face clearing.

"Nothing, no reason. Please continue."

"Okaaay," she said. She opened her mouth as if to ask a follow-up question, then shook her head and moved on without comment. "Well. I know you're busy these days. You probably already have several jobs lined up after… whatever it was you were doing on Oblitus."

"Only legal things, I assure you," Peter said. Someone

scoffed behind him, but Peter's full-on charm smile stayed determinedly in place. Drax ruined it by barking a harsh laugh.

"We actually have no work whatsoever and will likely starve within a few rotations," he said.

Peter propped his elbow on the armrest of the pilot's seat and covered his eyes with one hand.

"Dude, can you be cool for like... a second?"

"What?" Drax asked, looking around at the others. "What?"

Gamora strode back to her own station and sat back down, arms folded. "Can you just... tell us more about this job? Please? Before anyone says anything else?"

Mox's gaze flicked over to Gamora, her eyes momentarily narrowed, then looked back over to Peter. She took in a breath and sighed it right back out, seeming to age ten years with that one motion.

"I'm sorry to bring up old memories, Peter, but I'm afraid this has to do with the war."

Peter tensed up, immediately on his guard. Old memories were *not* Peter's jam, unless they involved cassette tapes or a lack of clothing. He hadn't had the same level of direct involvement in the war as Gamora or Drax, but he wouldn't be out among the stars at all without it. His mom was killed because of it, because the Chitauri decided the thirteen-year-old half-breed son of Spartoi's emperor would be the perfect collateral to keep the Spartax Empire out of the way of their little expansion plan. He'd been minding his own business on Earth, being a grumpy teenager obsessed with his music and action figures, until some asshole lizards in another galaxy had decided to go all evil empire.

Mox gave him a beat for the flurry of memories to die down, then laid it all out.

"The old Resistance base on Mercury where we fought back the Chitauri… it was abandoned in a hurry when the tides of the war turned, not too long after you left," she said. "Everything was deactivated, anything of value got packed up, they shipped us all off to other fronts, and they locked the door on the way out."

She smiled ruefully. "Not well enough, though, apparently."

"Let me guess. Not so abandoned anymore?" Rocket asked.

Mox nodded. "Exactly that. Mercury Base has a squatter who needs evicting."

"Any clue who it might be?" Gamora asked. "Pirates? Chitauri nationalists?"

Mox's mouth hardened. "No, no idea. And Nova Corps won't do anything about it. Even though the Corps was essentially rebuilt from the ranks of the Resistance after the war ended, it's still not technically *their* facility, and they don't have the resources to devote to it. It's been nearly a cycle and this *invader* shows no signs of leaving."

"Wait, wait, wait," Rocket interrupted. "Wouldn't a base like that have military-grade weapons systems and security?"

Mox looked to Rocket and nodded. "You see the problem. It was an intelligence facility that saw a lot of action toward the end of the war, and it's got a heavy-duty defense grid.

It's dangerous to have it in the wrong hands. Not just that, but…"

Mox trailed off and looked away from the camera, her jaw tightening. When she looked back, her eyes were steel.

"So many people died there, both before and during your time with us, Peter. To a lot of us who were stationed there, it feels like a violation."

"Like walking over a grave," Gamora said quietly.

Mox's eyes flickered to Gamora and briefly narrowed, then she continued.

"There's a group of us who fought in the war who chipped in to pay a hundred-thousand-unit bounty. Once you all clear out the security systems and traps, I should be able to meet you there, assuming my current investigation wraps up in time. There are some files I need to recover."

Her mouth pressed into a hard line and she shook her head.

"I don't suppose you remember that whole security leak situation?"

All at once, Peter *did* remember, and all the hundred-thousand-unit excitement drained right out of him.

"Oh. Uh, yeah. Weren't… *you* one of the suspects?"

Mox laughed wryly. "I sure was. It still bothers me, if I'm honest, that I was one of the accused. But I know the commander had no way to tell which one of the three of us it was, so I don't blame her. I do still want to solve that mystery, though. Whoever it was nearly got me killed, and *did* kill more than half our force. When I meet you there,

I'm going to download all our old data. I think our Nova Corps analysts will be able to figure it out."

She sighed.

"I know it's too late for any sort of real justice. Last I heard, Tasver was dead in prison and Suki had fallen in with some church. But just knowing the answer will bring at least a little peace, you know?"

Rocket kicked his feet up on the dashboard and tugged thoughtfully on the beads threaded over his beard. One of the beads was an adorable likeness of his best buddy Groot's head, and absolutely no one mentioned it. Ever.

"Is that really it?" he asked. "For a hundred thousand units? *Of money?*"

Mox nodded in acknowledgment. "Yes... and no. I want to be clear about what you're walking into. The person turning that base into their new home will be at the very heart of the facility, in the command hub. That's also where I'll need to meet you to retrieve the files. It will mean fighting your way through traditional security, picking a few locks, you know... but the final lockdown security measures are more like booby traps. Do you remember all those bizarre security droids we discovered after the Chitauri counterattack?"

"Vaguely?" Peter admitted. "I never actually saw them myself, just heard people grumbling about twisted engineers."

Booby traps, though. Peter briefly imagined himself with an Indiana Jones-style hat and whip, swinging on a rope over a pit of snakes. Gamora may or may not have been there.

Awesome.

"Hundred thousand units, huh?" he said thoughtfully. Mox nodded.

"And… again, just to be clear, we're talking about units of money?"

Mox made a face, but nodded again. "Yeeees?"

A long, awkward pause. Then:

"Can you hold on a sec?" Peter asked.

He muted the feed and cut the visual before she could reply, then stood to get everyone's attention.

"So, yes? Right? Any objections?"

Rocket climbed out of his seat and stood on the armrest, all the better to glare at Peter.

"Didn't we just do a job with booby traps and security systems that wanted to kill us? Am I the only one remembering that?" he said, looking around for support.

"I am Groot," Groot said. Rocket pointed at him for emphasis.

"Exactly. It sucked, and though it was incredibly funny to watch Star-Jerk turn blue holding his breath, there was an awful lot of almost dying. I ain't doing it again."

"I agree," Gamora said. "This sounds way too much like another Hark Taphod situation."

"It has nothing to do with that douchebag!" Peter said, throwing his arms up. "Come on, guys, this will be so easy! I know that place like the back of my hand. We'll get in, wave some guns around—"

He glanced at Gamora and Drax, both standing with arms folded, looking skeptical.

"—*and swords*, help Mox set right an old wrong, and boom. We're heroes with a hundred-thousand-unit payday. Actual units. Can't argue with that, right?"

Silence.

Then Drax. "We stop for food first or I eat the rodent."

"Yesss!" Peter held his hand up for a high five, then brushed it over his hair instead when Drax left him hanging. "That's what I'm talkin' about!"

Rocket produced a gun from somewhere and leveled it at Drax's head. "Call me a rodent *one more time*, meat head, and I'll give you another scar right in the middle of your—"

"We'll take the job," Gamora said, one finger still pressed on the comm control screen. "We want twenty-five percent up front. Peter will send you the account details. And if you need any other assistance once this job is complete…"

Gamora looked over at the others. Rocket pointing a gun at Drax. One of Drax's arms cocked back, blade aimed for Rocket's throat. Groot with tendrils wrapped around Drax's wrists, holding him back. Peter silently motioning for the others to calm down.

"…my services may be available. *Alone*," Gamora finished, then turned on her heel and stalked away.

"Gamora, wait!" Peter called after her, then sighed. "Yeah. That's about right. So uh… anything else we need to know?"

Mox's eyes flicked over Peter's shoulder to the minor struggle happening behind him, then shrugged.

"You probably remember this from when you and the Ravagers showed up back then, but landing on Mercury is…

challenging if it's the wrong time. The whole time you were there, it was essentially early morning sunlight. Right now, the sun is directly over the base, and will be for the next few cycles. You'll need a way to land inside the base."

"I know a way," Rocket said, but Peter hurried to cut him off.

"Right," he said. "We'll definitely find a way that *doesn't* involve blowing a hole in the side of the base and announcing our arrival *as loudly as possible*."

"Oh," Rocket said, his ears drooping.

"Do you still know any of the engineers who used to work with us?" Mox asked. "One of them might still know the transmitter code to access the landing bay."

Peter smiled. Finally, a break.

"You know, I actually know just the person. I'll send you the account details for the units transfer. Let us know how to contact you, and we'll get right to work."

"Pleasure doing business, Quill," Mox said before her hologram faded out.

Rocket flopped back in his seat, dropping the gun over the side (but still within easy reach) and looking up at Peter.

"So, Quill, do you *actually* know someone who can get us in, or are we blasting the door down?"

"Oh, I really do know someone. She might even be happy to see me," Peter said with a grin. He turned back to the controls and revved the engines up. "Set course for Knowhere."

INTERLUDE: 12 YEARS AGO

MERCURY – 7789

KO-REL stared out the viewport at the nondescript gray planet below and did her best to tune out the grumbling around her. The journey had been short, thanks to the Sol system's local jump gate, but the troop transport was small and frustrations were running high, like a fog constantly recirculating throughout the ship's ventilation system.

She *did* understand the resentment her people were dealing with, and even shared it to a degree. Just one rotation prior they'd been at the heart of the galactic war against the Chitauri, serving under Richard Rider himself as he led the offensive. He was practically a living legend, the only member of the Nova Corps to survive the Chitauri's attack on Xandar.

It was a defining moment of the war—that the Chitauri were able to wipe out an entire galactic policing organization powered by the Nova Force meant the rest of the galaxy could no longer write off their expansionist campaign as someone else's problem. Sure, most members of the Nova Corps only had access to a small amount of that vast energy store, but the higher ranks, Centurions like Rider, could fly and manipulate energy fields and so much more. And they were just... gone. All but Rider, who now held the entire Nova Force and used it to rally the Resistance, harassing Chitauri warships and helping threatened systems fight back. Ko-Rel respected him immensely, and if he were ever to rebuild the Nova Corps, she would be first in line to join up.

Then word had come in that the Chitauri were sniffing around his home planet of Earth. So, Ko-Rel and her small force had gone from shoring up the defenses of a planet next up on the chopping block, right at the center of the action, to... this. A small dusty rock near Earth's sun, home to a covert intelligence outpost and a few forward monitoring stations. And nothing else.

Ko-Rel was honored to be entrusted with ensuring the safety of Rider's home, but she felt her people's frustration, too. Fending off a few Chitauri scout ships to discourage a full-scale attack was important work, but not nearly as satisfying as actively fighting back, putting in the work to force the Chitauri out of Kree space or pushing the front line toward Chitauri Prime. She hadn't had the time to get to know her crew personally, yet, but some things went without saying. They'd all lost people to the war. Some had lost everything. *She* had lost everything.

They all wanted blood in return, and defending this rock wasn't going to do it for them.

"Commander, we're ready for our final approach," the pilot said, turning her face up to Ko-Rel. "Shall we hail the base?"

Ko-Rel sighed and nodded. "Transmit the codes and get the base commander on screen. Let's see who we'll be working with."

She strode to the comm station and stood over the Terran man's shoulder, waiting for the connection to go through. Below, the tiny gray planet grew larger in the viewport, its meteor-scarred surface eclipsing the black void of space around it as they neared. The silence stretched until Ko-Rel, frowning, laid a hand on the back of the officer's chair.

"Any response, Officer Tasver?" she asked.

"None yet, Commander," he replied, his fingers dancing over the glowing display. "I'll keep trying."

The pilot sat back in her chair and looked over. "Should we wait to land?"

Ko-Rel scanned the surface of the planet and glanced down at the sensor display; nothing of note. The back of her neck prickled with *something*, a faint sense of warning... but there was no sign of anything to warrant concern. The base was at full power, there was nothing visibly wrong from the outside, and there was no evidence of Chitauri presence in the vicinity. Ko-Rel pursed her lips, then shook her head.

"No, they should be expecting us. Let's go ahead. We could be arriving in the middle of their night cycle."

Officer Tasver snorted. "Whoever's supposed to be monitoring comms probably got bored and fell asleep."

Ko-Rel suppressed a huff of laughter. She may sympathize with their frustrations, but she couldn't show it, or morale would spiral down along with her attitude. She'd lead this crew in focusing on their duty and performing with excellence... even when excellence meant sitting around so Mercury (and Earth) looked like slightly less appealing targets. Not exactly the stuff of glamorous war dramas, but vital nonetheless.

The pilot announced their approach, and Ko-Rel sat down at her own station to strap in for landing. She brought up the personnel roster, though she practically had it memorized. It wasn't particularly large. A handful of intelligence officers, both analysts and field agents; a small combat unit; and a bare minimum of support staff. Many people were doing double duty, such as Intelligence Officer Tasver running comms, or Captain Lar-Ka staffing the gunnery console as well as commanding the ground troops. Mostly, they'd be relying on the existing crew at the base. Ko-Rel's people were just reinforcements.

She forwarded the list to the base commander in preparation for their first meeting, then looked up just in time to watch the landing bay doors separate and withdraw, allowing them entrance. The pilot expertly lowered them through the opening and into the landing bay, the descent smooth and controlled—until she yelped and pulled back on the controls, throwing them all against the backs of their seats.

"There are... bodies," the pilot said, her voice tight, and

Ko-Rel threw off her restraints to get a better look out the front viewport.

"Captain—"

Captain Lar-Ka didn't even need her to finish the sentence. He leapt to his feet and sprinted for the door.

"Combat unit, report to the docking ramp, gear for drop," he barked into the comm, his words fading out as he followed his own orders. Ko-Rel turned back to the pilot with a grim expression.

"Find a spot to set us down and brace for a fight."

The "Yes, commander" was swallowed up in the cacophony that erupted on the bridge as Ko-Rel ran for her quarters. Too many terrible scenarios ran through her mind, and too many memories. The bodies on the ground, the *people*—did they have families? Spouses? Children? (She'd had such things, once, but pushed them out of her mind. She needed focus, not a wave of pain that would wash her out to sea if she let it.) She grabbed her sidearm and tactical vest from her tiny box-like quarters and rushed for the docking ramp, stumbling as the bump of an uneven landing jarred her steps.

Ko-Rel arrived just as Captain Lar-Ka called his people to attention. A small force, just eight four-person squads, though they were fine soldiers. All stood at the ready, pulse rifles in hand, body armor perfectly fitted. One would never know that they'd been grumpily lounging in the mess hall bare moments earlier. Ko-Rel and the captain made eye contact and exchanged a nod. A wordless ready check.

Ko-Rel hit the door controls, and Lar-Ka was the first down the ramp, rifle held at the ready and with his squad on his heels. The second squad followed, and Ko-Rel slipped into step with the third, heading down the ramp and scanning the landing bay over the barrel of her own gun. The landing bay was dimly lit, on the night cycle as they'd predicted. Two other ships took up berthing, a small Kree-made light attack ship and a slight, nimble-looking scout ship of unknown make. Piles of supply crates and gear were stacked near each ship and in tidy rows near the doors that led to the rest of the base. A dual-purpose space, both landing bay and storage facility, as these small installations sometimes necessitated. Her brain processed this first scan of macro-level information in just a few ticks. Then her gaze snapped to the critical details.

There were four bodies in the immediate vicinity. All were face down, humanoid, and wearing Resistance colors.

The soldiers, with all their cool professionalism and detachment, fanned out and took up defensive points around the room. Each body was carefully flipped each over and checked for a pulse. The calls came in quickly: "KIA. KIA."

Killed in action. No survivors. Yet.

Ko-Rel caught a flash of movement out of the corner of her right eye. She whipped her gun around to sight on a humanoid man emerging from a small door marked *Infirmary*.

"Identify yourself," Ko-Rel barked.

"Don't shoot!" he shouted back, throwing his hands in the air. "There are others coming behind me. Please, help us."

Ko-Rel lowered her gun a fraction and studied the others

who followed the man into the landing bay. Mostly Kree and Xandarian, a few others, all wearing the uniforms of support staff. Cooks, nurses, maintenance... but something niggled at the back of Ko-Rel's brain. Something was off.

"What happened here? Why isn't your commander responding?" Ko-Rel snapped at the man who'd spoken first.

The man lowered his hands and glanced over at the crew who had followed him, then turned back to Ko-Rel and smiled.

"There was an attack," he said.

Then a gun appeared in his hand. He fired.

Ko-Rel threw herself to one side, already in motion before the gun even went off, her gut two steps ahead of her brain. Fire erupted into the air above her as she rolled behind a stack of crates for cover, the shouts and screams of battle echoing through the space. Around her, each squad leapt into practiced action, calling commands and setting up patterns of fire.

That same battle calm settled over Ko-Rel, too. The world narrowed and slowed. Training kicked in, both academy study and the trauma that had shaped her nervous system's reaction to threat. For better or worse, her body knew exactly how to protect itself.

Ko-Rel leaned around the crates to squeeze off a few shots and get the lay of the scene. The number of people in the bay had multiplied, but everyone wore Resistance identification: unit patches, arm bands, cheaply printed work shirts. That crucial extra tick required to ID a target—friend or foe?— would cost lives.

Ko-Rel leaned out again, prepped to fire on their leader,

but a body came crashing down nearly on top of her as soon as she edged out. She toppled backward out of the way of a bleeding man, his head hitting the deck with a sickening thud, a hole burned in his chest… and right before her eyes, his flesh melted from medium copper brown to a leathery, scaly green.

Chitauri.

Suddenly, everything made sense.

"We've got Chitauri shapeshifters," she called out over the comm. "The base has been infiltrated."

That was why no one had responded to their calls. Why no one was there to greet them. Why there was no sign of Chitauri presence out in the system.

They were already here.

"Squad one is down," Captain Lar-Ka called. "Three wounded, one dead."

"Squad two is at half, two critical," the next unit reported.

"Squad three, one KIA."

One by one, the rest reported in, painting a bleak picture. They weren't a large force to begin with, only thirty-two combat soldiers in total. The ambush had cost them dearly. She scanned the landing bay, ran the numbers in her head, and made her decision.

"Fall back to the ship," Ko-Rel said, moving to follow her own orders. "As soon as the last person is on board, get us out of here."

"What about the people stationed here? We can't just

leave them," one of the young squad leaders protested, though she was quickly admonished by Captain Lar-Ka over the comm.

"If we were able to be ambushed like this, they're likely already dead. Squad six didn't report in, and they were scouting in toward the command center. This facility is under enemy control. Commander Ko-Rel is correct. We need to retreat."

Though her orders shouldn't have to be explained, Ko-Rel was still grateful for the backup as all surviving squad members came charging up the ramp. As soon as the last boots hit the deck, Ko-Rel called up to the pilot, "Get us in the air!"

The ship lurched, soldiers knocking into each other as they lifted back into the air. The engines had never even had a moment to cool off. Around her, wounded soldiers groaned as the two medical officers they'd brought flitted among them, triaging the wounded and skipping over the dead. Time no longer mattered for them, after all.

As soon as the ship was clear of the landing bay doors, the pilot punched the throttle—then an explosion rocked the ship so hard, Ko-Rel fell to her knees. She stumbled, tried to climb to her feet, but the ship lurched to one side, sending her tumbling against the port side wall. She slammed her shoulder hard and bounced off, cracking her kneecap on the way down. Panicked shouts echoed from every corner of the ship as gravity seemed to change directions constantly, taking Ko-Rel's heart along with it.

"What—" was all she managed to get out before another

series of thuds pummeled the ship, the last one blasting a fingernail-sized hole in the hull directly to the left of her face. The whine from the engines ramped up in pitch, and Ko-Rel's stomach lurched as the ship took a hard dive… then never pulled back up.

"We're going down!" Ko-Rel shouted to the soldiers around her. They couldn't be too far off the ground. Maybe the damage wouldn't be too bad.

"Brace for impact!" the pilot shouted over the comm, before she was cut off by a horrific *CRUNCH*. The shriek of tearing metal drowned out the screams Ko-Rel knew must be there. Bodies tumbled, slamming into Ko-Rel, into the walls, the ceiling, the world tumbling end over end. Brief glimpses: mouths open, crying out, eyes wide in terror, bright blood and spittle and sickening cracks.

Then silence.

Stillness.

Nothing.

PRESENT DAY

EN ROUTE TO KNOWHERE – 7801

IF the entire crew of the *Milano* arrived on Knowhere without any murders committed or grievous wounds inflicted, Peter thought it would be a true and honest miracle. He'd let Rocket have the helm to get them headed for the ass-end of space, with Groot up there for company and supervision, so Peter could keep an eye on the other half of the crew.

If a murder were imminent, this would be the scene of the crime: the *Milano*'s common area, the roughly circular room that all the crew quarters branched off from, and that led straight to the aft airlock. Not an ideal arrangement for sleepwalkers, but it had only been a problem once. To be fair, the girl was unlikely to ever visit the *Milano* again *anyway*, so it was still a wash in Peter's eyes. Peter had a portable display screen propped up on the table and had tried bringing up a variety of fun entertainment vids to distract his murder pals.

Alas, nothing could overcome the dark influence of the protein paste.

It was, in a word… *revolting*.

"How can they have the audacity to call this food?" Drax raged, squeezing a packet of it so hard that it exploded. The disgusting gray goop splattered all over the table and those sitting at it. Including Peter. But mostly Gamora.

Gamora, with quiet and deadly calm, pulled a blob of the paste from the clean white material of her body armor and wiped it on the yellow cushions lining the seating around the table. Then she looked up at Drax with a glare that would have made Peter's testicles retreat to safety.

"Will you please," she began quietly, "go literally *anywhere else on this ship* and leave the d'ast protein paste alone?"

By the end she was shouting. Peter winced and stuck a finger in one ear.

"I will *not*," Drax shouted back, shaking the exploded packet at Gamora. "This *paste* is an insult to the very idea of sustenance, and I will not abide its presence on this ship."

With that, Drax picked up one of the crates and hauled it over his head, turning toward the rear airlock.

"Hey, no, Drax, buddy," Peter said, leaping to his feet and looping around in front of Drax. "Let's just put the paste down, okay? That stuff could come in handy on Knowhere."

"It will not," Drax said. "Because it will be drifting through space into the heart of the nearest sun."

"No, no, no!" Peter protested, but he was summarily

shoved aside as Drax mercilessly spaced the first crate. "Aw, man, come on. That was our payment."

"We've been over this, Peter," Gamora said, kicking her feet up onto the table. She pointed at the ramp leading down to the cargo area and airlock, where the ninety-nine remaining crates were stacked. "*That* does not count as payment. *If* we actually manage to secure any units from this little wartime memory lane job of yours, *then* we can use words like 'payment.'"

"I'm not in this for the fond memories of rotting in a Chitauri prison," Peter said, voice heavy with sarcasm and deliberately not thinking of said prison. "I'm *trying* to get us paid enough to keep us in the air."

"And fed," Drax added, picking up another crate.

"Will you *shut up* about food?" Gamora snapped.

Drax dropped the crate and took a step toward Gamora. "Yes, I'm sure you've never worried about food in your life. You slaked your thirst with the blood of your enemies as you murdered for Thanos and the Chitauri."

Gamora rolled her eyes. "Yes, that's exactly what I did. And you, of course, have perfectly clean hands, no serial murdering of any kind! How lucky we are to be in the presence of such a pure-hearted *hero*."

"At least I acknowledge my past sins," Drax snarled. "I am here with this contemptible crew *because* of those sins. *If* Thanos is truly dead, then I must find something else worthwhile to do with my existence. You, Daughter of Thanos—*you* walk around here like we should all bow in thanks because you turned traitor."

Peter held up a finger. "Actually, her defecting to the Resistance *did* kind of change the course of the war, and—"

Drax turned to stare coldly at Peter.

"—*and* I will shut up and sit down now," he finished.

Gamora stood and, in a blink, was right in Drax's face.

"I do not do that," she hissed. "I know full well that I will never atone for my past. But I *can* try to do better with my future."

Gamora broke off and looked at Peter, then back at Drax, shaking her head.

"Though it's looking more and more like maybe I'm in the wrong place for that. Most of the time, I have no idea why I'm here."

Drax crossed his arms and nodded. "Yes. Me as well."

"Hey now," Peter said, eyes going wide. "We've come a long way. We're professionals now! We're registered with Bagoo! and the Nova Corps, we have a name, we even have *business cards*. How many teams have you been part of that have actual business cards?"

"I don't *do* teams," Gamora said, retreating back to the other side of the table. "And I'm starting to think I should have stuck with that model."

"No other team would ever accept you anyway, assassin," Drax shot back.

Gamora's eyes narrowed. "Yes, and how many were lined up to greet *you* as you were released from the Kyln? Don't pretend you are any more virtuous than the rest of us. You are just as alone as I am."

Peter was struck silent at that. He spent a lot of time aggressively *not thinking* about things like that, and there Gamora went, just… saying it. They were trying, but trying wasn't working out, and Peter could see the edges of their little Guardians of the Galaxy scheme starting to crumble. He really would be alone again if he couldn't fix things.

He'd tried to fly solo after selling out Yondu to the Nova Corps and leaving the Ravagers. Despite the cost, he still thought it was the correct decision; Peter had lines he wouldn't cross, and kidnapping children was one of them. Call it a sore subject. But after spending his entire adult life as a Ravager, he'd been adrift.

He bounced aimlessly around the galaxy until he hit on the "hero-for-hire" idea, pulled the name Star-Lord from his favorite heavy metal band, and started asking around for work of the more heroic variety. It definitely felt better than being a pirate, but life was far too quiet without dozens of Ravagers around to bring the chaos. The bounty Yondu had put on his head had been almost a gift, in that it had brought him, Rocket, and Groot together. Or rather, it brought Rocket and Groot to him, wanting to collect on said bounty. Thankfully, fate (and Peter) had other plans.

Drax had agreed to join with reluctance, but only because he was using the team as a substitute Kyln—a source of control to keep himself from being the Destroyer. Gamora… well, Peter had no idea why she'd joined them after bumping into their nascent group on a mission. And ever since she had, he'd been playing referee between her and Drax, who just could not believe that Gamora wasn't somehow hiding her dead father. Rocket and Groot were the most stable members of the team… and even thinking that brought a flicker of despair to Peter's heart.

"Hey, are you idiots strapped in?" Rocket called back. "Because we're hitting the jump point whether you are or not. Have fun."

The *Milano* lurched as Rocket gunned the throttle, and Peter, Drax, and Gamora all stumbled at the distinct wobbly feeling of going through a jump gate.

"I loathe you," Drax said, bracing himself on one edge of the table.

"I loathe you as well," Gamora said from the opposite side.

"Can we all just think peaceful, non-murdery thoughts?" Peter said, largely to himself.

"I am Groot," Groot said from the flight deck.

"Yeah. I thought not." Peter had not suddenly learned to interpret Groot's language, but sometimes Rocket's questionable translations weren't needed. No doubt Groot could see the same thing Peter did: the cracks in their foundation. The shifting sand underneath. The whole Guardians of the Galaxy thing was due to collapse any rotation now, unless there was some kind of breakthrough.

Some twenty-six jumps later, Rocket called out their arrival, and Peter reluctantly turned his back on Drax and Gamora and headed up to the flight deck. Through the front viewport, Peter saw the severed head of a Celestial floating in the near distance, perched on the edge of the known universe and surrounded by ships like buzzing flies.

Knowhere. Mining colony, port of call, home to a famous market and myriad denizens of the galaxy.

They had arrived. Mostly intact, even.

Well.

Peter poked his head back into the rec area. Gamora and Drax were nowhere to be seen, but there was no blood, and the ninety-nine remaining crates of paste sat intact. Peter breathed a small sigh of relief.

At least the protein paste was safe.

Peter's neck, and the Guardians as a whole?

TBD.

INTERLUDE: 12 YEARS AGO

MERCURY – 7789

HUMMING, whining. Bright light. Hissing.

A groan, then another.

Weeping.

Ko-Rel shifted in place, moving her arms, then her legs, doing a full body scan without moving her aching head. Nothing broken, she thought. Her eyes, though—she tried to crack them open, but tears flooded her eyes at the intensity of the brightness. Everything was blurry, floating, even after the tears broke over her cheeks, leaving her eyes clear. Had she hit her head that badly?

"Commander?" a voice warbled somewhere off in the distance. Ko-Rel hummed an acknowledgement, turning her head gently from side to side. Someone needed to turn the sun down.

"Commander? Are you hurt?" the voice said again. A hand landed on her shoulder, rough and urgent. That shook something loose. Ko-Rel blinked again, and again, her vision clearing and head pounding with each pass.

"How long was I out?" she asked, already trying to force her addled brain into a situation assessment. Captain Lar-Ka knelt over her, a bleeding cut over his eye leaking a trail of dark blue down the side of his face.

"Only a few ticks," he replied, looking her over for serious injuries. "Can you stand?"

Ko-Rel held out a hand, which he took and used to haul her up to her feet. Her banged-up knee protested fiercely, and her head swam, but she held out a hand to belay any call for help.

"See to the wounded," she said. "We could have Chitauri breathing down our necks to finish the job any tick. I'm going to check on the bridge crew."

"Yes, Commander," Lar-Ka said, and turned to help one of the medical officers disentangle herself from the cargo netting.

Ko-Rel limped down the long hallway to the fore of the ship and winced when she saw the ladder leading up to the bridge. She managed a one-legged climb, mentally thanking her career military parents for a lifelong dedication to peak physical performance as her arms bore the brunt of the strain. When she neared the top, a hand reached down to meet her, and together they managed to coordinate her ungraceful flop onto the bridge deck. Ko-Rel got to her feet and shook out her suffering leg with a nod of thanks for the Xandarian officer who'd helped her up.

The officer who stood completely alone on the bridge with her arms hugged tight around herself.

Her nose was clearly broken, oozing blood, and her pale brown face was streaked with tiny blue-blooded cuts. She stared straight into Ko-Rel's eyes blankly, refusing to turn around and look at the rest of the bridge. And Ko-Rel could see why.

No one else on the bridge was moving.

Ko-Rel moved from person to person, checking for signs of life. The pilot was dead, her throat cut by shrapnel. The chief engineer. The navigator. When she reached the comm station, though, a strong pulse fluttered in Officer Tasver's neck. Knocked out cold, but alive. She paged the medical staff so they could fit him into their triage plan, then used the next console along to pull up a diagnostic report for the ship.

Most of the vessel had locked down due to hull breaches. More important, though, was the fuel leak. If they managed to take back the base and repair the tanks, they could refuel using whatever stores the base had on hand. Until then, they were essentially sitting in a giant puddle of explosives just waiting for a Chitauri infiltrator to light a match.

Not good. They couldn't stay.

Ko-Rel took a moment to collect herself. Knocking around at the edge of her awareness was the memory of another crash, far deadlier than this one, and the weeks of horror that followed. She acknowledged it, looked those memories in the face and simply thought to herself: *I see you. I don't have time for you right now, but I see you.*

The acknowledgement calmed some of the clamor in her mind, and she nodded to herself, then turned back to the silent Xandarian woman who had helped her up the ladder.

"What is your name and posting, officer?" Ko-Rel asked. She knew, but thought the rote recitation of information might help the woman find a way back to herself. Sure enough, the officer seemed to shake herself and come back to the present moment.

"Adomox. Intelligence. Part of the field team."

Ko-Rel nodded. "Thank you for your assistance, Adomox. Return to your quarters and pack up your gear. We're going to need to seek shelter. Understood?"

Adomox took one deep breath, blew it out slowly, then nodded. "Yes, Commander."

"Good. I'll see you at the docking ramp in five."

Adomox turned and retreated, stepping aside to allow a medical officer up the ladder, then disappearing a moment later. Ko-Rel relayed the same orders over the comm to the rest of the ship. They needed to find shelter, and quickly. If the mission briefing was anything to go by, they were in for a hot rotation.

WHEN Ko-Rel returned to the boarding ramp with her gear bag slung over her shoulder, the sight that greeted her made her stomach twist. Bodies were lined up all along one wall, covered with bedsheets pulled from the now useless crew quarters. The assembled crew were mostly finished donning their enviro-suits, same as Ko-Rel wore, and hasty patches had been thrown over any hull breaches that weren't closed off by bulkheads. Crew ran back and forth, packing up critical gear, prepping the wounded for transport, sidestepping each other with focused intensity on their tasks. Tasver, the comm officer who'd been knocked out on the bridge, sat atop a crate with a chemical cold pack held to his forehead, looking pained but otherwise well.

They were as ready to go as they were going to be. No time to waste; a Chitauri mop-up squad could arrive at any tick to finish them off. Ko-Rel intended to be long gone by the time they got there.

She got Captain Lar-Ka's attention with a quick gesture, and he waved her over to where he was in deep discussion with a junior officer.

"Do we have a rendezvous point?" Ko-Rel asked. Lar-Ka motioned for the young officer to speak up, and the woman cleared her throat nervously.

"Intelligence officer Hal-Zan, Commander. I did some training as a navigator before switching to intel, so the Captain had me analyze our position."

She drew a portable display from her vest and pulled out the screen, displaying a map of the base and the surrounding area.

"We'll need to take the heat into account, as the sunrise will be hitting soon and we can expect dangerous temperatures,"

Hal-Zan began. "The ship went down *here*, about five klicks east of the base. If we head toward these hills over here, we can keep the ship between us and the base for cover, get some shade, and there might even be some caves that—"

"Perfect, good work," Ko-Rel said, cutting the woman off. "Lar-Ka, you and Hal-Zan take point. Get us moving in that direction and we'll adjust as we go."

"What about your leg, Commander?" Lar-Ka asked, gesturing to the leg she'd been limping on earlier. "Will you need assistance?"

She shook her head. "I walked it off. Won't be running any sprints today, but I can keep up. You worry about finding us shelter, I'll worry about getting myself there."

Lar-Ka and Hal-Zan saluted, then stepped back as Ko-Rel called the entire room to attention.

"If your suit is not sealed and pressurized, do it now. I'm opening this airlock in ten ticks and we are moving out," she called, looking over the people assembled to assess their readiness. A few were still fumbling with helmets and suit controls, but none so far behind that they couldn't catch up. She continued.

"Once we open that door, we don't know what's waiting for us. We have to be prepared for a Chitauri offensive from the very tick we disembark. Captain Lar-Ka is sending you all coordinates for a rendezvous point in case we're separated."

Ko-Rel took one slow, even breath, inviting the quiet clarity of battle into her mind.

"Weapons at the ready. Ten ticks, now."

She counted down, scanning the assembled crew. A stillness fell over them all, tense and taut like a string on her late husband's favorite instrument. As ready as they could be for what awaited.

Ko-Rel hit the ramp controls and held her breath.

The airlock hissed, and the ramp hummed and creaked as it descended, revealing the scarred Mercurian landscape beyond.

Empty. For now.

"Lead on, Captain," she said, motioning to Lar-Ka. He and Hal-Zan led the crew down the ramp and out into the field. A strained quiet hung over the group as they skirted around the nose of the battered ship. The beautiful, powerful piece of war craft that had been entrusted to them lay bruised and beaten in the dusty gray regolith, a sludgy puddle of muddy fuel soaking the back end. An explosion waiting to happen. Ko-Rel ran one hand along the underside of its nose as they looped around to the opposite wing. *Thanks for the ride. We'll be back for you.*

"Commander," Lar-Ka said over their private comm channel, and pointed back toward the base.

There, on the horizon, a wave of Chitauri soldiers surged toward them.

Great. She'd hoped for at least a small break, but she should have known. Hope was nothing more than disappointment in waiting.

"How far out?" she asked, tightening her grip on her pulse rifle.

The captain tapped the side of his helmet, adjusting his long-range sight. "About one-point-five klicks."

"Let's move, then," Ko-Rel said, turning to Hal-Zan. "Your hill strategy is a good one. We could use some high ground right about now."

"Yes, ma'am. I'll get us there," Hal-Zan said with a salute.

"Move out!" Lar-Ka ordered, taking off toward the foothills with Hal-Zan at his side. The rest of the intel officers, including a much more fierce and determined-looking Adomox, jogged up to run alongside her. One of the other intelligence officers—Yumiko, she thought —was practically glued to Hal-Zan's side. It was nice to see the intel team had each other's backs. They were in for some tough hours, rotations, and cycles.

Ko-Rel looked around until she found Tasver, the wounded intel-turned-comm officer, and waved him forward. He jogged up alongside her, matching her pace.

"Are you okay?" she asked, gesturing to his bandaged head. He nodded automatically, then winced.

"I can function," he said with a rueful expression. The dark brown skin of his forehead was marred by a wound patch and a smudge of dried blood. Under different circumstances, Ko-Rel would tell him to rest, head to medical and take time to heal. Unfortunately, the Chitauri had taken that option from them. She pressed on.

"We need to get in touch with the forward ops posts and warn them," she began, but Tasver shook his head before she could finish.

"I've tried. No response, not from any of the outposts. There are signals coming from the stations, but they're encoded. I think—"

"—that they've been infiltrated, too. Right," Ko-Rel said. She lifted her gaze to look up at the sky as she jogged, willing her racing heart to steady. This wasn't supposed to be a high-casualty posting, but here they were, already down to two-thirds strength and without any of the backup that was supposed to be on the planet. They needed to send word back to the war front. They needed to take back the base, and all the outposts.

But first?

They needed to survive the next rotation.

A shout went up from the rear of the group, and Ko-Rel risked a glance over her shoulder… just in time to see a Chitauri ship that had appeared out of *nowhere* fire on the stragglers at the back of the group.

"Scatter!" she shouted, whirling around to bring her gun to bear on the ship. The flurry of energy bolts pinged off the ship's force shield, useless and weak. Not nearly enough to bring it down. It provided a moment of distraction, though, for the group to fan out and create less of an easy clump of targets.

"Squad four, blinding crossfire!" Captain Lar-Ka called. "Heavys, focus fire on the port side engines!"

Captain Lar-Ka's second-in-command, Lieutenant Chan-Dar, let out a mighty "Hooah!" that her fellow heavies returned. She swung the enormous pack off her back to use as a tripod, then joined her squad members in a textbook field assembly of the biggest ordnance they'd brought along. While they charged up their first blast, Ko-Rel scanned the foothills ahead of them, looking for a heavy outcropping, a valley, anything to provide a little cover for their most vulnerable.

Then she saw precisely what Officer Hal-Zan had been hoping for—a cave. The opening was nearly large enough to admit a ship, but it looked deep. Exactly what they needed. Typically, she'd prefer to stay in the open when being pursued by an enemy. They'd have options, at least; could retreat further and avoid getting trapped. Right now, though, they needed shelter, a point they could control, a bottleneck to focus their fire.

"Make for the caves ahead!" Ko-Rel called over the comm. Someone, probably Hal-Zan, was a step ahead of her, and the coordinates for the cave system flashed on her suit's heads-up display. The Chitauri ship roared overhead, looping around for another pass, but that wasn't what struck true terror into Ko-Rel's heart.

It was the three other Chitauri ships racing up to meet them, and the distant dots of more ships following right behind.

Scenarios flew through her mind, each quickly discarded. The chances of taking down four ships, much less all the ones on the horizon, were slim to none. But they couldn't just lie down and wait to be killed.

If nothing else, they'd go down fighting.

"Heavies, go mobile," Lar-Ka ordered, reading her mind. "We'll set back up under shelter."

At the mouth of the cave, Ko-Rel turned and waved her people forward, firing over their shoulders to discourage the Chitauri ships. Those at the front of the pack flooded into the cave, their breaths heaving with both exertion and terror. At the rear of the group, a few brave souls assisted the wounded despite how it slowed them down.

And behind them, the ground was littered with the casualties of the Chitauri ship's first pass. Five lay abandoned in their wake. Ko-Rel distantly hoped they'd be able to retrieve the bodies later, but realistically, she knew there likely wouldn't be anyone left alive to retrieve them in the end.

"Erect the barrier pylons and form a line, weapons ready," she said, her voice firm. "This is where we make our stand."

On the horizon, all four Chitauri ships joined in formation, bearing down on the cave system that hid all that was left of the Resistance forces. The energy barrier could withstand one ship, for a while, but setting it up against four ships was an exercise in futility.

At least they'd die trying, and hopefully take out a ship in the process.

Ko-Rel joined the line of rifleman and knelt, bracing her rifle and setting her sights on the lead ship.

"Hold," Captain Lar-Ka shouted. "Fire on my mark!"

Sweat prickled on her forehead, dripping into her eye inside her helmet. Her heart seemed to swell with this, her last moment, her last stand. If she was to die, she wanted to die not with fear in her heart, but with the memory of her family fresh in her mind.

Her sweet baby son, Zam, gone far too soon. His chubby little hands grabbing at her shirt. His feathery soft hair tickling her chin as he climbed over her like she was a playground. The quiet moments as he nestled into her, warm and sleepy, while she hummed to him before bed.

And her husband. Talented, brash, brave Tar-Gold. His heart had been so full of music, his mind so free and open. He'd opened her up to a whole new world she'd never thought she'd want or have. He'd changed the entire course of her life.

And they were both gone, thanks to the Chitauri. Soon she would be, too.

She held their faces firm in her mind and heart as her finger tightened on the trigger, her gaze narrowing until everything faded but the target in her sights. Her breath echoed in her helmet, ears, chest, a rasping draw in, out...

"FIRE!" Lar-Ka shouted.

The lead ship exploded.

BOOM!

Ko-Rel lowered her rifle in confusion, looking around at her people. They'd barely fired a handful of rounds, certainly not enough to take out a whole ship. The heavies hadn't even gotten their shot off yet.

The other three Chitauri ships veered off course, revealing the host of ships that had been on the far horizon.

Not Chitauri ships after all.

A dozen—no, *dozens*—of M-ships sporting varied and eccentric paint jobs swarmed the sky, chasing down the remaining ships. In the far distance, more ships ran strafing runs near the base while others settled down nearby. Ko-Rel adjusted the vision enhancement in her helmet to zoom in on the figures on the ground. They were still barely visible from such a distance, but they all seemed to be wearing mismatched coats and gear, and sporting an incredible variety of weaponry.

"Officer Tasver," she called. "Can you get us on their channel? I want to know who these people are."

"Already on it," Tasver said, crouched over the portable field comm unit he'd carried. He tapped furiously at the display until he sat up with a little "Ah-ha!" and patched the signal into her suit.

"Whoooo hooooo!" an unfamiliar voice shouted. "Get them lizards, boys! Let them know the Ravagers been here!"

PRESENT DAY

KNOWHERE – 7801

AH, good old Knowhere. It wasn't home, exactly—that was the *Milano*, always—but it was maybe the next closest thing. Peter had found all his best black market Earth goods at the famous Knowhere market over the years, from action figures to cassette tapes to the guy who kept him supplied with Earth liquor whenever it mysteriously became available. Knowhere never failed to provide either the goods he needed or the *something interesting* he always sought.

Peter hoisted his bag onto his shoulder as he approached the *Milano*'s aft airlock, passing Rocket and a truly impressive collection of weaponry along the way.

"You aren't planning to start a fight, are you?" Peter asked, eying the pile of detonators Rocket was lovingly packing into his bag one at a time. "We come in peace, you know. Get in, get what we need, then off to score our easy payday."

"Maybe *you* come in peace," Rocket said, checking over one of his many guns before stashing it in one of the chest pockets on his orange armored jumpsuit. "But me 'n Groot? We never take Knowhere for granted. Got some history here. Can't be too careful."

"I think careful and paranoid may have gotten crossed in your brain at some point," Peter said. "We're just hitting the market. We'll be here half a rotation at most."

"No, *you're* hitting the market. Groot and I ain't going anywhere near that place. The Collector has his nasty little fingers in everything there, and we've got old blood with him. I saw his ship docked on our way in, so he's around here somewhere."

Peter leaned back on the rec room table and folded his arms. "What exactly is your beef with Tivan? You're always so weird when he's in the neighborhood."

Rocket paused in his packing to point a tiny raccoon finger at Peter and snarl. "It ain't none o' your business. Suffice it to say, Groot was in trouble, I saved him, and—"

Rocket gestured expansively to his collection of custom boom toys.

"—it involved some rather spectacular acts of thievin' on my part. The rest is history. *Private* history. So, no, we ain't goin' to the market with you."

Rocket flipped over some complicated contraption, fiddled with some wires, then set it aside rather than pack it for the trip. "Anyhows, you said you wanted new suits for the team to help with the branding, so me 'n Groot are gonna pay a visit to a guy I know. A designer, real good with this kinda thing, and respectful of my personal genius as comes to the bells and whistles. Lay low until we're ready to leave, you know?"

Peter was… oddly touched. He'd mentioned the suits in passing, assuming they were a fancy pipe dream that would cost way too many units to be feasible anytime soon. Leave it to Rocket to make the shiny toys happen.

"Hey, man, that's really great of you," Peter said. "Glad someone around here still believes in the Guardians."

"Yeaaaaaah, about that. Seriously, Quill, you gotta know it's gonna take more than suits and business cards ta hold this team together. At this rate, I'm pretty sure we'll be leaving Knowhere with only four members."

Peter covered his eyes with one hand and shook his head.

"Look, Drax and Gamora will both live through this trip, I promise. I'll be with them the whole time."

"I wasn't talking about them," Rocket said with a raised eyebrow. "Better watch your back while you're strollin' around with them stabby types. I'm still of the personal opinion that we were better off just you, me, 'n Groot, but if you want us to be a fivesome, you gotta watch yourself."

Peter blinked.

"Oh. Right."

Rocket zipped up his bag and stood, slinging it over his shoulder and nodding at Groot as he joined them by the airlock. "Just don't screw this one up, Quill. I'm not saying it's your *last* chance to make this work, but… actually, yeah, that's exactly what I'm saying. Last shot, buddy. You got this. Probably."

Rocket strode over to the ramp and leapt up onto Groot's arm, scrabbling up to the shoulder harness he'd built for himself. Ostensibly it was to give him a better vantage point for shooting-type situations. Peter thought it was more that Rocket and Groot just liked to stick together and watch each other's backs. Groot raised one vined hand to Peter in farewell, a tiny green sprout blooming on the tip of one finger, then serenely turned toward the bustle of Knowhere. Rocket chattered at Groot as the two of them stepped out into the crowds together, remaining visible for quite a while on account of Groot's towering height. Peter watched them go thoughtfully.

"Last chance, huh?" Peter murmured—then shoved the thought aside for Future Peter to deal with. "Well, guess it's just me and the two who want to murder each other. And me. Cool."

"I have no plans to murder Drax," Gamora said as she exited her quarters. "At the moment."

She said nothing about not murdering *him*, Peter noted, but decided it was implied. Drax appeared over Peter's other shoulder and huffed, grumbling grumpily. Peter nearly jumped out of his skin.

"Do not trust the murderous sorceress, Peter Quill," he said. "She has changed sides before and can do so again."

Gamora sighed. "I thought we were past the 'murderous sorceress' thing."

Peter hit the airlock controls and stepped out with a friendly wave at a nearby Xandarian woman. She looked him over with an assessing gaze, her eyes flicking from his (awesome) jacket to his jet boots, then kept right on walking. Ah well. He was here on business anyway.

"She's not going to change sides, Drax," Peter said. "First of all, there are no sides, the war ended *twelve years ago,* why is it coming up so much all of a sudden?"

There was a moment of awkward silence.

"And second of all?" Drax finally asked.

Peter blinked. "What?"

"You said, 'First of all,'" Drax said. "You cannot say 'first of all' unless you mean for there to be a 'second of all.'"

"He's right," Gamora said. "It doesn't make any sense."

Drax gave her a sidelong glance. "I do not believe there is a 'second of all' in this case. Once you've committed treason, future betrayal is always a possibility."

"I do not need absolution from a serial murderer," Gamora snapped, stalking ahead and shoving her way into the crowd.

"I'm in hell," Peter said to a random passing Skrull. He received only a strange look in reply. It was fine; no one could truly understand the suffering of Peter Jason Quill.

Through the rainbow sea of skin colors and feathers and at least one dog tail, Peter and Drax eventually caught up with Gamora, just as they crossed into Knowhere's famous marketplace. The main drag was lined on either side with storefronts and market stalls. Some were draped with fabric canopies, others bolstered by laser-cut metal signs, some crowded and others near deserted. Proprietors hung out in front of many, calling to passersby and hawking their wares. All around them, bodies pressed together in the crowd, weaving around each other and batting away the questing fingers of pickpockets. When Peter appeared at her shoulder, Gamora turned to glare at him briefly, then returned to scanning the crowd for threats.

"Where is this engineer friend of yours?" Gamora snapped, clearly still pissed. Peter sighed internally and scanned over the heads of the crowd, looking for the shop's sign. It had been a bit, but he was pretty sure it would still be here. Ten-Cor was a successful entrepreneur and her shop did good business selling both secondhand tech and artwork made from repurposed tech scraps, unless something drastic had changed. Finally, he spotted the three-dimensional piece of welded metal art that was the shop's sign, made by Ten-Cor's own hand. It read *TC'S TECH* in big block letters, with broken-down gears, circuitry, and wiring artfully affixed around the border. Very eye-catching.

"There, it's that one across the street," he said, gesturing with his chin.

Drax perked up. "The one with the hanging meat?"

"No, the one next to that."

"The one with the dancers?" Gamora said, razor sharp and deadly.

Peter winced. Scantily clad performers lounged around a cheap sign out front reading, *WIGGLES: all genders, all species, all the time!*

"*No*, next to it on the *other* side," Peter said, hands held up to protest his innocence. "And to be fair, that club hires only professionals. No indentures. I hear the pay and benefits are great."

Gamora relaxed at that, her instinct for protective murdering tamed for the moment. No one in need of saving.

"Frequent client, are you?" she asked instead, raising an eyebrow.

Peter shrugged. "I've been a time or two. Great buffet."

Peter cut across the crowd, leading the way through a maze of people to Ten-Cor's shop. As they drew closer and more details of the shop became visible, Gamora and Drax both tensed, their hands drifting toward the hilts of their various blades.

"*That* one? The one that says, 'Kree only, all others will die?'" Gamora said with deadly calm.

"Hey, whoa, now, it's a joke! It's a—hey, put those away," Peter said, laying a hand on Drax's arm. One look from Drax and he whipped his hand away, smoothing it through his hair instead. "Look, Ten-Cor just has a warped sense of humor. She thinks she's hilarious. The war affected us all in different ways, right?"

"And how did it affect you, *Star-Lord*?" Gamora asked with an eye roll.

Peter looked back toward the shop without replying.

"Oh, look, here she comes now. Ten-Cor!" Peter waved. He hadn't actually seen her in at least two years, but that was honestly a point in their favor. Hopefully time would have dulled the memory of the complete and utter ass he'd made of himself the last time they'd seen each other. "What a delight to see you! You're looking lovely as always."

Ten-Cor had just stepped out of a squat windowless building that, at a quick glance, appeared to be packed to the brim with junk bits of tech from every civilization in this galaxy and the next. The main part of the shop was out front, where a long bench was squeezed between two pillars that held up an awning with the same *TC'S TECH* logo as her fancy sign. Behind the bench, Ten-Cor flopped back into a chair and put her boots up on the worktop. She looked Peter up and down and rolled her eyes theatrically.

"Oh look, it's the pink ape," she said. "What do you want this time?"

"Here to ask a favor of an old war buddy," Peter said, spreading his arms wide and putting on his most charming smile.

Ten-Cor folded her arms and leaned back farther in her chair. "I don't do favors. Try again."

Peter knew he'd have to work for this one, but he'd hoped they'd get off to an easier start than this. He took a step closer, holding his hands out in supplication. "Would it help if I asked you to marry me again?"

That got a barked a laugh from Ten-Cor, and she dropped her feet to the ground and stood, leaning forward over the bench and thawing a bit. "Not even a little. Though I'm flattered you aren't drunk this time. I'm not going to fall for your games, Quill."

"What games? I'm an honest businessman these days," Peter said, reaching into his inside jacket pocket for a business card. He held it up for her to see and flicked it to… show off how sturdy the cards were, he supposed? It was a thing he saw someone do in a movie once.

"Guardians of the Galaxy. Heroes for hire. We're here because we have need of your particular unique expertise on our current job."

A little flattery never hurt. He slid the business card across the bench to her, and she took it with the air of someone about to file it in the nearest trash can as soon as she walked away.

"You can skip the preamble, Quill. Let's get to business. What are you—"

She cut off suddenly, her eyes locking onto Peter's companions. In half a tick, there was a gun in her hand. A very large Rocket-sized gun, produced from absolutely nowhere.

Her eyes had gone very, very hard.

"Awfully murderous company you're keeping these days, Star-Lord."

She cocked the gun and aimed it straight between Drax's eyes.

INTERLUDE: 12 YEARS AGO

MERCURY – 7789

KO-REL emerged from the cave with one arm shielding her eyes from the slowly rising sun. Her suit beeped a temperature warning, but she ignored it. It was getting hot beyond the temporary force shield they'd erected, but not dangerous. Yet. The real danger, it seemed, had ended. For now.

The small fleet of M-ships that had appeared out of nowhere settled to the ground outside the mouth of the cave system, their engines flaring and wings folding in. Not Resistance ships, but not Chitauri, either. *Ravagers* was the name they'd used. Each ship sported a small white flame logo on it somewhere, presumably the symbol of the group.

A few of her people had heard of them before: a band of pirates who'd been hitting both Chitauri and Resistance supply caravans since the start of the war, among their other piratical activities. The intelligence officers (Hal-Zan, Adomox, Suki Yumiko, and Tasver) had immediately gathered around Tasver's portable field comm unit to listen in, research, and gather as much information on the newcomers as possible.

They'd caught some of the battle chatter over the comm, enough to know these people weren't here to kill them, that they'd cleared the infiltrators out of the base Ko-Rel and her people had been sent here to defend. That they'd arrived *too late* to defend.

Whether these *pirates* would demand payment for their assistance, or simply leave them here to die while they looted the base, remained to be seen.

The closest ship, a blue and orange one with a white flame logo stenciled near the nose, whirred as its aft airlock opened. A humanoid wearing a helmet with glowing red eyes stepped out, looked around, then walked toward Ko-Rel with his thumbs hooked in the loops of his gun belt. His gait was casual, his manner calm and loose, not at all like someone who had just done battle. He stopped several yards outside the energy barrier and lifted one hand in a wave.

"Took care of your little Chitauri problem," the humanoid said, shrugging one shoulder casually like it was no big deal. "Your base is a bit of a mess, though. Dead lizards everywhere. Sorry about that."

He pointed at the shimmering barrier and sketched out the rectangular shape of a doorway with one finger. "Mind if I come in?"

Ko-Rel looked him over in silence. He was one person,

and she was surrounded by her troops. If he tried anything, he'd be dead before he could pull a trigger. She punched a command into her wrist unit. A door-sized area of the shield glowed blue, and the man stepped through, keeping his steps slow and deliberate like he was afraid of spooking her. Maybe he should have been. After the rotation she'd had, her trigger finger was feeling twitchy.

"Thought we were too late," he said, stopping a few feet away from her. "When all we saw were lizards, we thought they'd already taken everyone out. Then we saw those Chitauri ships chasing y'all down and, whew, what a relief! It's not Lizard City after all."

He tapped something behind his ear that made his helmet retract, revealing the face of a young humanoid man, maybe Terran, who couldn't be more than about twenty. Every inch of him was in constant motion: bouncing on the balls of his feet, swiping a hand through light brown hair, shifting his weight from one leg to the other. He was spilling over with energy. With life.

Around Ko-Rel, what remained of her squad worked at the business of survival: packing up gear, limping on injured legs, holding dislocated limbs protectively to their chests, assisting wounded comrades. So few. Barely enough to hold the base, once they had a chance to retake it, much less recapture all their forward outposts and root out the Chitauri still on the planet. They'd have to send word to Rider for reinforcements, take stock of the equipment that had survived the attack—

"Hey, you in there?" the guy said, cocking his head and taking a step closer. "Hellooooo?"

She snapped her eyes to his and narrowed her gaze.

"Who are you? Who sent you?" she snapped, completely unable to rein in her anger and completely not caring. Who did this man—this *boy*—think he was, walking up to her like he hadn't just walked over the corpses of her people? Like she hadn't just been prepared to go down with the memory of her dead husband and child in her heart? Like his help entitled him to smiles and gratitude and praise? All she had to give was exhaustion and anger. She didn't owe him a d'ast thing.

After everything that had happened… anger was easier.

"Whoa," he said, holding his hands up in the universal 'don't shoot' signal. "I'm on your side, okay? The Ravagers…" He gestured to the ships behind him. "We hit a convoy of Chitauri supply ships and heard about the plan to infiltrate the base here. I convinced Yondu—that's the blue guy over there, he's our leader—to come help and turn over the supplies we scored. I'm from Earth, you know, so I didn't so much love the idea of those garbage lizards knocking on my front door. Not that I'm planning to go back or anything, but—"

"Enough," Ko-Rel said, cutting off his babble with a sharp gesture. This Terran talked a *lot*. "Were there any Resistance survivors at the outpost? *Anyone* from our side left alive?"

The guy kicked at the slate-gray regolith and avoided her eyes. "Nah. Only Chitauri in there. But we took care of that for you, right?" he said, brightening. "You should have been there. It was nuts! There was this one moment, it was totally like a Han Solo gunslinger moment. I had my guns out, right, and there was this Chitauri in front of me, and he was a *big boy*, and I—"

Ko-Rel rushed forward and grabbed the guy by the front of his coat.

"Look—what's your name, Terran?"

"Peter Quill?" he offered, like a question.

"Look, Quill," she said, giving him a little shake and pointing back toward the base. "Those people in there? They *died*. They lost their lives to those Chitauri murderers. Their families—"

She broke off, her throat suddenly too thick to speak.

Their families would never see them again. Just like she would never see hers. Thinking of her baby and husband in what she'd thought would be her last moments had broken the seal she'd welded over that part of her heart, and now she couldn't stop. Her baby boy, who she'd grown and nourished from her own body. Who she'd watched over as he learned about the world, every leaf a wondrous discovery. Her bright and silly husband, the center of Zam's world. It was true, what they said about parenthood. It changes you.

It had changed Ko-Rel more than she'd known was possible. And she'd loved every tick. Right up until it destroyed her.

Ko-Rel tore her gaze away from Peter Quill and let him go, looking toward the distant sunrise instead. She had no time for boys playing hero.

"This isn't a game," she said finally. "This is war."

Peter turned to look, too, deliberately ignoring the shouts of his comrades trying to get his attention.

"Believe me. I know."

And there was something in his voice... a weight, a resonance. Something that spoke of scars. There was more buried beneath the bravado. Ko-Rel gave him a second look, studying closer this time.

She believed him.

Perhaps he was more than a brash boy after all.

THE golden sun crept ever closer over the pockmarked ground toward the Ravager fleet and the bustle of rescue. Captain Lar-Ka was in talks with Yondu, the two of them gesturing emphatically and standing far closer than a discussion over a comm channel required. Ko-Rel observed for a moment before deciding the posturing was non-threatening and actually quite amusing.

"Commander."

Lar-Ka's voice over the comm startled her out of her study.

"Go ahead, Captain."

"I've negotiated our transport back to the base. Yondu and his Ravagers are offering us a full load of supplies stolen from a Chitauri convoy. There are weapons, medical equipment, and rations, enough to replace what we lost in the crash and then some."

Ko-Rel felt a cautious hope blooming in her chest, but hesitated.

"And what payment does he ask?"

"That's the thing, Commander," he said, disbelieving. "He keeps referencing some guy named Quill, a member of his crew, who talked him into just... giving them to us, free of charge. Called it his 'good deed for the millennium.' Should we accept?"

It seemed an obvious decision, but Ko-Rel understood his hesitance. Nothing ever came without strings, especially in a wartime universe, and *most* especially from pirates. What choice did they have, though?

"We aren't in much of a position to say no, Captain. Please tell Yondu we accept his offer with gratitude. If he comes to collect my skull for it later, I'll deal with it then." After a beat, she added, "Don't repeat that last part."

"I figured as much," Lar-Ka said with a chuckle.

Ko-Rel replied in kind, the laugh sounding hollow and worn. "Just making sure."

The captain put out the call for the troops to begin loading the wounded onto the Ravager M-ships, and her people leapt into action without hesitation. Good. Rotations on Mercury were long, but they were at a tipping point—the temperature would be rising quickly, and soon. Much longer and they'd have roasted to death, no matter how good their energy barrier was and how deep the caves.

How amazing and terrible, the way a mere fluke of timing determined life and death.

"Come on. Let's see these supplies you brought," Ko-Rel said, and strode toward Peter's ship. "It's about to get very warm outside."

"Great, I could use a tan," Peter said, trotting alongside her. "You would not believe how pasty white my ass has gotten being in space all the time. Hey, do Kree tan in the sun?"

"I don't think you'll want to be lying out in the sun here," Ko-Rel said with a wry smile. "Unless your idea of a tan is burning the top layer of your flesh clean off."

Peter sucked in a breath between his teeth. "Ooh, yeah, I'm gonna pass on that, thanks."

Ko-Rel nodded. "Smart choice. And thank you, by the way. Captain Lar-Ka said you were the one who convinced Yondu to give us the supplies without charge."

Peter looked over at her with a relieved grin.

"Oh, he did it, good! I was really doubting it there for a bit. Yondu's a good guy, but he's not always the most… *giving* soul in the universe. I'm sure he'll want me to make up the loss somehow." He waved a hand vaguely at his future self. "I'll deal with it. Do you want to talk to Yondu now, or can I give you a ride back to the base?"

Ko-Rel glanced over at Captain Lar-Ka and Yondu, still deep in their discussion, and decided that for once she'd just let someone else handle the details. There was a bigger picture that needed tending to. She opened a comm channel to Lar-Ka.

"Sorry to interrupt what I'm sure is a fascinating negotiation, but I'm hitching a ride back to the base with Quill to evaluate the damage. I'll see what I can do to prepare for the wounded arrivals. Can you oversee the transport operation?"

"Yes, Commander," he replied, then lowered his voice. "Are you sure you trust this Quill guy enough to fly solo with him?"

Ko-Rel glanced over at Peter, who was rubbing at a smudge of something on the underside of one of his ship's wings. He stared at his fingers for a long few ticks, rubbed them together... then licked them.

Okay then.

"I don't know about *trust*," she said. "But I'm pretty sure I'll be fine. All else fails, I can take him. I'll report back once we're in."

Ko-Rel closed the channel and looked back to Peter. "So, are we going to board your ship, or just lick it?"

Peter laughed sheepishly and rubbed at the back of his neck.

"Sorry. I don't spend a whole lot of time looking at the outside of her, and she's a little more banged-up than I realized."

"You really love this ship, don't you?" Ko-Rel asked.

"She's my home," he said with a shrug. At that, he lowered the docking ramp and waved for her to follow.

"Welcome aboard the *Milano. Mi casa, su casa*. Just... don't look too closely at anything."

INTERLUDE: 12 YEARS AGO

MERCURY BASE – 7789

KO-REL constantly marveled at the resilience of soldiers. Not even twenty-four hours ago, her people had been fleeing the wreckage of their downed starship, carrying each other to one last desperate hiding place. Covered in each other's blood, exhausted, but taking one step after another with rifles at the ready and arms wrapped around those needing support. Incredible effort, and an incredible drain on physical and mental resources.

And yet, now, here they were: lining the tables in a mess hall, sitting shoulder to shoulder with a bunch of pirates, laughing and fighting and shouting and generally being... alive. Taking up seats that were formerly populated by a completely different crew of people, all of whom were now stacked three deep, held in stasis in the infirmary until they could all be given a final ritual and send-off. Of course, the chaplain officer had been killed in the infiltration as well, so one of the more religious members of Ko-Rel's reinforcement crew had offered to step up and do his best to honor the dead.

That had been a dark conversation, trying to figure out what to do with the bodies and what level of respects they could offer them without putting everyone in danger with the delay. It was important, though. Honoring was part of healing, and it was necessary for everyone to feel okay sitting in a dead person's seat, sleeping in their bunk, and eating in their mess hall. It was their duty, but that didn't stop it from being weird.

Despite it all, despite the fact that they were only alive because of a series of coincidences and good luck, her people were doing... well. Part of it was sleep, Ko-Rel assumed. They'd broken up their crew into shifts, and one third slept while the other two thirds got to work on cleaning up the mess and returning the base to operational status. Ko-Rel herself hadn't slept yet, but she planned to, as soon as the very late dinner was over. For now, she felt it was important to take a meal with her people and observe the slowly returning morale.

Some were doing better than others. Captain Lar-Ka sat with a long table of combat troops, holding court as they quietly basked in his presence. Everyone under his command adored him, and Ko-Rel felt lucky to have him here. The camaraderie the combat units shared went a long way toward easing some of the shock of the past rotation.

The support staff seemed to be doing okay as well.

They'd been well protected by the soldiers, so their casualties had been minimal, but they'd also been the least combat experienced. And yet they, too, showed their resilience. A bold young Kree woman named Ten-Cor held court at a table full of medical and technical staff, her guffawing laughter pulling smiles and chuckles from everyone around her. She was one of the engineers who had erected the energy barrier around the cave entrance just in time to stop the first round of fire from the Chitauri ships, and she'd hardly blinked in the face of the threat. She may not have been a soldier, but she had nerves of steel.

Ko-Rel worried more about the intelligence officers. The nature of their work made them more naturally isolated from the others, and sometimes from each other as well. Adomox sat alone, picking at the healing scrapes on her face. Tasver sat nearby, muttering to his portable comm unit. Neither one looked up, each lost in their own heads. Not a good sign. Suki Yumiko and Hal-Zan sat together, at least, their heads bent together as they talked quietly. Once their plates were cleared, they stood and left together, still deep in conversation. Probably time for them to take over watch in the command center.

And Ko-Rel? She had somehow ended up spending much of the last twenty-four hours in the presence of one Peter Quill. He'd acted as something of an unofficial liaison between Ko-Rel and Yondu, smoothing things over when military and mercenary clashed and generally keeping the mood light. He'd gotten his hands dirty right alongside the

Resistance forces, bumping shoulders as they hauled crates of supplies and patched up the damage done during first the Chitauri attack, then the Ravagers' rescue. He wasn't quite the lazy, lackadaisical pirate she'd thought him at first meeting.

"Okay, so tell me more about your Ravager friends here," Ko-Rel asked Peter, forcing herself to take in some of the levity in the air. "They seem like an… interesting bunch?"

"Oh, you don't have to be all nice about it," Peter said, gesturing to the assembled Ravagers with his spoon. "We're a bunch of frickin' weirdos and we know it. Well, most of us know it. A few are in denial."

He paused to take another bite and chewed thoughtfully for a moment, then gestured with his spoon at a girl with black hair. "That's Sera. She claims to be some kind of angel or something? And she got separated from her girlfriend, or her girlfriend got kidnapped, or something like that, so now she's with us. I don't know how much of her story I really believe, but I try not to get in her way."

"What about that guy there?" Ko-Rel asked, gesturing with her chin.

"The guy with the bug-eye helm? He never takes that thing off, I swear, looks like some kinda freaky praying mantis thing like—" Peter held up his arms bent at the wrist and elbow, she assumed like this "praying mantis" thing.

"I see you over there—*tik*—doing the arm thing again, Quill," the bug man said.

"Sorry!" Peter said, dropping his arms and shrugging

sheepishly. "He's not actually a Ravager, just hitching a ride for a minute."

"I meant the guy next to him, anyway, in the armor with the giant pile of desserts in front of him," she corrected.

"Ooh, that's Torgo," Peter said, tucking back into his food. "It's not armor, actually. That dude is literally made of metal. And yet, he has a wicked sweet tooth. Don't ask me how that works."

Ko-Rel took another bite and chewed thoughtfully, watching the bug man draw laughs out of his tablemates. There was a whole ecosystem out in the universe that she had no idea about. She was only twenty-five, and she'd spent most of her life being raised by military parents, attending a military academy, or serving as an officer in the military. The thought of drifting through the universe, joining up with a crew of pirates, seeing the edges of this galaxy and the next… she couldn't truly imagine it.

She could see how perfectly it suited Peter, though.

"I'm curious," she said, looking over at Peter with her head propped up on one hand. "Tell me how a Terran ends up with the Ravagers. There aren't many of your kind out here."

"Yeaaah," Peter said, cutting his gaze away. "Wish I could say it was a funny story, but—"

An echoing *BOOM* cut him off mid-sentence, and the lights flickered. Ko-Rel was on her feet in an instant.

"Report," she barked over the open comm channel, even as she sprinted out of the mess hall, Peter right on her heels.

"Chitauri ships are making strafing runs on the Ravager

ships parked outside the landing bay," Yumiko replied from the command center. "One of the smaller ships caught some concentrated fire, but shields are holding up on the others so far."

"Nooo, what color was the ship?" Peter wailed from somewhere far behind her. Ko-Rel pursed her lips.

"Weapons officer to the command center. This base had some defensive weaponry, so let's get it online ASAP. Captain Lar-Ka?"

Lar-Ka came over the comm, firm and collected as always. "Heavy specialists to the landing bay. All other squads, set up at the access points. Squad one at the landing bay entrance. Squad two at the east entrance, three at the south, four at the west. Intelligence field agents and all other troops to the landing bay. Go!"

"I…" Peter began, and Ko-Rel whirled around to find him stopped in the middle of the hallway, hesitating.

"Get to your ship," she said. "Shoot some of those Chitauri bastards down."

"Right," Peter said, and he walked backward for a few steps, nodding his thanks before turning to run the other way. Adomox and Hal-Zan jogged past, too, reporting to the landing bay as ordered. Ko-Rel itched to join them, to get a rifle in her hand and take some blood, but it wasn't her place this time. She needed to be the commander, at the center of it all, directing the battle while her people risked their lives. That meant being where she could see the whole battle unfold.

She burst into the command center, where Officer Yumiko

sat alone at her station. She grabbed one camera feed after another, dragging the projected images through the air in front of her until they were arrayed in a grid, the whole exterior of the base visible. She pulled one and gestured to make it bigger, zooming in on what looked like a bare stretch of outer wall.

"Oh *no*," she said.

"What's wrong?" Ko-Rel asked.

Then she saw it. A panel hanging half open, revealing a maintenance shaft. Where did it lead? She didn't know the base well enough yet, though it was similar to every other hastily constructed prefab base she'd ever been in. If it was close to the western side of the base, then that maintenance shaft likely led to...

A door banged open, and an energy blast whizzed right past Ko-Rel's ear, striking one of the glowing displays. She whirled around and grabbed for her sidearm, desperately wishing it were a pulse rifle instead.

"Get down!" she shouted at Yumiko. She threw herself behind a pile of collected rubble cleaned up after the last attack and leaned out to fire, managing to bullseye the lead Chitauri right between the eyes. She immediately swept her gun to take out another one... only to find him grappling with Yumiko.

Yumiko ducked and managed to get her pistol up under the Chitauri's ribs. A flash, a roar of pain, and Yumiko was flung backward into a pile of debris. She cried out and didn't get up.

Ko-Rel took her shot. As soon as Yumiko was clear, she caught the Chitauri attacker with two more pulses in the shoulder and throat, just to make really sure he'd go down. She darted over to the next console, moving steadily toward Yumiko's unmoving form, never taking her sights or her gun off the maintenance entrance. But nothing came.

Yet. On the camera feeds, Ko-Rel saw a Chitauri shuttle setting down just outside the pried-open hatch. A shuttle big enough to hold a whole squad.

"Ravagers, the western side of the base!" she called out over the open comm, hoping the Ravagers were listening in on the same channel. "Lar-Ka, we need reinforcements to the command center!"

"We've got no one to send from the landing bay," Lar-Ka replied, shouting over the sound of gunfire and a distant explosion. "Anyone who's available, go!"

"Squad two is pinned down," one of the lieutenants called.

"Squad three, same," said another. And another. And another.

No help was coming.

"I've got you, Ko-Rel," Peter said over the comm. "Making my run now. Kraglin, you coming?"

"Hell yes, brother, let's toast some lizards," one of the Ravagers replied. "They shot at my ship!"

Ko-Rel ran the rest of the way to Yumiko's side and knelt down beside her, gun at the ready. The woman's cheek had a huge gaping wound down the side, deep and bleeding heavily. There was an emergency med kit across the room with wound patches, but there could be Chitauri breathing down their necks at any moment.

Ko-Rel paused next to Yumiko and listened to the sound of her breath as it moved through her, finding calm, keeping her ears attuned for the smallest indication that further threats were incoming. In the far distance, the rhythmic pounding of energy weapons on metal and ground reverberated through the walls. Nothing closer, though.

After a moment, the noise died away.

"Sitrep?" Ko-Rel called out. An uncomfortably long beat of silence later, Captain Lar-Ka's voice came over the comm.

"Enemy forces are retreating," he said, sounding winded. "I don't think they were aiming to retake the base. This was a quick strike to weaken us while we were still recovering, and to try to scare off our reinforcements."

"And it worked," Yondu said, breaking into the conversation. "No offense, folks, but this ain't our fight. Ravagers, pack it up. We're leaving."

"What? No!" Peter protested.

"Don't you talk back to me, boy," Yondu admonished. "We lost ships today, and that was never part of the plan here. Land, refuel, and be ready to go in one hour."

Ko-Rel's heart turned cold, her eyes locking on to Yumiko's dripping blood staining the shoulder of her own uniform. "Udonta, please, let's meet and talk this over. I'm sure—"

"I'm sure there ain't nothin' you can say that'll change my mind, but if you wanna talk *at* me while I load my ship, have at it," Yondu replied.

Ko-Rel wouldn't beg over an open comm channel and further demoralize her people. The world felt like it was closing in on her from all sides, but she forced herself to close her eyes and breathe. She was all too aware of Suki Yumiko sitting beside her, a splatter of Chitauri blood on her forehead and her own red human blood oozing down the side of her face. Ko-Rel needed to keep it together until she was alone, until Suki was seen to. She leaned down and wrapped an arm around the woman's waist and hauled her up, letting the woman's uninjured cheek loll onto her shoulder.

"I'm escorting Officer Yumiko to the infirmary," Ko-Rel said over the comm. "Meet me there with a casualty report, Captain."

"Hal-Zan," Suki murmured into Ko-Rel's neck. Right, good idea.

"And have Officer Hal-Zan meet us there, please," she added.

The trip to the infirmary was a long and awkward stumble until Ko-Rel gave up and swept Suki up into her arms, carrying her the rest of the way. She forgot sometimes that Terrans didn't have the strength of the Kree. Chaos greeted them at the infirmary doors, medical staff running from bed to bed, working to triage the most critically wounded. Ko-Rel threaded her way through the crowd, doing her best not to knock Yumiko's injured face into anyone.

Finally, an orderly flagged Ko-Rel down and directed her to sit Yumiko in a chair shoved against one wall, out of the way of the more serious action. Her injury, though painful and vicious-looking, wasn't in any way life- or limb-threatening. Unlike those of the people around them. Far too many people.

"Where is Hal-Zan?" Yumiko murmured, eyes half closed as a nurse administered a painkiller and wound patch to her cheek.

"I'll find out," Ko-Rel said, scanning the infirmary for Captain Lar-Ka. She spotted him fending off a nurse, who was waving his hands in irritation as he tried to get the captain to sit down and submit to treatment. Lar-Ka gave him the slip, ducking under the man's arms and walking toward Ko-Rel. She met him halfway, and they leaned on a wall out of the way of the essential work of keeping people alive.

"How bad was it?" Ko-Rel asked.

Lar-Ka winced. "Pretty bad. Not as bad as it could have been, since they were clearly targeting the Ravager ships, but we had three KIA, two badly wounded. Our numbers are dwindling."

Ko-Rel did the quick math and her heart sank. If they lost the Ravagers, they were looking at a force barely big enough to staff the base, much less run any operations against the Chitauri.

Then Yumiko's voice rose above the general din of the infirmary, edged with panic.

"Where is she?"

"Step back, officer," the orderly said in a calm but firm tone, his hands held out to block Yumiko from going any farther.

Lar-Ka met Ko-Rel's gaze and shook his head.

"This is for me to handle. Get some rest, Commander. Don't think I don't know you haven't slept yet."

Ko-Rel held her hands up to admit defeat, and took one last look back at Suki Yumiko as Lar-Ka approached her. Yumiko latched on to him immediately.

"Where *is* she?" she pressed, her voice rising, tearing ragged at the edges.

Lar-Ka's voice was soft, but its low rumble carried far. "I'm sorry, Suki—"

"No," she cut in. "She's not a soldier, someone should have been with her. Who was protecting her? *Where is she?*"

A quiet murmur in return, then Yumiko's wail filled the command center.

Ko-Rel squeezed her eyes shut against the wave of second-hand grief. She knew that cry. She'd danced on that edge herself, mixing madness and heartbreak and staring into the long void of after. She wondered who Officer Hal-Zan had been to Yumiko. Sister? Lover? Friend? Wife?

Ko-Rel's brain skittered away from thoughts of spouses and children. *Not now.*

Lar-Ka and the orderly struggled to gently restrain Suki as she thrashed against their hold. "I hate this! I hate this place! I hate Richard Rider, I hate the Chitauri, and I hate *all of you*. *You* should have died, not her! *Not her!* You don't deserve to live!"

It was like a knife lodged in Ko-Rel's breastbone, a sharp pressure threatening to cut off her breath. The words were fueled by the darkest of despair, and that was a place Ko-Rel was all too familiar with. She'd been there, lived it, drowned in it. Without the purpose of the Resistance to pull her out of it, she might have stayed there.

That meant she was the best person to talk to Suki right now. And she completely did not have it in her. She needed a minute. Just a beat of silence before the next miserable task. She ducked out of the infirmary and looked for somewhere, anywhere...

There, a supply closet. A bit stereotypical, but it would do.

Ko-Rel closed the door behind her and leaned up against it, then let go of the great wracking sobs she'd been holding in. In five minutes, she'd go find Yondu and try to convince him to let the Ravagers stay. Beg, if she had to.

But first, this: the grief of yet more losses, of command mistakes, and of the only reinforcements they had abandoning them while Richard Rider stayed silent on the matter.

Five minutes.

Then she'd be Commander Ko-Rel again.

PRESENT DAY

KNOWHERE – 7801

DRAX raised his blades, scarily large arm muscles flexing under red-orange tattoos, completely unfazed by the size of the gun currently pointed at his head. Gamora frowned, reaching for her sword hilt but not yet extending the blade. The situation was barely ticks from spinning wildly out of control, so Peter did the only thing he could think of.

He threw himself between Drax and Ten-Cor, arms up in surrender… and immediately wondered what the hell he was thinking. What a *terrible* plan.

"Whoa now, okay, let's just *hold on* a tick," he said, trying to buy time to think. "So, Ten-Cor, clearly you're familiar with Drax—"

"The Destroyer? Yeah. I'm familiar. So's my wife's father. He was on board one of the *many* ships full of people you slaughtered because you thought they were hiding Thanos."

To Peter's surprise, Drax took a step back and sheathed his blades. He inclined his head to Ten-Cor in acknowledgment. "My apologies. I was not in my right mind."

Ten-Cor sputtered in disbelief, the muzzle of the gun dipping slightly. "What, that's it?"

Drax nodded. "Yes."

Peter glanced between the two. Drax's expression was matter-of-fact, calm. Ten-Cor's mouth gaped open, occasionally starting to say something, then cutting off. Her medium-blue skin darkened over her cheeks, and the volume of her half-formed words rose with each one. An explosion was imminent. Time for intervention. Fast.

"No, okay, I get that Drax killed a lot of people. And that was... awful. But he *did* also kill Thanos."

"Allegedly," Drax interjected.

"Now's not the time for splitting hairs, buddy," Peter said under his breath with a significant look.

"Why would I split hairs?" Drax said at full normal volume, looking quizzically at Peter. "And whose hairs would I split? I am hairless, myself, even around my—"

"*Yes*, okay, that is so very much more than enough," Peter said with a grimace matched by everyone close enough to overhear. "Look, Drax, Gamora, maybe I should just handle this one on my own, yeah? Just... go find someone who'll trade with us for some food and fuel and I'll meet up with you when I'm done."

Ten-Cor, who had let the muzzle of the gun drift down

further during the exchange, snapped it right back up. "Oh, no. I don't think so. My wife would never forgive me if I let this one go."

"And I get that, but wouldn't you lose your shop when Cosmo comes barking up here to investigate a murder?" Peter said in his most calm and logical "let's put our weapons away" kind of voice. "Come on, you know me. I wouldn't be hanging out with Drax if he were still... you know..."

"Serial killing?"

"Yes. That." Peter took in a slow breath to compose himself. "A serial killer who turned himself in, to *the Kyln* of all places, to stop himself. So that's, you know. Something."

The light glinted off the gun menacingly.

"It's a lot, actually. It's life-changing, you know. Really... sort of..."

Ten-Cor sighed and lowered the gun. "They're gone, Quill. You can quit with the begging."

Peter looked over his shoulder and saw Gamora's and Drax's retreating forms being swallowed up by the crowd, Gamora's hand clawed around Drax's forearm, their heads bent together as they bickered. Well, that wasn't good. He'd be lucky if they both turned up on the ship later, alive and un-murdered.

"It wasn't *begging*," Peter clarified. "It was... manly protection of my team members."

Another Kree woman poked her head out of the shop door, eyes locking onto the gun in Ten-Cor's hand. Her blue skin was a shade darker than Ten-Cor's, and though she wore a soft, flowing dress, the body underneath and exposed arms said military, and definitely not an engineer like Ten-Cor had been. Great. Ten-Cor's new wife could totally beat Peter up, and he'd brought her father's murderer straight to her doorstep. The morning was not looking promising.

"Everything okay?" the woman asked, looking Peter over.

"Nothing I can't handle," Ten-Cor said, setting the gun aside. She tipped her head back to receive a forehead kiss and a squeeze on the shoulder, then the other woman disappeared back into the shop.

"So… wife, you said?" Peter shoved his hands in his pockets. "You're married now, huh? Bummer, I always kinda thought we had something."

Ten-Cor rolled her eyes. "Get over yourself, Earth-born whelp. I can't believe Ko-Rel ever lowered herself to be with you."

Peter opened his mouth to protest, then snapped it shut with a nod and a shrug. No, that was fair. Ko-Rel was *way* too good for him, especially back then when he had barely popped the lid on age twenty and didn't know scut about scut. He was a different person these days. Not necessarily wiser, but at least a little less naïve. And keeping much different company. Back then, he'd been a Ravager, a pirate, even when he took a break to play war hero. He'd been that person until embarrassingly recently.

Now, he was part of a very different team. The Guardians of the Galaxy were supposed to be "heroes" for hire, a group that did *heroic* things to earn their profit. Maybe they didn't stand on the *highest* of moral ground, but they were at least a step above robbing both sides of a very bloody war, and they had standards about the type of jobs they took. There may have been some pretty big body counts in the past for each of them, but they'd all joined the team for the promise of a different sort of future, and Peter aimed to deliver it.

If he could keep them all from killing each other, at least.

"That was a long time ago," Peter murmured.

Ten-Cor sighed and ran a hand through her hair, shaking her head.

"Not nearly long enough," she said. "What do you *want*, Quill? You buying something or what?"

How to say it without sounding suspicious? Peter thought for a moment… then decided straightforward honesty would have to do.

"I actually need to get back into our old stomping grounds," he said. "Got a job to remove an unwanted visitor from what's left of the Mercury base, and it's gonna be hotter than Satan's balls planetside."

"And you need a code transmitter to open the landing bay doors so you don't fry."

"Mmm, yeah. Yep. Pretty much."

"I *should* let you fry," she said. "But for the right price, I'll let someone else have that privilege in the future."

Peter scoffed in protest. "Come on, now, do you really hold *that* much of a grudge?"

"You nearly got me arrested, Quill," Ten-Cor said.

"By accident!"

"You got me drunk."

"I got *me* drunk. It's not my fault you started slamming my drinks."

"You didn't once wonder where it was all going?"

"I see an empty glass, I fill it."

"And the bar fight?"

Peter hesitated.

"Yeah, okay, that one *was* my fault. But to be fair, I didn't know they were married, and I—"

"Okay, okay, enough," Ten-Cor said, waving away Peter's justifications. "It was two years ago and I learned my lesson."

"What lesson was that?"

She glared at him. "To never drink with a man who calls himself Star-Lord unironically."

She dropped back down into a rolling chair and slid over to a bin full of tiny drawers. She opened three of them before she found what she needed: a palm-sized transmitter, a bit worn and scuffed up, but with a functioning display. Ten-Cor took her time inspecting it, turning it over in her hands, prying off the casing and fiddling with the hardware. After a few silent moments, she snapped it back together and handed it to Peter.

"Should transmit the code reliably, but you can manually display it on the screen here if it's not getting through and you need to do a work-around with your ship's comm."

Peter took the device with a quiet sort of reverence. The last time he'd made an entrance on Mercury, there'd been no polite knock on the door. The Ravagers had blasted in, guns blazing, like they were raiding another supply caravan instead of saving a doomed squad from certain death.

If only the dying had stopped there.

"Thanks, Ten-Cor," Peter said, pocketing the device. "I owe you one."

She leaned back in her chair again, staring off into the middle distance for a long moment.

"You're braver than me. I wouldn't be able to go back there," she said quietly, then seemed to shake herself. "But you don't owe me scut because you're *paying* me. Ten thousand units."

"Ten—" Peter cut off at the look on her face. He tipped his head back with a sigh, paused… then perked up.

"Yeah, okay. Fair enough. Gotta pay to get paid and all that. I'll make it happen. I'll have hard currency delivered shortly."

"Don't make me regret this, Quill," Ten-Cor said with a wary look.

Peter beamed an innocent smile.

"Why would you regret it?" he asked.

PETER opened a channel to the rest of the team once he was out of the market as he half-jogged back toward the *Milano*, transmitter in hand.

"Alright, folks, we gotta head back to the ship and be in the air. Like, soon. Really soon. As soon as possible."

"Me and Groot ain't done yet, Quill. You can't rush

creative genius," Rocket said over the comm.

"I am Groot," Groot added.

"Genius is *exactly* the right word," Rocket protested. "There's a lot of fine detail to be worked out here!"

Peter groaned, glancing back over his shoulder to make sure he wasn't being followed. "Just... tell your designer buddy you want us to look like a badass crew of heroes for hire who are totally worth the money and be done with it!"

"No respect for the creative process," Rocket grumbled.

"What did you do, Peter?" Gamora asked over the comm.

He decided it was in his best interest not to answer that, instead making a beeline for where the ship was docked. And yet, he could only avoid his fate for so long. Gamora appeared over his left shoulder as he all but fled, jogging to keep up. "Peter. What. Did. You. Do?"

Damn. How'd she find him so quickly? At least Gamora was alone. He couldn't handle the combined disappointed disapproval from both her and Drax simultaneously.

"I got us the transmitter and codes we needed," he said as the *Milano* came into view. A cargo bot was in the process of hauling away five crates of protein paste, heading back toward the marketplace. By the looks of it, they'd just finished up.

"Oh, Peter, you *didn't*," Gamora said, a hand over her face. "Rocket, Groot, Drax, ETA?"

Drax rounded the corner carrying a very large box labeled *Steaks*.

"This is a much earlier departure than planned," he said. "I suspect you have once again done something dishonorable that will prevent us from returning."

"You really are only out for yourself, aren't you, Star-Scut?" Rocket said over the comm. "You never stopped to think, hey, maybe the others on my team want to stay a little longer. Maybe they want to shop for food, or get some spare parts, or, you know, work on getting the fancy uniforms *you* wanted made. But nooo. You always gotta—"

"Hey, look, I am doing what needs to be done for the *team*," Peter shot back. "This is not about me."

His comm beeped urgently at him. He silenced it, and it started back up again. And again. And again.

It was Ten-Cor.

"We should leave," Peter said. "*Now.*"

PRESENT DAY

IN ORBIT AROUND MERCURY – 7801

BEING back in the Sol system was... weird.

Peter had no desire to go back to Earth, really. His mother was dead, and there was no one else there he cared to visit. Might be nice to see what music was like these days, what new albums Star-Lord had released...

Except the band had probably broken up. It had been, what, twenty years since he'd last been on Earth? A few more years since his mom gave him the money to buy his first Star-Lord cassette? The band members were probably pushing fifty, drinking too much, playing terrible solo gigs or getting back together for the inevitable has-been reunion tour that everyone would go to and everyone would hate. Or, they could have all gone on to lead totally normal boring lives with spouses and kids and fond, hazy memories of their eighties rock days.

No, Earth was definitely better left behind. But he still felt its presence hanging in the space many million of miles behind him, and looking right over his shoulder at the same time.

The *Milano* approached Mercury from its dark side, hovering in its shadow. Peter hadn't expected to feel much of anything upon seeing the dusty gray planet. He did, though. A lot. Some kind of tangled mix of pride and dread and… almost nostalgia? It had been a weird time in his life. He'd done a lot to be proud of down there. He'd also seen some bad scut that he had no particular desire to relive. His hands slipped on the controls, and he wiped his sweaty palms on his pant legs.

"What are we waitin' for?" Rocket said. "Let's get this over with."

Peter shook himself out of his daze and forced a half smile for Rocket.

"The base is on Mercury's day side right now. It's hot. Like, *really* hot. You wanna serve yourself up barbecued for Drax?"

"Oi!" Rocket protested.

"So, we're waiting for the rotation to bring it around to the night side?" Gamora asked.

Peter shook his head. "No, Mercury's rotation is painfully slow. It's like… fifty-eight standard rotations. We have no choice but to land while it's on the day side, but the heat is going to wreak havoc with the sensors. Once we start in, we are *committed*. So, you know, we just gotta be ready."

Drax folded his arms. "So we are waiting on nothing, and you are wasting our time."

Peter scowled.

"Geez, okay, I didn't realize we were in such a hurry. I'll take us down."

Peter leaned down to rummage in the satchel next to his seat, then handed Rocket the transmitter from Ten-Cor. "When we get in range, hit that button on the side—"

"I know how a code transmitter works, Quill," Rocket snapped, and Peter held up his hands in defense. He felt like he was doing that a lot these days.

"Fine, fine, we're going. Geez."

Peter wrapped his hands around the controls and stared down at the bleak, pockmarked gray surface of Mercury. No point in putting it off. Peter turned on some music (Star-Lord, of course), and gripped the controls again.

"*Mama she said, son, you'll always be on the run,*" Peter sang under his breath, finishing the verse at a hum as he throttled up, taking them in.

Peter squinted against the intense sunlight as they moved out of the planet's shadow to begin their approach. The *Milano*'s viewport adjusted, but not quite quick enough to keep Peter from taking a blast of way-too-bright rays of 400-septillion-watt sunlight straight into his eyeballs before it could compensate. The *Milano* protected them from the quickly rising heat, but it was all too easy to think back to those first few hours on Mercury, as the planet slowly rotated into the light.

"*Tonight we ride straight into the fire,*" he murmured, then dove into the wispy excuse for an atmosphere Mercury managed to hold onto.

At first, everything was just fine. A simple landing approach. Nothing to worry about.

Then the sensors went haywire.

Then the shooting started.

"What the flark?" Rocket shouted, his nimble little hands dancing over the controls as he fought the traitorous sensors. "You didn't say anything about anti-air weapons, Quill. Where is it coming from? I can't get a target lock."

"From the base, *obviously*," Gamora shouted over a very concerning whine coming from the port side sensor package.

Peter winced and ducked automatically as a barrage of fire came way too close to landing smack in the middle of the front viewport.

"I didn't think of it, okay?" he said. "The guns never got used against *me* while I was here. I was one of the good guys! And I think they got used, what, one time that I saw? Twelve years ago? Give me a break!"

The distant speck of the base grew larger as they approached, marked by the stream of energy bolts streaking across the sky toward them.

"We should be close enough for the transmitter to work," Peter said, readjusting his grip on the controls. "Do it!"

"I *am* doing it," Rocket said, mashing down on the button over and over again. The base, much closer now, close enough to see the landing bay facility tacked on the side... stayed stubbornly closed.

Peter began to sweat, and a little creeping suspicion niggled at the back of his brain. "Are you sure you're doing it right?"

Rocket let out a scornful "Tch!

"Am I sure I'm pressing a button right? Yeah, pretty sure, Star-Nards. You wanna push it instead?"

As much as Peter wanted to fire back over "Star-Nards," the base really was getting concerningly close, and the force shields were taking a hell of a beating.

"Just bring up the code so we can send it manually!"

"I did, but—flark!"

The transmitter went flying from his paw as Peter pulled a particularly tight (and awesome) maneuver. Gamora, quick as the deadly assassin she was, leapt from her seat and plucked it from the air. As soon as she was strapped back in, though, she gave a skeptical hum.

"This code can't be right, Peter, it's—"

"I—agh!" The *Milano* dipped dramatically, throwing everyone to the side. "Gamora, just read the code out to Rocket!"

"No, really, Peter, I don't think this is going to work."

"Just give it here," Peter said, reaching a hand back. As soon as he felt the transmitter hit his palm, he transferred control of the *Milano* over to Rocket's console and looked back to Gamora.

"Okay, send over this code: F – U – P – E – T – E… oh."

A beat of silence.

"The code is F U Peter Quill. I'm pretty sure that's not going to work."

Gamora rolled her eyes.

"I am Groot," Groot said from behind Rocket's seat.

"Yeah, no kiddin'," Rocket said. "Did you not realize

these codes could be changed remotely? You obviously did something to piss that engineer off."

"Yes, Peter, whatever could it be?" Gamora said with the absolute maximum amount of sarcasm possible.

"It was obviously the fact that Peter Quill paid her in protein paste," Drax said. "I know you are a morally corrupt and soulless beast, Daughter of Thanos, but I did not think you were also stupid."

"I have had enough of your judgment, Drax the D-Bag," Gamora snapped. Peter barked a sudden laugh, then shrank down in his seat. Too late, though.

"What is a d-bag?" Drax asked.

"It is an Earth term for one who is without honor," Gamora snarled. "I learned it from Peter."

"You called me a d-bag?" Drax said. Peter swore he could hear a note of hurt in his voice.

"I didn't call you specifically a d-bag, I called us all a bunch of d-bags back during the Contraxia mission and that is *so* not relevant right now!"

"I am Groot," Groot said.

"Groot says you shouldn't be going to Peter to expand your vocabulary, but I disagree! The 'I'm a little teapot' song came in handy, didn't it?" Rocket said with a snickering laugh.

"Can we focus on the problem at hand, please?" Gamora shouted over them all.

Peter internally sighed at Rocket's impending joy.

"Well, there's really only one way in if the transmitter isn't going to work."

Rocket bounced in his seat. "Ooh, my favorite way. We should have done this from the start."

Yep, there it was. Peter sighed externally this time.

"Well, I was *hoping* for an element of surprise, you know, but that's clearly gone so far out the window it's practically on Hala. I guess there was no chance of doing this all stealthy anyway, considering we're already being shot at. Everybody hold on!"

The base grew rapidly in the front viewport as they raced toward it, dancing between the oncoming bolts of suppressive fire. Rocket, ever the expert on blowing very large holes in things that shouldn't have them, took aim on the landing bay doors.

"Knock knock," he said, and pulled the trigger.

An enormous missile streaked out from under the *Milano*'s nose, arcing out toward the domed landing bay doors. A tick later, missile number two joined its friend, and together they slammed into the retractable roof doors of the base landing bay, leaving two very big, very charred holes in it.

Holes that were, unfortunately, not big enough for a whole ship.

"Huh. Stronger than I thought," Rocket said.

"Pull up!" Gamora shouted.

Peter hauled back on the controls, bringing the *Milano*'s nose up, but he could already tell they were going to hit. The two missile holes were like close-set eyes, joined by a thin, creaky piece of blackened metal and undercut by an arc of blaster fire scoring. It looked like a smiley face.

"Yeaaaah, about that…" he said.

The *Milano* crashed through the center of the smiley face and into the landing bay below with the screeching sound of metal on metal. The ship's paint job was no doubt wrecked, but Peter was much more concerned about the ground rushing up at them. He hit the landing jets full power and winced, bracing hard as he put the thrusters in reverse, but it wasn't enough, and the landing bay deck came rushing up at them until…

CR-RRRUNCH!

The *Milano* creaked, and the lights flickered out.

11

INTERLUDE: 12 YEARS AGO

MERCURY BASE – 7789

KO-REL stood over the sink in the communal restroom nearest the landing bay and splashed some cool water on her face, listening to her steady breath in and out. The sterile recycled liquid dripped into the corners of her mouth and soaked into the hair framing her face, turning the near-white strands to a pale blue. Her skin prickled as the water dripped and dried away, taking with it the dried blood from Suki's wound and the tear residue from her miniature breakdown.

She looked at herself in the mirror and gave a small, rueful smile at her reflection. No amount of water would make her look any less like she'd been sobbing, but at least she felt a little more alive. And hey, anyone who wanted to say something about it could eat the live end of her pulse rifle. It had been a hell of a rotation/cycle/year/war, and she doubted there was a person on the base who hadn't felt like unloading today. Besides, crying was a healthy response. Much better than creepy silence (Adomox), sullen glaring (Tasver), death threats (Suki), and being aggressively *fine* all the time (Lar-Ka).

Ko-Rel dried off her hands, smoothed back the wet strands of hair, and stood up straight at attention. Good enough. She wasn't getting dressed up for a night out with her (late) husband or anything.

She was going to beg the leader of a band of pirates to please, please not abandon them to the Chitauri.

Yep. She was really looking forward to the conversation. So. Much.

Shoulders back. Head high.

She could beg with dignity.

The door whooshed open, and Ko-Rel stepped into the controlled chaos of the hallway. Ravagers heading to their ships. Newly patched-up troops heading to their bunks to recuperate. Officers reporting to watch posts to dread the next attack. And Ko-Rel, returning salutes with red-rimmed eyes as she stepped into the landing bay. She scanned the crowded space until her gaze landed on Yondu Udonta, the man who currently held their fate. Udonta spotted her and ended his current conversation with a back slap, then met her halfway.

"So, you got a speech prepared or something?" he asked, sticking his thumbs in his belt loops just like Peter did. Or, Ko-Rel now realized, as Peter had picked up from Yondu.

She shook her head with a rueful smile. "No, no speech."

Yondu gestured wide. "Well, by all means, ask your question so I can give you your answer and we can all move on with our lives."

Well, he could at least pretend he was going to consider it. Nevertheless, Ko-Rel stood up straight, looked him dead in the eye, and made the ask.

"I'd like you and the Ravagers to remain on Mercury until we're able to drive the Chitauri from the planet, or until we receive fresh troops from the warfront," she said. "We'll make room in the base for any Ravagers who want a real bunk, or you can remain in orbit until needed, or whatever other arrangement will work for you and your people."

Yondu nodded, running his tongue over his teeth behind closed lips in thought.

Very *brief* thought.

"No," he said.

Ko-Rel blinked.

"Just… no? That's it?"

"That's it," Yondu said, nodding again. "Very simple, clear cut, no unnecessary nuance here. Black and white. Yes and no."

He pointed at her with a grin. "But, in your case, just plain *no*."

Ko-Rel struck a parade rest stance to hide her balled-up fists at the small of her back.

"There must be something we can offer you," she said. "An incentive to stay on as reinforcements."

"Offer me?" Yondu barked a laugh. "Only things you

have here are things I brought you, lady. Anything I wanted from that I coulda just kept. You offering me my own stuff back is damn near insulting."

"Even though you know you're essentially condemning us to death."

"Like I said before," Yondu said, his voice lowering to a half-whisper. "Not my fight. Not my problem. You don't wanna die? Leave. Ain't no one keeping y'all here but *you*."

Ko-Rel grit her teeth to keep herself from snapping back. That wasn't how the military worked. They had orders to defend this critical intelligence lookout post. Their orders, and the lives at stake on Earth, did not allow for retreat. This man was not a soldier. He didn't operate on the same honor system as she and her people did. His loyalty was to his own people and his own profit.

And maybe... to Peter?

Well, there was an idea. Peter had been able to convince Yondu to turn over an entire raid's worth of supplies to the Resistance. Maybe, just maybe, he would have enough pull to convince them to stay, too.

"Well, I'm sorry you feel that way. I wish I had more to offer you. We owe you our lives, and we've appreciated having you here." Ko-Rel held out her hand for Yondu to shake. "Thank you for everything you've done for us."

Yondu met her gaze for a moment before taking her hand for a solid shake.

"Wish I could say it's been a pleasure doing business," he said.

"But this was neither business nor a pleasure, I get it," Ko-Rel said with a sigh. "Safe travels."

She spun on her heel and walked away before he could get another smart-ass word in... and before she could give in to the urge to punch that look right off his face. Peter had to be at the *Milano*, readying his precious ship for their next destination. Whether he was willing to make their case or not, Ko-Rel found herself wanting to say goodbye, see him one last time. Besides, she owed him thanks.

She walked among the parked M-ships as the Ravagers called back and forth to each other. Laughing, making bawdy jokes, already talking about their next score. Already moving on from the people they were leaving to die.

Everyone except Peter, that is. Ko-Rel caught sight of the blue and orange paint job of the *Milano* and spotted its captain under one of the wings, once again scrubbing at some bit of battle scarring. Discontent hung at the corner of his mouth, tugging it down even as other Ravagers tried to draw him into their banter. Peter ignored them all, picking up a bottle of solvent and tipping a bit onto a rag, then resuming his scrubbing, mouth hanging open in concentration.

"Quill," Ko-Rel said, announcing her presence.

Peter startled, dropping the rag into his open upturned mouth. He spat it out onto the ground, then spat a few more times for good measure.

"Augh, gross. Well, that stuff's probably poisonous, but what can you do?" He shrugged and shoved his hands in his pockets.

"You're awfully cavalier about possibly poisoning yourself to death," Ko-Rel said. She leaned up against the side of the ship and folded her arms, raising an eyebrow.

Peter crouched to retrieve the instrument of his potential death. The rag came flying at Ko-Rel's chest, and she snatched it out of the air. Even running on zero sleep, wartime reflexes didn't quit. She smirked, and Peter grinned right back and stood.

"Yeah, well, I've had worse."

He shoved the rag in his pocket and propped his hands on his hips, looking everywhere but at Ko-Rel. She sighed internally and chucked her last hesitation out the window.

"We'd be dead without you so, you know. Thank you for convincing Yondu to come here and give us the supplies."

Peter smiled almost bashfully and puffed out his chest. "Well, you know, I—"

Ko-Rel pushed on before Peter could get on too much of a roll.

"I just talked to Yondu. I tried to get him to halt his withdrawal of the Ravagers, but he shut me down with barely a thought. So you're leaving within the hour, right?"

Peter's mouth twisted unhappily. "Yeah. He just put out a call for us to 'wrap it up and say our goodbyes.' He wants us off the ground ASAP."

Ko-Rel folded her arms and studied Peter's body language. Everything about him showed glum reluctance. "You don't want to leave yet, though."

Peter shook his head. "No, of course not. We just got here!

We came to stop the infiltration, and we did that, sort of, but only halfway. Right? Because the Chitauri are still here. We didn't finish the job. No offense to you and your people, but I kinda still feel like Earth is going to get royally screwed by lizards."

"No offense taken," Ko-Rel said. "You're absolutely right. We sent word for reinforcements from the front, but all Rider could say is, 'We'll try. No promises.' I still haven't heard back."

She waited a beat for that to sink in, then made the ask. "I'm hoping *you* can talk to Yondu."

Peter shook his head and turned away, lolling his head back against the side of the *Milano*.

"He's not going to change his mind. That man is stubborn like you wouldn't believe. Especially about stuff like this."

"He listens to you, Peter," Ko-Rel said, insistent. "You're like his son. You have his ear in a way that none of the other Ravagers do, not even his second-in-command. I've known you all for barely a rotation and even I can see that. Please, at least try."

Peter opened his mouth to protest, hesitated, then snapped it shut.

"Fine. Fine, I'll try, but absolutely zero promises. Honestly, he'll probably laugh in my face. Like, big wave of stinking breath straight in my nose holes kind of laugh."

He gestured toward his nostrils with two fingers and wrinkled up his face.

"It's bad, Ko-Rel, I'm telling you. I have experienced it and lived to tell the tale, but I'll risk it. For you."

Ko-Rel rolled her eyes but couldn't help the small huff of laughter Peter drew out of her.

"Thanks, Peter. Truly. It is a noble sacrifice indeed."

Peter slapped the ramp controls to seal up the *Milano* and went to find Yondu. Ko-Rel followed, but at a distance. Yondu was near a long viewport overlooking the flat open area the Ravagers had been using as an overflow landing pad, deep in negotiations with the Resistance quartermaster. Probably arguing about how much fuel the Ravagers were taking with them, if she had to guess.

Peter inserted himself smoothly into the conversation, and Ko-Rel set up at the display panel nearby so she could overhear. She pulled up the most recent diagnostics for the base and grabbed one particular section, pulling it forward and zooming in. Something about the logs looked off, but in her exhausted state, it was little more than a jumble of letters and numbers. As soon as the quartermaster walked away from Yondu, he spotted her and came to unload his irritation, repeating every single thing Yondu had just said to him.

"Uh-huh," Ko-Rel said, watching Peter over his shoulder and trying to lip read. Eventually, the meaningless noise coming from the quartermaster stopped, and she looked down to find him watching her.

"Are you okay, Commander?" he asked.

She shook her head and forced a small smile. "Still haven't

slept. Sorry, Lieutenant, that was all brain static to me. Can we catch up in eight hours?"

She managed to usher the young officer along just in time for Yondu to lower his voice and step closer to Peter.

"Look, son," he said, putting a hand on Peter's shoulder. "I like you. And you know, I think it's pretty cute how you Terrans get all sentimental-like about things. But you been with us for two years now. You know our ways. And those ways don't include charity. You've pushed the line already, and I let it go, but I'm gonna say it again since y'all seem to have a hard time remembering. This. Ain't. Our. Fight. This isn't what we do. We don't take sides."

Yondu stepped back and looked away, out the long viewport that looked over the Mercurian landscape. Ko-Rel followed his gaze, watching as M-ships fired up their engines and ascended into the sky one by one, their engines glowing against the sky. Leaving Peter behind.

Peter balled up his fists at his sides and turned to look out at the departing ships, too. He lifted his right fist like he wanted to punch straight through the window, but instead just gently thumped it against the clear acrylic holding the Mercurian atmosphere at bay.

"Well, I'm staying," he said.

Ko-Rel suppressed a small gasp. Well, that wasn't the outcome she'd expected.

Yondu looked over at Ko-Rel, who didn't even pretend not to be listening now. She stared right back into Yondu's red eyes, daring him to step up, to summon some of the courage and purpose his protégé had found. A thoughtful look crossed Yondu's face, and he glanced back and forth between Ko-Rel and Peter for a silent moment. When he finally spoke, though, Ko-Rel's heart sank.

"Well, that's your choice to make, boy," Yondu said, shaking his head. "I hope you'll get your fill of this and get your head on straight quick, and you'll be welcome back with the Ravagers when you do. You remember, though, that we won't be in this fight. When you fly with us, it's as a Ravager, not as a Terran Resistance hero wannabe. Get me?"

"Got you," Peter said, refusing to meet Yondu's gaze.

A long, tense moment pulled taut between the two. Some kind of weight born of shared history swelled to fill the air between them, the severe awkwardness of two people definitively Not Talking About Something. Peter at least made an attempt.

"I don't understand, though," he said. "I really don't."

Yondu shrugged. "I don't expect you to, boy."

And that was that. Yondu clapped Peter on the shoulder affectionately and walked off, presumably to complete his own preparations for departure. Peter stood there and stared out the viewport for several more minutes. Regretting his decision, maybe? Changing his mind?

But a moment later, he turned and offered her a weak smile.

"Well, I tried. Like I said, Papa Smurf is stubborn to the max."

"At least he didn't give you the stink laugh," Ko-Rel said with a shrug.

Peter's smile turned genuine at that. "True. I dodged that bullet."

A quiet chime came over her comm, and Ko-Rel held up a finger to Peter while she answered.

"Yes?"

"We have an incoming communication from Richard Rider," Tasver said, his voice more full of energy and hope than it had been since before the crash. Ko-Rel's mouth broke into a grin, and her heart floated up into her throat. *Finally.* This was the break they needed. Maybe the Ravagers leaving wouldn't be the end of everything after all.

"I'll take it in my quarters in one minute," Ko-Rel said, waving for Peter to follow her as she jogged out into the hallway. Sure, she was supposed to be heading to bed, but sleep would have to wait just a little while longer.

Richard Rider, leader of the Resistance, was waiting on the line.

PRESENT DAY

MERCURY BASE – 7801

FOR a few long moments, the only sound was the ominous creaking of a recently crashed ship. Then, one by one, the Guardians sounded off.

"I am Groot?"

"Yeah," Rocket said with a groan. "I'm okay, buddy. Quill?"

Peter blinked a few times to clear his head and sat up with a groan.

"I'm alive. Ish." He turned to look behind where Gamora sat in the navigator's seat, holding her head in her hands. Beside her, Drax picked himself up off the floor with a grunt. "Any injuries?"

"Just my brain," Gamora said. "I'm assuming it's been damaged, since I'm still a member of this crew."

"No one is keeping you here, wench. You are free to leave," Drax said with a sidelong glare.

"Okay, okay, that's enough," Peter said. "No name calling."

Rocket laughed. "Oh, is that a new rule? Are we making you saaad, Quill? Are we too mean?"

"I mean, yeah, kinda," Peter muttered under his breath. He unbuckled from the pilot's seat and went to stand, then froze as a scuttling sound ticked from somewhere above him. A moment later, the same sound came again, a sharp tapping on the outer hull. Peter groaned internally. A space rat infestation was absolutely not necessary on top of everything else. Nothing that would keep them from getting into the base, but obnoxious, nonetheless. Rocket would probably try to bait him into a rat-shooting contest or something.

"I'm gonna go check that out," Peter said, standing and stretching out the post-crash aches. "Rocket, how's the *Milano*?"

"Should have power back in a minute," he said from up underneath the co-pilot's console, nothing visible but his feet. "Doesn't look like the engines were damaged. No hull breach. We were damn lucky, Quill. You break this ship, I'm gonna have to find something else of yours to hold as collateral."

"I never agreed to that," Peter called back as he made his way off the flight deck and toward the aft airlock. How long had it been since he'd first run into Rocket and Groot—months, definitely. Almost a year? Either way, long enough that he thought they were past the whole issue of the bounty. What, was he supposed to be grateful for the rest of his life that Rocket and Groot didn't turn him in on Malador? They wouldn't have caught him at all if they hadn't been, you know, a talking tree and a raccoon with a gun pointed at his crotch. Anyone would have laughed under those circumstances. And okay, so he hadn't exactly delivered on his promise to pay them double Yondu's bounty yet, but this Guardians of the Galaxy thing would earn out eventually. Right?

Peter stumbled down the ramp of the *Milano*, reaching up to tap the control behind his ear. His helmet reformed over his face, the red eyes glowing as they powered up, allowing him to see in the faint lighting of the landing bay.

And he immediately wished he couldn't.

The room was filled with creeping, crawling... somethings. On the walls, on the ceiling, clinging to the support pillars... and perched atop the *Milano*'s wings.

"Ahhh!" he shouted, tripping backward into Groot, who steadied him with a quick hand on his shoulder.

From somewhere behind him, the sound of a large gun being cocked echoed through the space. "What the hell are those things?"

"I am Groot?" Groot asked.

"I don't know if 'bug' is really the right word," Rocket said, squinting into the low light, which his enhanced eyes let him see through much better. "They kind of look like—"

With a horrific *SCREEEEEE*, one of the creatures flew through the air straight at Peter's face.

"Agh!"

He leapt off the *Milano*'s ramp and brought one of his guns up, firing two energy blasts in quick succession. The creature fell to the ground, smoking and crackling in a deeply unpleasant way, and a grossed-out shiver ran down Peter's spine. He nudged the crispy creature with the toe of one boot, his lip curling in disgust.

Then the room came alive with that horrific screeching, and all of the creatures that had been peacefully resting on the walls rushed toward the *Milano* in a cloud of skittering legs and screeching mandibled mouths.

"Flark!" Rocket shouted, leaping up to Groot's shoulder as he took aim at the first wave of the creatures. His gun made a threatening whine as it charged up, then released a massive missile that blew a pocket of the creatures to bits. The screeching got *angrier*.

"I shall break their bones!" Drax shouted, charging into the fray. He grabbed one creature in each hand, squeezed until Peter heard a CRUNCH, then threw the carcasses at two more, knocking them clear across the room. Gamora drew her blades and seemed to slip into the shadows. You'd never know she was there... except for the corpses that fell to the deck as she darted through the swarm, blades flashing.

"I am Groot!" Groot said, his voice urgent as he punched the ground, his branches re-emerging as vicious spears, piercing a dozen of the creatures at once. "I am Groot, I am *Groot*!"

"What is it?" Peter called, looking to Rocket for a translation.

"Yes, I saw your spikes, Groot, very cool, but now isn't really the time for—" Rocket cut off, tossing a grenade into a cluster of creatures. "—warm fuzzy positive reinforcement."

"No, Rocket," Gamora shouted over the screeching. "Spikes! These things are called spikes."

Peter ducked under a tangle of three critters—who, on second glance, did have a wicked looking spike protruding from their center—then turned and fired three quick shots after them.

"So, what exactly does that mean? What's a spike?" he called out.

The sharp metallic sound of blade on carapace rang out, followed by Gamora's voice loud and clear. "Do *not* let them sting you!"

"They would not dare sting me," Drax roared, leaping into the air with both blades out. "My flesh is mighty and virile!"

Drax's delighted cackle rang out over the screech of the spikes, going on for a good twenty ticks straight.

One might not think an awkward silence could occur in the middle of a frantic battle against a swarm of space spiders with death spike boners.

One would be incorrect.

Thankfully, Rocket came to the team's rescue.

"I'll bet you fifty units I can off more of these things than you, Quill," Rocket said.

"Fifty units?" Peter asked. "Make it a hundred and you're on!"

"Units of *money*, Quill," Rocket clarified, then cackled maniacally as he peppered an entire half of the room with energy bolts, if not with accuracy, then at least with enthusiasm. Spikes fell by the dozen.

"Sixty-seven, ha! Eat it, Quill!"

"How could you *possibly* know how many that was?" Peter protested. "The count is rigged!"

"Guess we'll need to come up with a way to keep score," Rocket said with a tone Peter absolutely did not like.

"Whatever you're planning, Rocket—" Peter ducked as a spike flew at his face, then blasted it. "I'm counting the ones I've already killed, too!"

"Sure, Star-Loser, no problem. You'll need the help."

"Aaaaagh," Peter groaned, resisting the urge to take aim at Rocket instead of the spikes. He spun around and shot off a few random bolts to release some annoyance, then took a breath.

"Okay, Star-Lord," he said to himself. "Be a grownup. Focus on the mission. Keep everyone alive."

The shockwave from a small explosion buffeted the back of his head.

"That's ninety for me! How you doing there, Quill?"

"Oh, bite me, you little weasel," Peter grumbled. He flicked a switch on the sides of his guns and leapt into the air, hovering above the fray on his jet boots. "Suck on this, assholes!"

He squeezed the triggers, and his guns spat a burst of automatic fire that ate through a swath of spikes. Immensely satisfying.

"That's... thirty-four! I think! I'll catch up," he said with false bravado.

Then he felt a pinch in his right calf. A pinch... then a white-hot pain pouring through his entire right side.

"What thaaaaa—"

Peter trailed off as the side of his face sagged, like that time he'd gone to the dentist as a kid and gotten novocained all to hell. Then his right arm raised without his permission and aimed his gun at Groot.

"No!"

He let his left leg buckle, dropping him to the side and sending the shot wild. It didn't help for long, though. As Peter looked on in horror, his right arm grew a spur from his wrist, one that looked just like those the creatures had sticking out of their centers. Inside, it felt like those spurs were moving through his veins, crawling through his body, slowly taking control of his limbs one at a time. More spurs stretched his flesh at the elbow, knee, shoulder...

He staggered, managing one shuffling step forward.

"Gaaa-raaaah!" he called. "Gaaaaa—ugh!"

"Peter!" Gamora shouted. She appeared at his side just as he fell to one knee, her blade arcing toward him. Peter's eyes widened in horror, but the thing controlling him did what Normal Peter would never have been able to do—it dodged Gamora's blow.

"Orrr-eeeee," he managed from the one corner of his mouth still under his control, even as the spike's domination over his body solidified, forcing him into a surprisingly coordinated backward walk. Gamora ignored his apology, her eyes narrowing at the spike attached to his leg as she swung her blade to her left and right, cutting down the spikes that took her focus for distraction.

Peter's arms lifted, raising his guns toward her and thumbing the autofire switch. His mouth was fully out of his control now, so all he could do was scream deep in his throat, completely inaudible over the cacophony echoing through the landing bay. Peter wanted to scream for real, wanted to wrench his arm away, wanted to squeeze his eyes shut so at least he wouldn't have to *see*. But the spike's control was complete. And it was squeezing the trigger. Gamora glanced up, meeting his eyes for the briefest tick, her expression regretful.

Then, in a blink, she darted forward with her blade thrust straight out, straight for Peter.

Peter mentally braced himself for pain, for oblivion... and the pain came roaring up his leg, sure enough, as the spike fell off, Gamora's sword piercing its horrific little body.

Peter's legs went out from under him, and his knees hit the ground hard. His lungs *ached*, and his veins felt like... well, like they'd been filled with scraping spiked branches. Gamora stood at his side, guarding his back while he took a minute to get his breath back, then got to his feet with a groan.

"Don't let them sting you... got it," Peter wheezed.

Gamora gave him the side-eye, then darted away, blade flashing.

Right.

It was all mop-up duty from there. Drax and Gamora

sliced and diced, Rocket blasted, Groot smashed, and Peter...
well, he helped. A little.

Rocket won the bet.

Whatever.

When all was said and done, Peter limped toward the far
side of the landing bay, tuning out Rocket's gleeful crowing and
Drax's disturbingly sexual post-battle poetry. He kicked spike
carcasses aside as he made his way toward a partially hidden side
entrance to the main part of the base complex. A support beam
had partially fallen over a portion of it, but the red lettering
across the door could still be deciphered: *INFIRMARY.*

"Come on. In here. I know the way to the command center."

Rocket looked Peter over with disdain, holstering his gun
on his back and folding his arms.

"Do you, Quill? Do you really? Because I feel like we've
been doing an awful lot of stumbling around, losing money,
and almost dying on your watch lately."

"Hey, I'm the one who did the almost dying just now,
thanks!" Peter protested.

Rocket sneered. "Yeah, I'm not so sure that's the defense
you're looking for. You're supposed to be the leader of this
little outfit, but it sure seems like we've been the ones carrying
you. I let you use my ship—"

"*My* ship," Peter corrected automatically.

"—for this whole Guardians of the Galaxy outfit... but
I'm gonna be honest with you, *Star-Lord.* It ain't workin' out
so well."

"I am Groot."

Rocket threw his hands in the air. "I dunno, Groot, from where I'm sitting, it kinda *does* seem like his fault."

"I *am* Groot."

"He may not have put the spikes here, but we would have had a more controlled landing had we not had to gun our way in while dodging fire. But noooo, Star-Munch had to pull a scam on his old war buddy and piss her off. That *was* his fault."

Drax grunted an agreement.

"The protein paste was most definitely his fault," he said.

Peter groaned in frustration. "Are you going to hold that over my head forever?"

"It was disgusting," Drax said with intense sincerity.

Gamora glanced over at Peter with an unreadable look on her face. Then, without saying a word, she turned away.

And somehow that was the deepest cut of them all.

Peter turned and hauled the infirmary door open without speaking a word in his own defense.

13

INTERLUDE: 12 YEARS AGO

MERCURY BASE – 7789

KO-REL practically teleported across the room to her display as soon as she reached her quarters. Maybe it was the delirium-inducing lack of sleep, but she didn't care if she came across as too desperate. If by any chance Rider hadn't made up his mind about reinforcements, maybe her slightly unhinged appearance would work in their favor. She gestured for Peter to lean against the wall by the door, out of sight, then activated the display with a wave of her hand and accepted the call.

Richard Rider appeared on the display looking exactly as he had when she'd last seen him. In reality, it had been barely three rotations ago. Those three rotations, though, had felt like cycles. He was still wearing his Nova Corps Centurion uniform, as always, even though the Nova Corps was no more. They were completely wiped out at the beginning of the war, when the Chitauri made their opening gambit: a surprise attack against the planet Xandar. Rider, the only surviving Centurion, had teamed up with the Xandarian Worldmind to form the Resistance, and Ko-Rel had them to thank for the purpose that had driven her since losing her family. She was grateful to Rider, and she admired him.

She was also more than a little annoyed with him at the moment.

Rider ran a hand through his sandy brown hair and sighed, his pale skin washed even paler with exhaustion. Ko-Rel could relate.

"Ko-Rel. My apologies for the delay getting back to you. I've read your report."

He sighed again, holding a hand to his chest. "Condolences for the losses. I never imagined you would be hit so hard so soon upon arrival."

"Thank you," she said, keeping her voice even, though everything in her screamed *get to the point!*

"Has the situation changed at all since your last update?" he asked.

Off screen, Peter threw his hands into the air and turned to silently thunk his head against the wall. Ko-Rel bunched her hands into fists out of view of the display and calmly relayed the facts. The counterattack. The Ravagers' decision to leave. The situation had definitely changed—for the worse.

Rider nodded thoughtfully and tapped one thumb to his lower lip.

"I'm sorry to hear that. It's even worse than I knew. The

good news is from what we know of the Chitauri's tactics and movements, it does seem like no larger force is incoming. The enemy currently on Mercury are likely the only ones you'll face."

Ko-Rel's breath stilled, and she cut her gaze over to Peter, whose eyes had gone wide. She almost didn't want to ask, but this talking around the issue wasn't working.

"That's good to hear," she said. "Then once we receive your reinforcements, we should be able to retake the planet in its entirety."

Rider pursed his lips and, his expression grave, shook his head.

"Ko-Rel, I'm sorry," he said. "We won't be able to spare any reinforcements right now. We just began an operation to drive the Chitauri out of the Krylorian home system and our forces are stretched thin. I'm hoping we'll be able to send a small unit in two cycles—"

"Two cycles?" Ko-Rel cried. "Rider, we'll all be dead in two *rotations*!"

"You won't," Rider said. "Hold the base. You don't need to retake the rest of the planet yet. Just focus on holding the line. If we abandon Mercury altogether, the Chitauri will see it as an admission of weakness. Even if Earth isn't in their plans right now, they'll see the opportunity and jump on it. We can't take that risk. We have to show them that we plan to maintain a presence on Mercury."

Ko-Rel's mouth hung open as her exhausted brain cast about for something, anything to say in reply to *that*. Peter covered his face with both hands and tipped his head back against the wall in a silent groan. He was probably regretting his decision to stay, probably trying to find the words to tell her this was a lost cause and he wasn't available for lost causes.

"Sir, please," she tried, one last desperate time. "We barely have enough survivors to operate the base. My people are dealing with a lot from the last two attacks, and if I'm completely honest, some are probably not mentally fit to serve right now. They need time and counseling."

Ko-Rel herself definitely needed some time and counseling, but she left that part out. Rider winced, and the pain on his face was completely real. His pain meant nothing unless he backed it up with action, though.

"I'm sorry," he said again. "I truly am. As soon as there are available personnel, I'll send a unit your way. I would plan to operate as you are, though. Adjust your tactics to the situation and hold until we can provide more support."

Ko-Rel heard the words from a distance, like she was outside of herself, watching from the far corner of the room as her body stood in the light of the display screen, receiving these words. The blue and gold of Richard Rider's Centurion uniform cast a faint glow over her skin, and she curled in on herself slightly, shoulders sagging forward, eyes squeezed closed against the pain. It was not the look of a commanding officer at the head of a critical warfront. It was the look of a woman beaten, grieving, helpless to protect her people.

And yet, protecting her people was her duty. She would do it to the last.

She forced steel into her spine. Lifted her gaze, mastered

the hot pressure behind her eyes, and looked Rider straight in the face.

"We'll hold," she said. "But my people need support as soon as you can make it happen."

"And you'll get it," he agreed.

There was a long beat of silence.

"Well, I should go tell my officers the news," Ko-Rel said. Rider nodded, his mouth pressed into a thin line. Her chest felt like there was a mini war going on inside it right along with the real one. The part of her that wanted to be a good soldier fighting for the right things was winning out over the part that fantasized about pushing Rider out of an airlock... but only just.

He was doing his duty. Making the hard call. Now it was her duty to carry it out. She couldn't hold it against him.

Much.

She closed out the call and shut down the display, then just... stood there for a long moment. It was Peter who finally broke the silence.

"He wants you to just turtle up and try not to die, and that is some major bull scut," Peter spat. "We hate Richard Rider."

Ko-Rel wasn't sure what "turtling" or "bulls" were, but she agreed with the general sentiment.

"We don't hate *Commander* Rider," Ko-Rel said, despite having some hatred-adjacent feelings at the moment. "But we *are* going to have to come up with a new plan."

Ko-Rel sat down on the bed for a moment, then almost immediately got right back up. The allure of sleep was far too strong, and she was in danger of passing out on her face at any moment. Instead, she motioned for Peter to follow her out into the hallway. She made a quick call over the comm to get the intelligence officers and other senior staff to the command hub, then glanced over at Peter.

"I know this changes things," she said. "You don't have to stay."

"Hey now, I said I would stay, so I'm staying," Peter said. "Besides, if I go back to Papa Smurf now, he'll be insufferable."

"I don't suppose he'd change his mind about leaving if he knew our reinforcements were never coming?"

Peter barked a harsh laugh. "Honestly, I think it might make him leave faster."

Yeah, that was probably accurate.

"Well, I have to go deliver the news. You coming along?"

Peter gave her a bolstering smile. "I'm with you, boss."

When they arrived in the command hub, Adomox, Tasver, and Captain Lar-Ka all stood and saluted, looking at her expectantly. Surprisingly, Suki Yumiko sat at her station, eyes bloodshot and puffy from crying, but attention laser-focused on her display. Her wound had been bandaged, but she still looked in no shape to be on duty.

Ko-Rel caught Lar-Ka's eye and nodded at Yumiko with a questioning expression, but he shook his head in a "don't ask" kind of way. She eyed the woman skeptically, but moved on to the business at hand. She gestured for them all to sit, then propped one hip against the main console at the center of the room and folded her arms.

"We just got word from Rider," she said.

Lar-Ka brightened. "And? How many people are they sending? When will they be here?"

Ko-Rel's mouth hardened. She hated having to say it, but there was no use in softening reality.

"They won't be," she said. "They aren't sending anyone. We're all that's left."

Ko-Rel took in a slow breath and blew it out, trying her best to maintain her cool, for the sake of morale.

"Our orders are to hold the line," she said. "And so that's what we'll do. Protect this base. This system is still strategically important—"

"Important to *Rider*," Yumiko spat, standing up so fast her chair tipped backward. "I'm from Earth too, but you don't see me making it a priority over the lives of everyone else."

Tasver nodded along with every word, his expression darkening. He was Terran, too, Ko-Rel thought. Adomox stared at the far wall with a blank expression, not even appearing to hear the conversation around her. As a Xandarian who had already lost her home, she probably had some complicated feelings herself.

"Believe me, I'm frustrated too. We've been through a lot, and we need the help. They'll send it as soon as they're able. But Commander Rider is correct—this posting is critical to keeping the Chitauri from an easy expansion into yet another system."

Ko-Rel's eyes slid over to the station that had been destroyed in the earlier attack. The display projector had a giant hole burned through it, and the chair had enough sharp-edged debris piled on it to turn it into a decent improvised weapon. That maintenance shaft had been a big oversight, and it underscored one of their big problems—they didn't know nearly enough about their new base of operations. They needed to get the lay of the land.

"Chief engineer to the command hub," she said into the comm, then turned back to the rest of the room. "So. We're here. This is the mission. I need ideas. What assets do we have? What strategies might work for us?"

Silence reigned for a long moment. Tasver made a rude "Tch!" sort of sound and turned back to his comm station. Suki clenched and unclenched her fists, so hard Ko-Rel was worried she'd draw blood. Adomox continued her blank staring, nothing to contribute.

A young Kree woman entered the hub at a jog, then stood at attention and saluted Ko-Rel and Lar-Ka.

"Engineer Ten-Cor reporting, ma'am. The chief engineer is sleeping off his injuries, so I thought I'd see if I could fill in."

Ko-Rel nodded. "That's fine. I need you to coordinate with the other engineers to start learning this base top to bottom. I want to know every security system it has, every storage closet, every offensive and defensive feature, and every potential liability. I want you and your people to become experts."

Ten-Cor nodded. "Yes, ma'am. We've already discovered a few interesting things. It looks like there used to be some super soldier field test units stationed here, but they must have been killed in the initial infiltration attack like everyone else. There's a whole lab devoted to them. We'll work on access points next to look for liabilities. Anything else?"

"That's all. Thank you, Ten-Cor."

The engineer saluted again. "On it, ma'am!"

As she trotted away, Lar-Ka cleared his throat. "Back to the matter at hand. Is Rider expecting us to carry out an offensive? Because I can tell you, we don't have the personnel left for any kind of operation at-scale."

Ko-Rel shook her head, though what Rider *actually* wanted wasn't much better. "No. He wants us to hide out here and just hold the base and be a presence on the planet. I don't think he cares if we *do* anything so long as we stay."

Lar-Ka huffed an exasperated sigh and paced the length of the room.

"That doesn't sit right with me either, though I know I *just* said we couldn't go on the offensive. They're going to strike back at us again, though, and this base can only afford so much protection. Eventually, they're going to get through."

"So we strike back *small*," Peter said.

Silence followed. Ko-Rel chewed the inside of her lip in embarrassment, wondering what she'd been thinking, bringing along a civilian to a meeting like this.

"Peter, as Lar-Ka said, we're already dangerously low on personnel as it is. We don't have enough people to mount an attack when we don't even know what's waiting for us over there."

Peter held up a hand in acknowledgment.

"I know, but I'm talking guerrilla warfare, just like they're doing to us," Peter said. "Look, I'm no general or whatever, and maybe I have no idea what I'm talking about. But it seems like they aren't coming at us head on, for the most part, right?"

"He's right, actually," Lar-Ka said, pointing at Peter with a thoughtful expression. "This is the direction my brain's been going as well. They infiltrate. They hit hard and fast and retreat as soon as we start to mobilize. I've been wondering, actually, how many Chitauri there really are on the planet with us."

Adomox spoke up for the first time, turning to her station and pulling up a collection of video clips on her display. "We've been trying to figure that out. We've pieced together security footage from the original infiltration attack and determined there were no more than thirty individual Chitauri involved, though we have no way of knowing if there are more elsewhere who didn't participate in the attack."

Tasver stayed silent through the whole exchange. Ko-Rel met his gaze to see if he had anything to add, but he only stared back silently. Maybe a prompt would help?

"Officer Tasver, anything on the comms front that might help us evaluate the enemy's presence on the planet?"

"No, ma'am," he said, voice flat. "We already know where they are. Beyond that, what can comms tell us?"

Bad sign. Tasver was clearly burned out and struggling to cope after his injuries.

"We don't *know* where they are," Lar-Ka corrected, frowning. "We *assume* they're holed up in the forward listening stations. They could be hiding out elsewhere, though, or have erected some temporary shelter we've not noticed."

"Well then, it seems that's our first task," Ko-Rel said, a plan solidifying in her mind. "If we're going to strike the enemy, we have to *find* the enemy."

"Scouts to the forward posts?" Lar-Ka asked.

Ko-Rel nodded. "Do we have enough rested troops to fill a squad?"

"I'll go," Peter offered, and everyone turned to stare at him. Peter blinked and looked to Ko-Rel. "What? Should I not? Is that not how this works?"

"Field personnel is Captain Lar-Ka's purview," Ko-Rel said. "I defer to his judgment."

Lar-Ka gave Peter a long, thoughtful once-over, no doubt sifting through personnel records in his head and making up his mind about Peter's capabilities. He was an unknown quantity, for the most part. He'd shown courage and principle in convincing the Ravagers to aid the Resistance and deciding to stay behind, but that didn't make him a good combatant in the field. They didn't have a whole lot of choice at the moment, though.

"Fine. But only because I have too many people who haven't gotten enough sleep to be effective in the field," Lar-Ka said with a significant look at Ko-Rel. "We'll see how you do. I'll pair you with my second-in-command and you are to listen to every word she says without question. Understood?"

"Yeah, yeah, I got it," Peter said, blinking. He had no idea what he was getting into. He'd offered to stay and help, though, so…

Lar-Ka nodded. "I'll call a briefing in one hour, and you'll move out immediately after. Go see the quartermaster and get fitted for some armor."

"Sir, yes, sir!" Peter said with some kind of Earth salute.

"Good luck, then," Ko-Rel said. "I'm going to finally get some sleep, and I suggest you all do the same."

She looked over Adomox, Suki, and Tasver, making sure to lock eyes with each one. What a sorry, beaten lot they all were.

But then there was Peter. Bright, eager, ready to fight alongside them, and sparking the ideas that might actually be key to their survival. Maybe his energy would prove infectious, if they all lived long enough for it to propagate.

"Work out a watch schedule between the three of you. If you aren't on watch, I want you in your bunk asleep. It's going to take everything we've got to survive this, and I need you all at your best," she ordered. "And this goes without saying, but considering the state of things, operational security is paramount. I want radio silence outside of this base. No outside communications. Lock it down, Officer Tasver."

"Yes, Commander," all three murmured in response.

Ko-Rel turned to Lar-Ka and saluted. "Be safe, and good luck. Wake me when you return and report."

"Will do, Commander," Lar-Ka said, but a slight smile in the corner of his mouth betrayed him.

"You are lying to my face, Captain," she said, her own smile breaking through. "I mean it. Wake. Me. Up." She pointed at Peter. "Make sure he does, Quill."

"Yes, ma'am!" he said, doing his Earth salute again.

Lar-Ka rolled his eyes, but nodded. "Expect that report in about eight hours."

"Bring back good news, Captain. We need it." Ko-Rel clapped Lar-Ka on the shoulder and squeezed. "And come back in one piece. I don't need your wife coming down here to destroy me because I didn't keep you safe."

"Ah, she's not that scary. She's a tough woman, but the gentlest soul I know."

Ko-Rel gave him the side-eye. "If you say so. Professional athletes scare me more than soldiers anytime."

"I'll tell her you said so, ma'am," he said with a salute.

With that, she returned Lar-Ka's salute and left the five of them to finish their planning. It was up to them, now.

For her, duty called.

And duty was the name of her pillow.

PRESENT DAY

MERCURY BASE – 7801

THE infirmary was, if possible, even more stark and white than it had been twelve years before. Back then, it'd had the slightly off-polish look of frequent use. Now, it was dusty, but otherwise pristine. Not a speck of blood in sight. They paused just long enough for Peter to slap a patch onto the piercing wound in his calf, which numbed the pain and began knitting the flesh back together almost immediately. Ahh, Kree medical technology. Had to love it.

As Peter rolled his trousers back down over the wound, he snuck a glance around the room at the rest of the team. They were definitely pissed at him in a big way, and he just didn't get it. Yeah, the spikes had been annoying for them, but none of them had gotten taken over by one of the little bastards. He was the one suffering the consequences. They were all safe.

The mission could continue. The payday was still coming. They were all being totally unreasonable.

Especially Rocket. Rocket, who had been aboard the *Milano* the longest (though it was still Peter's flarking ship, thank you very much. Rocket liked to *think* it was his, but that was not at all how it worked). He'd thought Rocket was finally buying into the Guardians of the Galaxy thing, with the suits and all, but it seemed like nothing would ever really get him on board. None of them would just... believe.

Ah well. Nothing he could do about it but get this job done, get the payday, and hope that would be enough for them to stay on board for just a little while longer. It would work. Eventually, the heroes for hire thing would catch on, and they'd all see the benefit.

A light touch on his shoulder made him jump, but when he turned, it was only Groot smiling peacefully down at him. The others all had their backs turned, but Groot held out one hand and grew a tiny sapling. It was nothing more than a twig with a pair of leaves, but he picked it off his palm and handed it to Peter, then turned and lumbered away.

Well. Maybe there was at least one person in his corner after all. And if he was going to win over the rest, he had to step up and get this job done.

Peter yanked down the hem of his trouser leg and stood straight, looking over the others.

"Okay," he said, getting their attention. "Once we go through that door, we'll probably start encountering security systems almost immediately. We should be ready."

"What kind of security should we expect?" Gamora asked, because of course she did. Peter thought about faking it for half a tick, but sighed instead and went with the truth that would get him in trouble.

"I have no idea. Obviously, I was with the Resistance when I was here, and the Chitauri who infiltrated this base were shapeshifters, so they never tripped any alarms. The engineers were only just starting to understand what was here when I left."

Rocket climbed up onto a gurney to stare Peter in the face at eye level. "What exactly *do* you know about this place? Do you remember *anything* useful?"

Peter had a brief flash of blue Kree skin and stiff military issue bedsheets… which was extremely *not* useful. He cleared his throat and looked at the ceiling. He'd been barely twenty, only two years out of Chitauri prison, still seeing everything in the galaxy for the first time, stretching his legs, exploring… things…

Yeah, now that he thought about it, twelve years was a very long time ago and he hadn't been paying great attention at the time to begin with.

"I definitely remember the engineers talking about weird robots. We can expect drones and droids." Peter lifted his chin, trying to project some confidence. "I can get us to the command center from here. I remember there being some kind of computer issue… like, the computers in the infirmary here aren't connected to everything else, maybe?"

Gamora nodded. "Standard practice. Keep the medical

systems isolated in case the rest of the base is compromised."

"Get me to another terminal, then, and I can get us some real information," Rocket said, leaping off the gurney and scrambling up to his harness on Groot's back. "Let's get moving. The sooner we start, the sooner we can be done with this."

"And the sooner we can get paid our hundred thousand units," Peter added before he could stop himself.

"Tch, right," Rocket said. "We'll see."

Peter sighed. "Come on."

He waved a hand in front of the door control, the door swished open—then he leapt back and ducked as a genderless, distorted voice boomed out from nowhere.

"Hello, Star-Lord," the voice said. "So nice to see you again. You really shouldn't have come. But since you're here, let's have some fun, shall we?"

From somewhere deep within the complex, a whirring started up, followed by several ominous thuds.

"Can't have you slowing me down. I'll be watching," the voice said.

In the silence that followed, four pairs of eyes turned on Peter.

"Don't look at me like that," Peter said, holding his hands up in protest. "We all knew there was someone here who wasn't supposed to be, *and* that there would be security and traps of some kind. This is not a surprise and you all can't be mad."

"We can be whatever we want," Gamora said. "Do you recognize the voice?"

"What? No. How could I possibly recognize it?"

"They greeted you by your silly fake title," Drax pointed out. "And said it was nice to see you *again*, which is clearly a lie, but also means they've seen you before."

Peter nodded. "You're right. And if you'll give me a tick to think back over the entire thirty-three-ish years I've been alive, I bet I can pinpoint exactly which old acquaintance has decided to take over a random abandoned intelligence monitoring station on a tiny planet in my home solar system I haven't been to in over twelve years, because there's definitely no chance that this person is just, you know, *lying to mess with us*. No one *ever* does *that*."

"If they do, it's usually your fault," Rocket quipped, and Peter shot him a dirty look.

"Whatever, man," he said, walking out the open infirmary door.

He promptly fell into a pit. It was only the fact that he remembered his jet boots about twelve inches from the bottom that made the landing merely awkward and painful, rather than bone-breaking and possibly deadly.

Drax's laughter echoed down from above, soon joined by Rocket. Gamora didn't laugh, but she didn't need to.

"Hey, Peter," she said. "I don't know if you remember, but on that Hark Taphod mission with all the security systems, we all got dumped into—"

Peter scowled. "Yes, I remember the bunker, Gamora, but thank you *so* much for the *reminder*."

"Are you sure?" she asked sweetly. "Because it would be

so tragic for you to miss out on the irony of this situation. I just want you to enjoy this moment as much as I am."

Honestly, it was like this rotation was designed as a greatest hits reel of their worst moments as a team. It was entirely possible that, once all this was over, even 100,000 units wouldn't be enough to keep the team together. Peter wouldn't even blame them at that point.

With a sigh, he activated his jet boots again and lifted himself out of the pit. At least it was just an empty shaft and not a pit of snakes, or filled with lava, or covered in spikes. Or infested with the other kind of spikes. As far as traps went, it was pretty harmless. If things stayed this tame, maybe they'd be able to wrap this up quickly and he could find them another well-paying job before everyone decided he was more trouble than he was worth.

There was still a chance, however minute, that they could come back from this. They just had to focus and get this job done.

When he popped out of the pit, the others were already halfway down the hall, standing before a door.

"In here," Rocket was saying, staring down at a device in his furry little hands. "There should be an access point for the security systems that we can—"

It wasn't until the door to the lab had already slid open that Peter saw the nameplate next to it, the one Rocket had been too short to read:

The Halfworld Project — Rak-Mar Labs.

"No, Rocket, wait—"

Too late.

"Oh, I am *absolutely* going to blow this place up," Rocket said, standing stock still in the doorway. "And I'm starting right now."

INTERLUDE: 12 YEARS AGO

MERCURY BASE – 7789

IT was supposed to be a reconnaissance mission. No enemy contact. Not even within striking distance of the forward outposts. Just a handful of troops gathering some intel out in the field, having a look around.

Then the call had come in, wrenching Ko-Rel out of a deep sleep: all medical staff report to the infirmary. Casualties incoming.

Now: Ko-Rel felt the man's blood seeping through the thin shirt she'd worn to bed, foolishly thinking she'd finally be able to get a full six hours. The operation had launched just a few hours ago, and the team wasn't due to report in for another five. Some rest had seemed in order.

Then the team came back early. Very early. Bleeding, broken, and missing one member of their six-person unit.

Someone had screwed up, and Ko-Rel had a sinking suspicion it was her.

The human in her arms gave a pained groan as she shouldered past the orderly who held the infirmary door open. She winced and readjusted her grip, trying to take some of the pressure off the injured man's bleeding shoulder, but when she looked down… no, it was clearly no use. The shoulder was a mangled mess of burn and shrapnel, and she knew all too well the pain that came with a wound like that. Ko-Rel had started her career as an assistant medical officer aboard a battle cruiser patrolling the edge of Kree space, right before the start of the war. She'd seen plenty of these injuries in those rotations just before the war came to the Kree.

(She would absolutely not think about the deepest loves of her life with such blackened, marred wounds on the hour of Hala's fall, when they whisked her heart away into the void along with their own lives, cut brutally short.)

Too much. Sleep had brought her guard down, let too much of the old pain in. She needed to focus, but her head was a mess.

Back at the beginning of the war, after her cruiser had been damaged and crash-landed on Drez-Lar, it had seemed like rotations, cycles, endless ticks filled with blood and sickness. She'd done her best to keep the crash survivors organized and alive. She'd done her best.

It hadn't been enough. One thousand, eight hundred and sixty-five had died in the crash, but those deaths she couldn't prevent. It was the thirty-three lives lost afterward that would always follow her every step. Her responsibility. Just like these people right now, injured, dying, dead on a mission of her own design.

She laid her patient down on a gurney just as Peter Quill came stumbling through the door, bearing another wounded operative. He had the woman's arm slung over his shoulder as he kept her weight off her bloody mess of a left leg, though she barely seemed to notice he was there. Shock. She called for a nurse, instinctually dropping into triage mode as she coordinated the arrival of the rest of the team. All told, only Peter was relatively unscathed, probably because the troops had treated him like a civilian. The rest of the team would be down recovering from their wounds for weeks.

It was a blow they really couldn't afford. There were so few of them already.

Once the entire unit had been unloaded from their blackened shuttle and prioritized for care, time shifted from an aching drag of horror-filled minutes to the sort of timeless flow of emergency medical work. The medical staff were talented and efficient, but Ko-Rel stayed all the same, lending help where her training could be of use and freeing up more experienced staff to deal with the worst of the injuries. To her surprise, she looked up some ticks-minutes-hours later to find Peter Quill still there as well. She flagged him down as he flitted back and forth to the supply closet.

"You okay?" she asked. The question felt asinine, but she wanted to check in, and her brain couldn't come up with anything better. Peter summoned a smile that would have been far beyond her in his situation.

"I'm fine. Been through much worse. The others wouldn't even let me fight, just shoved me down and fired over my head."

The rest went unspoken, but guilt hung on every word, emphasized by the smears of dried blood on his forehead and cheekbones. He held up his handfuls of supplies and nodded at one of the doctors.

"Catch up with you in a bit?"

She nodded and watched him go. He'd been drafted as an amateur aide, fetching wound patches and scanners and whatever else was needed, and making quiet conversation with the least injured patients in between. He seemed to feel her eyes on him, because he looked up and flashed her a tired half-smile. She didn't have anything left to give in return. At that, Peter patted the shoulder of the Xandarian man he'd been speaking with and took his leave, weaving his way between the occupied beds toward her. He stopped by her side and put his hands in his pockets, cocking his head at her.

"You look pretty wiped," he said. "Take a break?"

"Such a charmer," Ko-Rel said wearily, with no real push behind it.

Peter summoned up a grin. "Hey, look, if I were charming you, you'd know. Right now, all I'm trying to get you to do is sit down. You seem like you could use a nap."

"I tried the nap. What I could use is a drink," Ko-Rel corrected, lifting a hand to wipe away the sweat about to drip into her eye... then catching herself before she could smear someone's blood all over her eyebrow. Ugh.

"Hey, that can be arranged, too. I've got a bottle in my quarters. Wanna come over to my place?" he asked, doing some funny eyebrow waggle. She quirked a small smile.

"My quarters are nicer."

They walked together, and she let him fill her silence with energetic chatter. Somehow his brightness hadn't been completely dulled by the evening spent witnessing the horrors of a combat action gone wrong, then helping to patch up the wounded. If she didn't know better, she'd think him callous, or oblivious. Lacking empathy.

She didn't think that was it, though. She didn't know *what* to make of Peter Quill.

They grabbed the bottle from Peter's room (something called "wild turkey" from Earth that he'd found on the black market somewhere), along with a handful of what he called "action figures." They were little recreations of creatures both human and non, none taller than her hand. Peter said they'd come in handy later... somehow. Until then, all they seemed to be good for was getting Peter to make funny voices.

"Mmm, stay and help you I will," he said in a strange high-pitched gravelly voice, waggling a small green figurine as they arrived at her quarters. Once inside, he took up a different one with lots of fluffy hair and a jacket identical to the one Peter wore everywhere. It even said Star-Lord on the back, just like his.

"Tonight we ride straight into the fire," he sang in a

dramatic voice, gesturing with the figure. "Are you ready to go, go, go? We'll make our stand, don't give a damn, this is our time to go from zero to hero!"

"Yeah, okay, Star-Lord," Ko-Rel said, snatching the figure from him and laying it face down on the table beside her. That brought a funny little secretive smile to his face, but he didn't say anything in reply, just popped the bottle open and waggled it at her.

"Got any glasses?"

Ko-Rel's eyes caught on a small painting hung over the desk, one of the very few personal effects she'd brought with her. It was one of the last works she had painted before she shipped out in the early cycles of the war. She'd felt silly, at first, putting the painting in her bag along with a tiny shirt that hadn't fit Zam since he was barely a year old. Her husband, Tar-Gold, had opened her rigid world to the arts, though, much to the chagrin of her career military parents, and she would forever associate him with all things passionate and creative. She'd only begun to paint at his encouragement. Though the painting had been created by her hand, the message it sent was all Tar-Gold: You are more than military. You can be as many things as you choose to be.

And chose she had. She'd achieved top marks at the military academy. She'd also spent her weekends painting, and listening to Tar-Gold as he rehearsed for his concerts… and being a mother to the sweetest little chubby-cheeked boy on Hala.

"Yeah, I have a glass right here," she said, grabbing the bottle and taking a swig straight from it. Peter barked a surprised laugh.

"Now that's what I'm talking about," he said. He took the bottle back and took a sip too, then sat on the floor with his back against the wall. Ko-Rel slid down the wall beside him, and they passed the bottle back and forth as Peter chattered. She had no idea what a wild turkey was, but its juices burned on the way down in a most pleasant way. Maybe it was that, or the way her brain was stuck on numbers, that made her suddenly question everything.

Nineteen: the age she'd been when she met Tar-Gold. Twenty: the age they'd gotten married. Twenty-one: the age her life had turned upside down with the birth of her son.

And then: twenty-three.

The age she'd been when the Chitauri came to Hala. The age when she'd lost it all.

Twenty-five: here and now. Two years out and still fighting that war.

Numbers, liquor… whichever it was, she suddenly needed to know more than anything else in the universe if Peter Quill could be trusted.

"Why are you here, Quill?" she asked, interrupting him in the middle of some lengthy story. He paused and blinked.

"I just thought you could use some time to relax," he said finally. "You were amazing back there. I didn't even know you knew doctor stuff. You just jumped right in and—"

She cut him off, inexplicably embarrassed. "No, I mean,

what are you doing *here*. As in Mercury. Why didn't you leave with the rest of the Ravagers? *Not your fight* and all."

"Hey, Yondu said that, not me." He took a longer pull from the bottle and stared at the opposite wall for several beats before continuing. "Yondu says the Ravagers are neutral. We raid everyone, Resistance and Chitauri alike. But, I just don't get that."

He thunked the bottle down hard between them and turned toward her, his eyes more intense than she'd ever seen them.

"Do you know where Yondu and I met?"

She shook her head, silent.

His mouth twisted into a smile, but there was something *wrong* about it. Something bitter she'd never seen from him before.

"In a prison on Chitauri Prime," he said. "They came to Earth, killed my mother, and kidnapped me on my thirteenth birthday, then held me in prison. For four years."

"Peter... I'm so sorry, I had no idea." She moved to lay a hand on his arm, then pulled back, afraid to break this fragile honest mood. "Why did they hold you? I thought they put all their prisoners through their sick gladiator arena."

"They do." He bounced his fists off his knees, drumming out the pent-up memories. "Not me, though."

"Why?"

The simple question provoked a reaction she'd never seen from Peter before. Anger. Swiftly covered up, but there all the same. He deflected.

"So, not to brag or anything—but, you know, feel free

to be impressed and maybe a little turned on—did you know I'm an actual prince? I know, I know, I'm certainly handsome enough for the part, but the bit where I run with space pirates might have thrown you off. I don't blame you."

Ko-Rel blinked. "What would the Chitauri want with an Earth prince?"

Peter gave her a wry smile. "Only *half* from Earth, it turns out. Old Pops is from Spartax, has an empire and everything. Never met him, but he sounds very important."

Ko-Rel stared openly. "Your father is King J'Son of the Spartax Empire?"

"That's the guy." Peter took a long pull from the bottle at that, with a long *ahhh* at the end. "The Chitauri seemed to think I'd be valuable or something. Joke's on them. I never even got a phone call. No idea why they bothered keeping me around so long. I watched so many people come and go. No one ever lasted. Learned not to get attached pretty quickly."

"Until Yondu?"

Peter sighed and thunked his head back against the wall.

"I guess. Yeah. I don't know if it was just the right timing, or… I mean, you met Yondu. There was just something about him. I'd been rotting in that cell for four years, and before they took me, I didn't even know that aliens and spaceships existed. I spent so much time dreaming about getting a ship of my own and just getting *out* of there and never looking back. And then this blue dude lands in my cell and tells me he leads a band of space pirates with dozens of ships who travel all over the galaxy and rob the Chitauri every chance they get.

I'd made so many possible escape plans, but I never thought any of them would work. Once he was there, though…"

"You did it."

"Yeah. We made it out. We stole a supply ship, sold it to the Kree, then hooked back up with the Ravagers. And I stayed with them. I didn't realize…"

He averted his eyes.

"It wasn't just the Chitauri they were raiding. They were equal opportunity pirates, playing both sides. I managed to get Yondu to focus on the Chitauri instead for the past two years, but getting him to come here… he almost didn't."

Peter fell silent and looked over at her. Ko-Rel nodded. He didn't need to say any more. Her unit would have died if they hadn't shown up. *She* would have died. She laid a hand on his knee and squeezed once, a show of gratitude… and a shock of contact that left her palm tingling and warm. How long had it been since she'd touched another person with affection? Not with medical detachment or the practicality of battle coordination, but real connection? Peter stared down at her hand for a moment, then shifted minutely closer, letting his smallest finger barely brush against the side of her wrist.

"So anyway… Yondu. After being in that prison, I didn't see how he could still come out and even think about playing both sides. How he couldn't just want to hit the Chitauri over and over and over until they're *gone* after being in that prison."

Ko-Rel turned more fully toward him, her knee pressing against his.

"He wasn't there as long as you were. He didn't suffer

like you did. It was bad, yeah, but maybe not bad enough for someone like Yondu. Definitely not four-years-level of bad."

"Yeah, well, it was plenty bad for me. No more. No thanks." He drained the last of the bottle, then grimaced. "I think he just can't stomach the idea of having any kind of allegiance. God forbid anyone think he might have ties to anything but the Ravagers. May as well be in prison."

"But you don't feel that way?"

Peter set the empty bottle on top of the desk, next to the pile of action figures he'd brought. When he sat back, he was flush with her side, warm and alive, eyes full of fire.

"This place right here… this is all that stands between the Chitauri and Earth. And just because I don't want to go back there, doesn't mean I want those lizardy bastards stomping all over my mom's grave. I'm here to take back Mercury with you. And we *will*. Beyond that… who knows?" He leaned in closer, a tiny quirk at the corner of his mouth. "I'm more about the here and now."

The answering simmer under her skin was both surprising… and not. Peter Quill was something wholly new in her wartime world. Brash. Brave. *Alive.* Present in his own life in a way she hadn't seen since…

Well, since her husband.

Tar-Gold was two years gone, and she wasn't over it. Not even close. But maybe she didn't have to be. The grief, the pressures of command, the constant cycle of adrenaline and crash, was like a pressure buildup with no release valve. Her chest ached with it. She was *tired*.

Maybe this is exactly what we need on this planet, she thought. *Someone who hasn't been beaten yet.*

Exactly what *she* needed, too. A bit of relief. A jolt to the system.

Besides, how often did one end up with a real-life handsome pirate prince in one's quarters?

"Here and now sounds good to me," she said, and closed the distance between them.

PRESENT DAY

MERCURY BASE – 7801

SOME who didn't know Rocket well might think his threat was exaggerated. Amusing hyperbole.

Those people would be wrong. Rocket did, in fact, already have a bomb in one hand, a detonator in the other, and deadly intent in his heart.

"No, Rocket, wait, just—"

"Back the flark off, Quill," Rocket snarled, waving the bomb at him. "You didn't tell me you supposed 'good guys' used Halfworld soldiers here."

"Because we didn't!" Peter said, gesturing placatingly. "I swear, I would have remembered if there were any super soldier raccoons in the ranks."

"Right, because they were probably all cannon fodder who died defending this dump from the lizards," Rocket roared. He stalked into the room and scrambled up onto the nearest table, unloading a frightening number of explosive devices from his pack. Though the medical instruments and machinery that were the tools of Rak-Mar's vile trade were all long gone, the evidence of his works lingered nonetheless. The lab was one long room whose back wall was lined with a series of cages and sealed cylinders large enough to house a Drax-sized humanoid. Many of the holding cells were marred from both the inside and outside by deeply gouged claw marks, scoring and burns from energy blasts, and in at least one case, hinges that had been completely ripped off.

"I'm serious, Rocket. I had no idea Rak-Mar was ever here, or I never would have brought us here," Peter said.

"Yes, you would have," Rocket said with a scoff. "You just would have made sure I never found out. That's the *only* reason I know you aren't lying."

With that, Rocket swept his practiced gaze over the room, no doubt looking for structural weak points. He picked up a particularly nasty looking bomb and made to leap onto a support pillar... only to be caught up in a tangle of thin, twining branches.

"Let... me... GO!" Rocket shouted, thrashing in Groot's gentle but solid grip.

"I am Groot," Groot said softly.

"I don't care! It could be fifteen *hundred* years ago and I would still want to blow this place to dust and leave a giant turd on its ashes!"

Rocket struggled for another few ticks, then resorted to biting.

"I am *Groot*," Groot insisted. "*I* am Groot. I... am Grooooot."

By the end, Groot's words—such as they were—had grown so soft Peter could barely hear them. Whatever he said, though, finally seemed to have an effect.

"Fine," Rocket said, looking away. "Whatever."

At that, Groot lowered Rocket back onto the table next to his laid-out explosives and released him. The spindly new growth retracted back into Groot's arm until all that was left was his usual hand, which he laid gently atop Rocket's head. Rocket's shoulders rose and fell as he sighed, then he began collecting his explosives with his back to the rest of them.

"Rak-Mar himself was never here. He never left Halfworld. Liked to tinker with us himself," Rocket said, his voice rough. "These poor bastards were sent out here for field testing. Guess the test failed."

Gamora dragged her fingers gently over the bars of a cage, a pained look on her face.

"I'm sorry, Rocket," she said. "I know what it is to be twisted to someone else's purpose."

Rocket's ears drooped. "Yeah. Well. There are a lot of messed-up people in this flarkin' galaxy."

With the last of the bombs stashed back in his bag, Rocket turned, avoiding everyone's eyes. "I'll try the terminal and see what's what."

"No point, man," Peter said, pointing to the display panel

built into the wall. It looked like it had been punched very hard, very many times, by a being with fists the size of Peter's head. "Screw the terminal. Let's just go."

"What, and rely on your twelve-years-out-of-date memory of what's where? Sounds like a terrible idea," Rocket said.

"Yes, Peter Quill, Mr. Starrrrrr-Lord," the voice from the intercom chimed in. "Listen to your raccoon. It's been a while. Your memory could be flawed. You wouldn't want to lead your team astray, now, would yooooou?"

Rocket drew his gun and blasted the nearest intercom.

"Ouch," the voice said, still perfectly audible. Gamora looked down at Rocket and sighed.

"What?" he said. "She called me a raccoon. Don't tell me you ain't tired of her already."

Peter couldn't argue with that.

"Look, I just want to point out one small thing," Peter said. "The fact that she *wants* us to access a terminal to find a map *might* indicate that it would be bad for our health if we did."

"You think it's a trap," Drax said, standing half in and half out of the room to keep watch on the hallway.

"I mean, it kinda seems like it, right?" Peter glared up at the scorched mark on the ceiling where the intercom had been. Who did this person think they were, judging his leadership like that? He sighed. "I've got this, guys. It's been a long time, but trust me when I say that the stuff that happened here wasn't very easily forgettable. I can get us where we're going, and if we come across a working terminal on the way there, we can decide then."

"Fine," Rocket said, cocking his gun. "But if she calls me a raccoon again, I'm blowing this whole place up."

And with that, he stalked out of the room.

A tick later: "Waaaaaaaah!"

Drax, Gamora, Peter, and Groot all locked eyes, then dashed out into the hallway.

"I am Groot!" Groot cried, charging into the lead, completely fixated on Rocket's crumpled form. Then his legs went out from under him.

Tim-berrrr! Peter's brain cried unhelpfully, right before his boot landed in something slick. His heel slid faster than if he'd stepped on a cartoon banana peel—then he was down and sliding, something wet seeping through his clothing and all over his side. Behind him, Drax yelped, and Peter glanced back to see him racing down the hallway, now a Slip 'n Slide of doom, with his knives in his hands... coming straight toward Peter.

"Drax, your knives!" he shouted, then activated his jet boots to get out of the way. Smart idea, right? Except that the jet boots jets apparently threw off just a little bit of a spark... and the floor was currently covered in oil.

The oil slick caught fire in a flash, the flames spreading so quickly they nearly reached Groot and Drax before Peter could react. Drax struck out with his knives, leaving long gouges in the wall to slow his wild tumble down the hallway. Peter's tactic didn't work quite as well.

"Yeaaaagh!"

He shut the boots off and threw all his weight to one side, away from the flames, but it was no use. He was *covered* in the stuff. His trouser leg caught fire just as he glanced up to see Groot and Rocket racing toward him—or no, him racing toward *them*, because the oil slick apparently had an end, and it was right there, and a literally-on-fire Peter Quill was about to crash right into them. Rocket, whose fur was soaked in oil, and Groot, who was literally made of firewood coated in lighter fluid. The two of them looked up just in time to witness a flaming Star-Lord come sliding into them.

All three of them toppled into the intersection with the next hallway, a pile of oily, burning hair and fabric and wood. Peter threw himself to one side and rolled around frantically, his kindergarten self parroting, "Stop, drop, and roll, stop, drop, and roll," over and over in his head. Apparently, no amount of rolling really helped when one was covered in flammable oil. The first tongues of flame were just starting to eat through the heavy material of his trousers and jacket when the air filled with a wet *whooooosh*, and Peter found himself covered in fewer flames, but many more globs of white foam. When the pain and heat fully subsided, he uncurled from his fetal position and looked up to see Rocket standing over him with a fire extinguisher.

"Now *that* is ironic," Peter said. "Never thought you of all people would be putting out fires."

"Look, when you carry around as many explosives as I do, it's just good business to carry a fire extinguisher. Not all of us are idiots, Star-Turd," Rocket said. "Besides, do you have any idea how many awesome things you can do with one of these? If you pierce the canister with a—"

"Yeah, okay, thanks buddy, that's cool. Hey, maybe let's get on with this before disembodied voice lady lets loose a giant swarm of killer bees next."

"What is a bee?" Drax asked.

Peter closed his eyes and experienced regret.

"It's a little bug that helps food grow by rolling in pollen," he said, knowing instantly it wasn't good enough. Sure enough:

"What is pollen?"

"It's how flowers have sex," Peter snapped, certain *that* would put an end to it. And, lo and behold, it did. Peter looked back to the head of the hallway, where Gamora stood, unsinged and unoiled, watching the proceedings with a faint smirk.

"You plannin' on joining us?" Rocket said, throwing his fire extinguisher aside and giving a wet-dog-style shake. Groot wiped a blob of foam from his cheek without comment.

Gamora backed up, cocked her head to analyze the oil-slicked floor, then took a running start. With a dainty little hop, she leapt onto the oil and rode it down the hallway like a surfer queen riding a sweet wave. At the end, she reached out a hand to Groot, who held her steady as she hopped back off the oil and wiped her boots on the floor until she could walk steadily again. Then she looked up at Peter expectantly.

"Well? Where to, Star-Lord?"

Peter scowled. "Oh, shut *up*."

He turned and stalked down the hallway, rounding the next corner with a huff.

INTERLUDE: 12 YEARS AGO

MERCURY BASE – 7789

SHOCKINGLY, the action figures did come in handy.

"Okay, so if the pillow is this base, and your knee is the forward outpost, what if Lar-Ka sent a platoon of soldiers—"

Peter held up a humanoid figurine covered in brown fur to represent the platoon, then marched it up her bare calf toward the "outpost." Ko-Rel shook her head and leaned forward to grab the Star-Lord figurine.

"No, because we know they have a contingent hidden away somewhere over here." She fluffed up the blanket to create a representation of the nearby foothills and plopped the figure on top. "Any troops that pass near this territory are almost certain to get ambushed. We can't afford more losses. I sent another report to Rider about the combat action, and his assistant confirmed receipt, but that's all I've heard. Not that I expected one botched operation to change his mind, but..."

She paused, then closed her eyes and sighed. "Actually, I suppose I kind of did. A silly hope to cling to, I guess."

"What if you sent a small force to harass them, draw them up this way—" He placed a small green creature with improbably large ears near the Star-Lord figure. "—so the other platoon can get through."

Ko-Rel opened her eyes and studied the "map," letting the battles play out in her mind... then shook her head.

"There's one big thing we're not taking into account," she said, flopping back onto her pillow. "I got the lieutenant's verbal report from your excursion, but she was injured and drugged up, so she might have missed something. Can you tell me in your own words what happened?"

Peter sighed and flopped down next to her. "There's not much to tell, honestly. We planned out our route in advance, just a quick out and back to the peaks to the west. As soon as we made it over the western ridge, there were Chitauri waiting in the valley."

"Did you take them by surprise?" Ko-Rel asked.

She knew the answer already in her gut, and Peter confirmed it.

"No. They were waiting for us."

Ko-Rel flopped one arm over her eyes and heaved an even bigger sigh.

"We have a traitor, don't we."

Not a question. Just a statement. Peter answered anyway.

"Pretty sure, yeah."

Ko-Rel hesitated before asking her next question, knowing it could alienate the only reinforcement she was ever likely to get. A commander had to do her due diligence, though.

"And it's not you, right?"

Peter barked a laugh. "Yep, that's me, big ol' lizard lover over here. Can't wait to call up my Chitauri buddy and tell him all about our next doomed plan. We can reminisce about my time in Chitauri jail. Such fond memories."

Ko-Rel cracked one eye open and stuck her tongue out at Peter. "Hey, look, how am I supposed to know? Maybe the Chitauri turned you into some kind of sleeper agent and that's why they really didn't throw you in the gladiator ring."

Peter stilled. "That's not a thing, right? They can't do that?"

Ko-Rel laughed. "No, Peter. Not that I know of, at least. You're not a sleeper agent."

She sat back up, doing her best not to disturb the carefully laid out battle plan hanging out at the foot of her bed.

"These plans are all well and good, but the mission security problem makes it all moot. We have a leak, and until we know where it is, we have to assume every operation is compromised. We either have to account for that and work around it…"

"Or catch the bastard who's got the Chitauri on speed dial, yeah," Peter said, which was half-incomprehensible to Ko-Rel, but she got the idea. They both paused to think, contemplating the problem in comfortable half-naked silence. Her mind was unusually calm and focused. Maybe blowing off a little steam and numbing a bit of the horror of war with some meaningless sex was exactly what she had needed. Borrowing a bit of that brash energy Peter brought to the base.

Peter huffed a laugh, pulling her out of her thoughts.

"I was just thinking," he said, searching through his pile of figures. "Some of these figures are from this movie called *Star Wars*. It's the story of this big intergalactic war between an evil empire and the Rebel Alliance trying to take them down."

"Sounds familiar," Ko-Rel said with a wry smile.

"Right? I was actually kind of surprised when I got out here and found out that big evil space empires actually existed." He took one of the action figures, a man wearing a black vest and dark blue pants with red stripes up the side, and raised the figure's gun arm to point it toward her with a silently mouthed "pew pew." "So this guy here, Han Solo, he's not actually part of the rebels *or* the empire. He's a dashing smuggler who wants nothing to do with the war but gets sucked in anyway. And Chewie, this guy is Han Solo's best friend. I actually had him with me when I got kidnapped from Earth. I found Han and a few of these others at some little booth in the Knowhere market, just total random luck."

There was an awkward silence in which Ko-Rel definitely did *not* point out how Peter clearly fancied himself a dashing smuggler type who got sucked into a war, too.

"So this Hanzolo character, and his friend. Did they end up winning their war?" she asked instead.

Peter looked up at her and smiled that charming boyish

grin that always seemed to promise everything would turn out okay.

"Yeah. They did win. Threw an evil old guy into a pit and everything."

Another brief pause, then Peter held the brown furry figure out for her to take.

"Here. You keep him," he said. "He'll look out for you. Any Chitauri try to mess with you, and he'll pull their arms out of their sockets. Wookies are known to do that."

Ko-Rel held her hands up and shook her head. "Oh, Peter, I don't—"

"Are you saying no to my incredibly thoughtful gift?" he asked with a sidelong glance. "Because I'm not saying it would be *heartless* of you, you know, I just…"

Ko-Rel sighed and took the figure. It *was* kind of cute, she guessed. Zam would have liked it.

"Thanks, Peter," she said.

"Don't mention it."

She looked down at the figure and turned it over and over. Chewie. A loyal best friend, always to be trusted. She *hated* having to be suspicious of everyone around her. In a military unit, trust was paramount. Even if you didn't like the person next to you very much, you still had to trust them with your life. Right now, she couldn't trust anyone.

In the last few rotations, the base had been infiltrated by Chitauri shapeshifters who killed nearly everyone right before Ko-Rel and her reinforcements were due to arrive; they'd fought off a devastating counterattack immediately after retaking the base; and, they'd had the absolute simplest of follow-up missions completely fall apart. An uncomplicated scouting mission, mounted with the utmost caution, that should have been so routine as to be almost boring.

They definitely had a traitor in their midst, and Ko-Rel intended to find out who. She rolled off the bed, riding a burst of energy borrowed from Peter.

"Come on. Get dressed," she said, grabbing a plain black undershirt and yanking it over her head. "We're going to get some more information."

"Ma'am, yes, ma'am," Peter said, hopping to his feet and stumbling as he struggled into his trousers.

In minutes, they were ready. Peter's pockets were stuffed with the spare action figures. Ko-Rel set hers back on her nightstand.

"Stand watch, Chewie," she said, then spun and stalked out of the room, a woman on a mission. Peter trotted after her, still wrestling with his shirt.

Ko-Rel led him through the darkened base with quick, sure steps despite the late hour. The lights were dimmed to night-cycle levels, and the hallways were near silent, echoing with every step. Many of her people were sleeping. There was one, she knew, who would not be. Ko-Rel wasn't certain she could trust her any more than anyone else on base, but she was willing to bet on it, and she'd be one of the easiest to catch in a lie if it came to it.

"Let me do the talking," Ko-Rel said to Peter as they entered the facility at the very heart of the base: the command hub, where all of their monitoring and analysis equipment resided… and where a certain talented young intelligence officer had been practically living since they'd retaken the base.

"Yumiko," Ko-Rel said, announcing her presence so as not to alarm the young woman. She'd been… jumpy since the attack that took Hal-Zan's life. Barely eating, not sleeping, glued to her station in the command hub even when she wasn't scheduled to be on watch as she pored over endless information. The wound on her left cheek looked to be healing badly, like she couldn't stop picking at it. It stretched from cheekbone to jawline, showing the jagged edges of the metal shrapnel she'd fallen on during the attack. Ko-Rel remembered that moment vividly, and probably always would.

As far as Ko-Rel was concerned, everyone who had survived to this point was under suspicion. This woman, though… losing Hal-Zan had affected her deeply, and Ko-Rel doubted she would aid the people who had caused that death, no matter how much she hated Richard Rider. Grief recognized grief. Ko-Rel knew that, at least, was genuine. She wasn't completely off the list of suspects, but she was near the bottom, and that was the best Ko-Rel could ask for at the moment.

The woman did, indeed, startle a bit at their arrival, but quickly swiveled around in her chair to face them. Her straight black hair was pulled back from her face, fully revealing the tired shadows under her darkest brown eyes. She wore a uniform that was at least a rotation overdue for changing, with *S. Yumiko* stitched above her left breast. Despite it all, she actually seemed more lively than she had since the attack.

Peter stepped forward to Ko-Rel's side and nodded at the woman.

"Yumiko… we haven't had a chance to talk yet, but that sounds like a name from Earth."

So much for letting Ko-Rel do the talking.

"Because it is. Suki Yumiko," she said, holding out a hand for Peter to shake, though her expression remained wary. "Good to meet someone else from the third rock."

"Likewise," Peter said. "Where'd you live?"

"Tokyo. I was just a grocery store cashier, but you know how these things go. One very strange series of events later… here I am, protecting Earth from another planet. Not that I'm doing a very good job of it."

"You are, though," Ko-Rel said firmly, laying a hand on the woman's shoulder. "You've given so much to this war. Hal-Zan… she would have been incredibly proud of you."

A flash of pain seemed to knock the breath out of Suki, and the skin at the corners of her eyes tightened. Ko-Rel's stomach twisted into knots of empathetic grief, but she forced herself to take a slow breath through her nose and re-center.

"Yumiko, I know you've been going over the data from the attacks for the last few rotations. Have you found any…"

Ko-Rel hesitated.

"…inconsistencies? Anything, even if it's minor."

Suki shrugged. "The data from the battles… no, there's really not much there. Even the transcripts of the battle chatter from every soldier's helmet mic. Nothing so far. I've been looking over other data sets too, though. Communication logs, door access logs, meal orders, supply requests…"

She paused and studied Ko-Rel as if unsure how much to say, then shrugged. "Honestly, Commander, the more I look at it, the more I feel like we might have a security leak. There's a pattern here, somewhere. Something is right on the tip of my brain, like the solution is staring me in the face."

Ko-Rel pursed her lips, but said nothing to confirm or deny that suspicion.

"Do you have any suspects?" she asked instead.

Suki's eyes slid to Peter, then to the empty comm station, before returning to Ko-Rel. "A few. None with particularly compelling evidence… yet."

She smoothed a hand over her hair, catching bits that had pulled free from her hair tie and tamping down a bit of its unshowered wildness. She needed rest, and a shower, and a good therapist, probably. It was clear she wouldn't be getting any of those anytime soon.

"I *will* find out who is responsible," she said, confirming the point. Her eyes shifted away then fixed on Peter again with a whole new intensity. "And when I do, I will do to that traitor what was done to Hal-Zan. Guaranteed."

Peter shifted uncomfortably, hands in his pockets. Ko-Rel didn't blame him. Suki clearly didn't trust him the way Ko-Rel did.

Because that?

That was a threat.

PRESENT DAY

MERCURY BASE – 7801

AS soon as Peter turned the corner, he was immediately assaulted by a swarm of bees. It was like the voice had been listening in, just waiting for Peter to say the wrong thing so they could hit the "deploy giant killer robot bees" button.

"I have got to stop saying scut like that," he said, dropping with the others to the ground so Rocket could do his thing. Rocket took a small device from his back and threw it into the air, where it released a lateral shockwave that spread out in a wide disk over their heads. All but a handful of the tiny bee-bots rained down on their heads, and Gamora quickly dispatched the rest with a few swipes of her blade.

"Ha, eat it," Peter said, shaking a fist at the ceiling. They called that a trap? No one even got stung.

"Can't blame me for tryyyyying," the voice replied. "Someone was very naughty during the war. Was it me? Was it *you*? There's so much *evidence* here. Data aplenty. Could get someone in very big trouble. I just need time, time, time. I knooow you, Peterrr. I know you."

Groot looked at Peter, head cocked quizzically. "I am Groot?"

"Good question," Rocket said. "Is there anything you'd like to tell us about your little wartime shenanigans, Quill?"

Peter kicked a bee drone down the hallway and stalked after it. "What's there to tell? I came here with the Ravagers to drop off supplies and stop a Chitauri attack. I stayed for a few weeks while the Resistance retook the planet. I left and joined back up with the Ravagers after that. The end."

"Not quite the end," the voice corrected. "There was the small matter of the treason."

Four pairs of eyes turned to Peter, and he held up his hands in defense. "Yeah, but it wasn't me. I didn't commit any treason."

"Hmmm, I don't knooow, Peterrr. Things started to go wrong right after you got here. How sure *are* you?"

"I mean, I'm me, and I can see inside my own head, you know, so... pretty dang sure," he said with an eye roll.

"Oh, Peterrr," the voice crooned. "War is complicated. So hard. You think you know a person. You work alongside them every rotation. They seem to have the same mission. They seem like they're helping."

The voice's tone grew sharp.

"But they aren't. They aren't helping at all. They are hurting and we want them *dead*."

A heavy *CLICK* resounded through the hallway.

"Get down!" Gamora shouted, just as the air filled with thousands of needle-thin energy bolts. Peter bellyflopped onto the floor, landing on top of Gamora's foot and letting out an *oof* of pain when one of Groot's arms whacked him in the shins. Worst game of Twister *ever*. A muffled string of swearing came from somewhere underneath Drax, who rolled to the side, revealing a rather flattened looking Rocket. Rocket spat and hacked, then looked up at Drax, his eyes haunted.

"Never in my life have I ever thought, gee, I wonder what Drax's ab sweat tastes like." He spat again, his eyes bulging as he gagged. "I'm gonna vomit."

"Do *not*," Gamora snapped, rolling away from the splash zone and staring up at the endless stream of bolts overhead.

"I am Groot?" Groot asked. He started to push himself up into a crawling position, then jerked back with a pained groan as one of the bolts sent a splinter flying from the back of his head.

Rocket scrambled for his pack, rifled through it for a moment, then withdrew a cobbled together device of some kind.

"I've got this. Cover your eyes," he said, then stuck the device in his mouth and ran on all fours to the head of the hallway. The bolts streamed forth from a dozen tiny muzzles, nestled inside narrow slits that had opened up in the wall.

So Indiana Jones... and so much less fun than it looked in the movie.

"Are bombs always the solution with you?" Gamora shouted down the hallway.

Rocket looked back, confused. "Of course. Why do you ask?"

And with that, he used a bit of tack to stick the bomb to the wall just below the slits, fiddled with it, then turned back and ran. The bomb exploded with the precise amount of force necessary to blow out the mechanicals in the wall, but without throwing any shrapnel back down the hallway.

"Effective," Drax said with a satisfied nod.

"Directional charge," Rocket said with the immense satisfaction of a job well done. He stood and brushed off his orange jumpsuit. "Lead on, Quill."

Peter sighed and poked his head around the corner, alert for the next trap that everyone would blame him for. The base layout was hazy in his mind, but he knew they were headed in the right general direction. Everything was built out from the command hub at the center. Spiraling hallways of personnel quarters and laboratories took up a significant portion of the real estate, with larger facilities like the dining hall, armory, and so on regularly interspersed.

Peter paused at the junction of the next hallway and looked back and forth, then turned left toward the wing of the base he thought held the mess hall. Maybe there'd be some unexpired rations tastier than protein paste that would make the crew happy and less likely to want to murder him. He scowled up at the ceiling as he led them on, the voice humming absently as they moved ever farther inward, eventually switching to a tuneless little song.

"Peterrr, little boy hero, Peter Quill-Quill-Quill you knooow who diiid the bad things. You say it wasn't you, you say, but sooo does everyooone—"

"Man, stop talking like you know me," Peter finally snapped. "There's only one person from that time who knew me well enough to talk like that and I know you aren't her."

"Why do I feel like 'know' has a very particular meaning in this case?" Rocket asked.

Gamora sighed. "*Why* would you ask that?"

Peter grinned.

"Yeah, you know. I had some good times in this base," he said, pulling out his best Michael Jackson pelvic thrust moves.

"Oh, please stop," Gamora said, averting her eyes to the ceiling.

Peter glanced at her over his shoulder and waggled his eyebrows, laughing as he walked through the doorway to the mess hall. The long cafeteria tables were neat and empty, save for the layer of dust left by the years of disuse. A few of the overhead lights flickered, and several others were dark. No need to replace them, after all. A small door was set into the far wall that Peter knew led to the food prep area; the head cook had appreciated the fresh supplies the Ravagers had brought so much that he gave Peter snacks anytime he wanted. Peter smiled at the memory and turned to mention his snack-raiding plan to the others.

Then he was whipped twice across the backside. He yelped in pain and whirled around.

"What the—"

Before he could even place the source of the attack, black cables appeared from nowhere in tight coils around his wrists and ankles, and in half a tick he found himself dangling six inches off the ground, face down.

Holding him up was a robot. Not even a cool, futuristic, kinda hot android-type robot—just a straight-up kill-all-humans box of bolts with a fetish, apparently.

"Okay, honestly," Peter groaned, "the engineers mentioned some strange droid security, but really, who designed these? Turning a military base into a BDSM club? Really?"

"What is a BDSM club? Is it a form of bludgeoning weapon?" Drax asked.

Peter let his head fall and thunk against the floor.

"I'll tell you later, buddy, but you aren't too far off. Can we focus on the problem at hand?"

The problem at hand got significantly worse as the robot's already tight grip began to twist. Peter's pulse beat with a heavy thrum in his quickly purpling hands. Around him, Peter caught glimpses of the others in similar predicaments. Drax with black cords wrapped tightly around his throat and wrists, Gamora with her wrists and ankles bound together, and Rocket and Groot tied together completely.

"Any ideas?" Gamora said, her voice tight.

"Oooh, poor Peter's friends," the voice of their tormentor said. "Pooor poooor friends. We should all choose our friends wisely. Friends, family, enemies, sooo many people in our lives and they all can turn traitor in the blink-blink-blink of an eye."

"I am not a traitor!" Peter raged as he lost all feeling in his hands. "Ooooh, I can't wait until we get to the command center and evict this son of a—"

A horrifically loud *BEEEEEEEEEEP* screeched over the intercom, the exact tone they used to use to bleep out swear words on TV when Peter was a kid. He almost felt nostalgic. Mostly, he felt murderous.

"I am Groot," Groot said, followed by an ominous creaking sound. Peter wrenched his neck trying to look back over his shoulder as Groot rumbled and the creaking increased. "I... am... GROOT!"

A wooden spike erupted from the floor mere inches from Peter's face, piercing the BDSM bot through its faceplate. Peter had just long enough to think, "Oh no," before the bot collapsed, releasing him, whose hands were too numb to let him catch himself. He smashed his face into the floor, and the taste of pennies slicked the back of his tongue. Around him, a chorus of groans joined his as they all picked themselves up, nursing bruised skulls and banged-up knees.

Peter looked around the group, taking in the tangled hair, scraped and bleeding flesh, and murderous expressions. No one said a word. Peter strode over to the kitchen entrance and poked his head in for a quick skim for something, *any*thing that would act as a balm—but there was nothing. Empty containers, shut down freezers... and one lonely crate of protein paste in the far back corner.

Peter shut the door quietly and wisely chose not to mention it.

"Let's just... move on," Peter said.

Drax stomped one enormous foot down on what remained of one of the robot's heads, releasing a shower of sparks and a horrific screeching of metal on metal. He looked up and met Peter's eyes, then nodded.

Peter swallowed hard and forced a smile. Everything would be fine. Juuust fine. They just needed to check in, take a breather, and get moving again.

He led them out a different entrance than the one they'd come in through, and they passed into a new area of the base that was significantly worse for wear. At first, the only noticeable change was the dust. Dust turned to pebbles of concrete, then larger shrapnel, until they turned down a hallway full of cracked walls and collapsing doorways. Here and there, chunks of roof had fallen away, revealing the shimmering force shield just beyond that kept the base's atmosphere from leaking away. Peter slowed toward the end of the hall, where entire rooms had been turned to rubble. One was so thoroughly destroyed that the dusty surface of the planet was visible through what used to be its outer walls.

"Whoa, what happened here?" Rocket asked, leaping into a giant hole blown in the wall.

"Chitauri attack. They did an air strike by night, maybe a week after I got here. Only got one good shot in before the air defense grid took them down, but that shot still killed three people." Peter paused in front of one of the blown-open doorways and put a hand on the crumbling wall. "It would have killed me if I'd been sleeping at the time. This was my room."

The sight of the rubble hit Peter in a way he completely didn't expect. At the time, it had barely registered. Sure, he'd been mildly disappointed at losing what few possessions he'd kept in his quarters instead of on the *Milano*, and regretful at the lives of his temporary neighbors lost in the attack. But, because he'd been younger and stupider, mostly he'd felt like dropping his trousers and mooning the Chitauri with some kind of quippy line like, "You missed, you flarking lizard brains!" Extremely effective, and not at all a regression to Peter's last days on an Earth school playground. He'd also reveled a bit in his smugness at having been busy getting laid when the Chitauri were trying to kill him. Well, not him specifically, but Peter didn't require that level of targeting to feel smug.

Now, though… Peter stepped forward slowly, the gravel crunching under his feet, and spotted a tiny plastic arm sticking out of the pulverized roofing. He leaned down, brushed some pebbles away, and pulled the arm free, holding it in the palm of his hand. It was melted and misshapen at the shoulder joint, like something molten-hot had fallen on the rest of the figure. The barest edge of a black vest peeked at the top of a white sleeve, and the arm ended with a pale hand clutching a blaster.

Peter knelt down and rummaged through the crumbled bits of structural material and splintered furniture, but the rest of the figure never turned up. There was a blob of green that may have once been Yoda, and a singed clump of twisted threads and plastic that might have once been the curly head of Steven, lead singer of the band Star-Lord. Only one figure was mostly intact, though melted past the point of recognition. Peter picked it up and inspected it, but dropped it again when no memories were forthcoming. Out of the corner of his eye, he saw Gamora pick it up and slide it silently into her pocket.

Peter chose not to comment. Instead, he took one last look around the room, sighed, and stepped back out into the hallway.

"Come on. We're close to the command hub. Let's keep going," he said.

"Are you sure, Peter Quill-Lord?" the Voice asked. "Don't you want to look some more?"

Peter had a brief mental image of a stately porcupine in a tuxedo. Quill Lord. Heh.

"Nah, I think we've done enough exploring," Peter said. "Maybe it's time for us to pay you a little visit."

"Oooooh, Peterrrrrrr. It won't end the way you think. Perhaps you'd better turn back."

"We've come this far. We'll finish the job." Peter grinned and looked over at Rocket. "Think of it as a bonus. A hundred thousand units and the opportunity to evaporate that loud-mouthed sadistic son of a—"

The screeching *BEEEEEP* rendered the rest inaudible.

It was probably for the best.

19

INTERLUDE: 12 YEARS AGO

MERCURY BASE – 7789

KO-REL sat bolt upright in the dark, the hair on her arms standing on end and her ears straining for a clue as to what had woken her. They'd managed five whole standard rotations without another casualty, but she hadn't allowed herself any sort of reprieve. Next to her, Peter's face was smashed into the pillow, and he mumbled a vague, "Wazzit? K'rel?"

"Shh." She sat absolutely still, and that, more than anything, seemed to finally wake Peter up. He sat up too, looking around Ko-Rel's darkened bedroom.

Then, they both heard it. Engines. Close. Getting closer *way* too fast.

"Everyone, take cover!" Ko-Rel shouted over the base comm. She shoved Peter off the bed and followed him onto the floor, wedging herself underneath it just as the base rocked with an echoing *BOOM!* The answering clatter of the base's anti-aircraft guns followed immediately after, prompting another, softer *boom*.

"Lar-Ka, report," Ko-Rel said into her comm as she pulled herself out from under the bed. She grabbed the nearest shirt and pulled it on over her head, probably backward, and grabbed the pants she'd flung over the desk chair the previous night.

"Lar-Ka, *report*," she said again, then shook her head. "I swear, when that man finally sleeps, he's dead to the world."

"Let's go wake him up, then," Peter said, appearing fully dressed at her side. He opened the door and poked his head out into the hallway, then gasped. Ko-Rel shoved past him, took a few running steps down the hall… then stopped.

The far end of the hallway was completely caved in.

"Oh, *no*," Ko-Rel whispered, then jogged toward the rubble, counting doors.

"Ko-Rel, wait, it could still be unstable down there!" Peter called after her, but she ignored him, jogging until she stood in front of the door that belonged to Captain Lar-Ka's first lieutenant. Pained sobbing came from within, and Ko-Rel triggered her command override and burst into the room.

The lieutenant lay in the remnants of her bed, pinned to the sheets by an enormous piece of debris. Her head was arched back against her pillow as tears streamed from the corners of her eyes, her sobs harsh and ragged in her throat. A shocking amount of blood dripped from the sheets into a small puddle forming on the floor.

"Medic to the officer quarters!" Ko-Rel cried into the

comm, falling to her knees beside the bed. "At least one critically wounded. Casualties likely. Is the attack over?"

"Affirmative," Tasver reported from the command hub. "It was just the one Chitauri bomber. We were able to take them down. No survivors, and no evidence of a follow-up attack so far."

Small miracles. Ko-Rel moved farther down the bed, accidentally planting her knee in the puddle of blood as she examined the rubble pinning the lieutenant down. Her right leg was completely crushed. Possibly her pelvis and right hip as well. It should be safe to remove the concrete slab without risking further injury, though.

"Peter, help me," she said, working her fingers oh-so-gently around the edge. "I can lift, just help me guide it off of her."

Ko-Rel sent an apologetic smile to the lieutenant. "I'm so sorry for your pain, Chan-Dar. Medics are on the way, but we need to do this part now."

Lieutenant Chan-Dar squeezed her eyes shut and nodded, taking long, deep breaths to get through the pain. Ko-Rel looked to Peter, counted down, and together they hauled the jagged chunk of wall off the woman's mangled body. Peter staggered, and they dropped the rubble with an echoing *CLUNK* just as the medic and an aide came rushing in.

"We'll take it from here," he said.

Ko-Rel nodded and squeezed the lieutenant's hand gently, then went back into the hallway, not ready to face what came next. Her whole being recoiled from the wreckage, but she steeled herself. Duty first. Duty to her people.

"Anyone available for excavation work, report to the officer quarters," she called out, though she sounded tired and beaten even to her own ears. Not exactly the motivating, confident orders she needed to be giving.

"There might be survivors," Peter said. His voice betrayed him, though. Bless him for always trying to bring the positivity—it was how he'd survived—but even he couldn't look at this situation and see anything but death. He walked over to the pile of rubble and started moving chunks of concrete away from a mostly covered doorway.

"Oh," Ko-Rel said, then pitched in to help. "This was… this was your quarters."

Peter nodded, not looking up from the task at hand. "Good thing I was otherwise occupied. Nothing in there but action figures and a change of clothes. I'm more worried about my neighbors."

Captain Lar-Ka. He'd been right next door. He'd wanted to keep an eye on Peter, so he'd stuck him in the empty room adjacent his, sandwiched between him and his trusted lieutenant.

Now…

The engineers and a few others arrived with equipment to assist with the excavation, which sped up the process considerably. Ko-Rel periodically checked in over the comm, calling out for any survivors to respond.

Silence in return.

When they finally uncovered the door to Lar-Ka's quarters enough for a medic to squeeze through, with Ko-

Rel following right behind, there was no surprise on the other side.

Lar-Ka was dead.

Of course he was. Ko-Rel stood to one side as the medical staff performed their examination.

Then, amidst the clutter, she caught sight of the one item on his desk that wasn't work-related: a white oblong ball with a signature scrawled on the side. His wife's. She played some Krylorian sport or other, good enough to go professional, and he'd always been so proud of her. She picked it up and turned it over in her hands, imagining her giving it to him before he was deployed. Imagining Lar-Ka watching her games, shouting at the top of his lungs with absolutely no embarrassment whatsoever. She'd seen pictures of their wedding. They were a beautiful couple, both of them fiercely independent and devoted to their own pursuits, yet never failing to give support and cheer each other on.

And now he was gone.

A gentle hand landed on Ko-Rel's arm and she flinched so hard the hand jerked back in surprise. Peter stood before her, concern written all over his expression, and it was only then that Ko-Rel realized how ragged her breathing was. How tense her muscles. How wide her eyes.

How deep and boundless and fierce her *rage*.

"I will find them," she said, low and dangerous. "I will find the traitor who is getting our people killed. And when I do, they will answer for every single death they have caused. I will find them!"

She was shouting by the end, but she didn't care. Let her people see. Let them spread the word in the mess hall and command hub. Let them *know*. She was coming for the traitor. No stone would be left unturned.

For Lar-Ka, a soldier through and through, to be killed in his sleep in his d'ast underwear was more than Ko-Rel could take.

Ko-Rel had spent rotations with the engineers going over the base from the landing bay to the hub to the toilets. Turned out the base had a whole host of strange security systems built in that had never been triggered during the Chitauri infiltration. There was a whole storage unit filled with strange security bots and drones that the system hadn't known to deploy, and the Chitauri had never made it deep enough into the base during their counterattack to trigger them then, either. If the Chitauri had tried to march the halls in their full lizard glory instead of shapeshifting like cowards, they would have had a very different experience.

Needless to say, they had changed the engagement parameters. Now, the bots would engage for anyone not currently registered in the Resistance personnel database, plus a special temporary override for Peter.

Of course, all the security systems in the universe couldn't do a damned bit of good unless the enemy actually set foot in the base. So they'd send a ship on a bombing run instead. It was almost like they knew.

Because, of course, they did.

The missile was targeted at the exact part of the base that

housed most of the highest-ranking officers. But none of the intelligence officers or engineers.

Ko-Rel moved to Lar-Ka's side and leaned down to retrieve his military ID tags, then wrapped them around the signed memento from his wife. She would make sure they were returned to her, the way she would have wanted her effects returned to Tar-Gold, were he still alive. She could do this one small thing.

She exited Lar-Ka's room into the destroyed hallway, watching the flicker of the force shield through a hole in the wall. Who could she trust in this hallway? All the engineers were hard at work, solemn and focused, until the way was clear for the medics to reach all the remaining rooms.

All told, three officers had been killed and two more were critically wounded. It was a blow she wasn't sure they could come back from. Their numbers were so few, survival seemed impossible. Even *trying* felt futile.

But there was one thing she knew for sure.

If she was to die on Mercury, she'd make sure that the traitor died first.

Ko-Rel spun on her heel and marched to her quarters. She needed her gun.

PRESENT DAY

MERCURY BASE – 7801

PETER was feeling pretty close to blowing out every speaker in the entire base.

"Peeeeeterrrrrr," the voice said as they neared the command hub. "I *know* you, Peeeeterrrrrr. Before you called yourself Star-Lord, you were just Peeeeeterrrrrr…"

"Yeah, okay, cool, that's great," Peter muttered, taking a shot at another one of the intercoms. It made him feel better for all of ten ticks. Unfortunately, the sound seemed to ooze from everywhere, enveloping them no matter where they went or how much of the intercom system they blew up.

"Your past follows you, Peeeeeterrrrrr," the voice continued. "Your present, too. Bit of a gap there. Twelve years. And now you lead everything right back to where it all started, where it almost ended. Oh, Peeeeeterrrrrr, I know you aren't the type to look back. But you really, really should. Really, really, really."

Peter scoffed. If there was one thing he *never* did, it was look back. He'd never been back to Earth. Never sought out Ko-Rel. Never thought about re-joining the Ravagers (if they'd even let him). And definitely never had any regrets about not sticking around for the end of the war. If he weren't being paid, he never would have set foot back on this miserable little planet. Sure, he had a few mementos from Earth back on the *Milano*, but that wasn't *looking back*. That was taking inspiration from an excellent band that totally held up.

And yes, okay, so he'd held out some *slight* hope that they'd come across some of his old action figures here, particularly Han Solo. A bit disappointing, but he *had* recovered Han Solo's arm, at least. Even more than that, he wondered if Chewie was still out there somewhere with Ko-Rel. Was he riding around with a Centurion, making arrests and threatening to pull people's arms out of their sockets if they resisted?

But that didn't mean Peter wanted to go back to any of it. It was about… knowing that time together had mattered. Or something. Yeah.

As they neared the next intersection, Peter held up a hand, pressed his back against the wall, then slowly eased his head around the corner.

Nothing. The huge double door to the command center was just down the hall, maybe twenty yards away, seemingly unguarded.

It was absolutely a trap. Maybe it was time for them to slow down, take a beat, and think.

"Okay, people, let's huddle up," he said, waving everyone forward. He pulled out his Walkman and hit play to give them some background sound for inspiration, and Star-Lord (the band, not the awesome hero and starship captain) sang about guts and glory. The others looked at each other skeptically, then reluctantly stepped forward to stand in a circle.

"So, this is it. How are we doing this?" he asked. "Without getting wrecked, I mean? Because I am absolutely assuming that door will try to kill us somehow."

Gamora looked up and down the hallways, chewing the tip of her thumb in thought. "I could try to find an air vent to crawl through, then open it from the other side."

"I will open the door," Drax said. "Let them come at me. I will destroy them."

"Bombs?" Rocket suggested. "There's always bombs."

As the others spoke, Groot stepped closer to the doors, paused, then stretched out an arm. Long tendrils grew from the tips of his fingers, stretching down the length of the hallway, until he could hit the door controls. Peter held his breath—but nothing happened. The door stayed firmly shut. Nothing tried to kill them.

O... kay.

Rocket took one step toward the door. Paused. Looked around, ears and nose twitching. Another two steps, then another.

Nothing.

Until Rocket touched the door controls, of course.

Above the door, a panel slid back, and a horrific screeching sound filled the air as three robotic sentries fell from the ceiling. Unlike the previous sentries they'd encountered, these ones did not simply wish to tie them up.

Instead, these ones were on fire, and they seemed to want everything *else* to be on fire, too.

"Yeeaaagh!" Rocket yelped, leaping back from the door and bringing his gun to bear in one smooth motion. Before he could fire, though, one of the sentries lashed out with long, fiery tendrils, each wrapping around one of Rocket's wrists. He cried out, and the smell of burnt hair filled the corridor until a swipe of Gamora's blade cut him free. Peter fired at the closest of the three drones, but they seemed to absorb the energy blasts without even the barest effort. Groot hauled back and punched one, but recoiled almost instantly, his bark singed black.

"Why fire again?" Peter whined. "Since when is fire our weak point as a team?"

The trio of sentries fell in line and set their flaming cords to spinning, reminding Peter terribly of his mother's aging weed whacker. She used to wield that thing like a spear, using it to scare off coyotes when they wandered onto the property. This whole job was filled with a confusing mix of nostalgia and fear for his life.

Groot punched the ground, sending up spikes like he did for the last bots, but these ones were much more nimble.

They dodged easily, then charged down the hallway straight for the Guardians.

Peter hit the deck, covering his vulnerable little human neck. The bots passed overhead with a blast of heat and a rhythmic *WHACK-WHACK-WHACK* sound. As soon as they had passed, Peter rolled over and brought his guns up, peppering the air with projectiles that *completely missed*, wow. Either these sentries were really agile or Peter was really losing his touch. Drax took a flaming lash to the face, and Peter locked eyes with Rocket.

"Crossfire?" Rocket said.

Peter nodded, flicked the switch on his guns, and aimed high, filling the air with a cloud of pink bolts. Rocket fired from the other direction, forcing the drones down, away from the ceiling. They managed to catch one in the web and blew a smoking hole in its side. The bots were too quick, though. Guns weren't the solution.

It was a job for the blade wielders, and they handled it beautifully.

The sentries dodged low, away from the bolts, only to drift perfectly into range of Gamora and her wicked sword. She sliced through the nearest one with a single clean swipe, while Drax dove onto the single remaining drone with his two knives held like fangs, stabbing down into the metal casing and ripping crosswise until the bot tore open with an eruption of sparks.

As the final sentry fell to the floor in a smoking, jerking mess, Gamora glared up at the ceiling.

"Okay, now you're just getting lazy," she shouted, her patience finally wearing thin. "You already did ropes once."

"And lit us on fire," Peter added.

Gamora glanced at Peter and shrugged. "To be fair, the fire was all you that first time."

"Look, where there's oil, there's gonna be fire, you have to plan for that—"

"I can't believe I'm the one saying it this time, but *can we please focus*?" Rocket said. "I would like to get through this door and say a *friendly hello* to the person who's been throwing all this scut at us."

"Credit where it's duuuuue," the Voice sang. "These security systems conveyed with the property. All I had to do was hit the on-on-on switch! Weird robots, remember, Quill?"

"Any chance you wanna hit the off-off-*off* switch now that we're right at your front door and it's pointless?" Peter asked.

"Awww," the Voice cooed. "That's adorable. No. But thank you for asking!"

Rocket stalked back over to the door and, with a quick glance at the ceiling, hit the controls.

The door slid smoothly open without protest.

"There," he said. "Was that so hard?"

He hoisted his gun in his arms and marched in. Peter steeled himself and followed.

The command hub looked exactly as it had twelve years ago. Six individual analyst stations arrayed around the edges of the round room, with one large central display for larger strategy coordination.

And at one of those six stations sat a woman with her back turned to the crew.

Rocket leveled his gun at her head and grinned.

"Okay, lady," he said. "I have been burned, stabbed, chased, tied up, and endured some *very* rude commentary from you. I'm gonna need you to step back from that terminal so I don't damage it by accident when I shoot you."

"Whoa, whoa, we aren't going to just kill her outright," Peter said. At the silence that followed, he looked around the group, brows furrowed. "We aren't. Right?"

Gamora drew her sword and tapped it on the ground beside her. Drax cracked his knuckles. Rocket's finger inched toward the trigger. Groot's fingers slowly began to stretch into tendrils.

"She shot at us, Peter," Gamora said. "A lot. With lasers *and* projectiles *and* fire."

"I am Groot," Groot added. Rocket nodded his agreement.

"Fire and trees, bad combo. Groot's pissed, and you ain't gonna like him pissed."

At that, Groot stretched his arms out, long tendrils vining toward the woman. In a blink, he had her bound and held six feet off the ground. Oddly, the woman didn't struggle. The curtain of her straight black hair fell across her face, but something about her still struck Peter as familiar. It could easily have been nothing more than the fact that she wore an old surplus uniform from around the base. Here, in this context, anyone wearing that uniform would feel familiar.

But then the woman tipped her head back so her hair fell away, revealing her features.

And down the side of the woman's face there was a ragged, badly healed scar stretching from her sunken cheek down to her knife-sharp jawline.

That scar, in this place, in that exact chair. Suddenly, Peter knew exactly who he was looking at.

"Suki? Suki Yumiko?"

The woman's head whipped around in his direction, and sure enough, there was no mistaking her. That straight black hair was still shoulder length and layered, though it was threaded with gray of late. Her face and body were the same shape, but haggard and gaunt. She looked like she hadn't eaten in rotations, maybe not since taking over the facility. The eyes... they were still that same shade of darkest brown, still filled with grief and pain and tortured by the lack of sleep. But they had a new shine to them. The same glint shared by warlords and religious zealots alike. Dangerous purpose.

And yet, her words held a softer edge.

"Ah, Peter. I've been expecting you."

"Well, *obviously*," he said. "You've been trying to kill us for the last half rotation, soooo..."

"Not *kill* you. Slow you down. I needed time. I knew you were here to take me away, but I needed to finish my work first. I mean you no offense, Peter Quill, but you and your *Guardians*..." She made air quotes, which Peter noted with both a thrum of nostalgia for Earth and mild annoyance at her obvious judgment. "Well. Your friends have a habit of..."

"Shooting things?" Rocket said.

"Stabbing things?" Drax added.

"I am Groot?" Groot noted.

"Not helping," Gamora said.

"Ah, yes," Suki said. "Such a team you've brought with you. Rocket the genetically altered super soldier. Groot the heir to an entire destroyed planet. Drax the Destroyer, slayer of Thanos."

"Allegedly," Drax muttered.

"And finally…" Suki turned to the last member of their party.

Then she lunged for Gamora's throat.

INTERLUDE: 12 YEARS AGO

MERCURY BASE – 7789

"KO-REL, wait! Ko— Damn it, wait up!" Peter called, jogging to catch up with her.

She did not wait up. She was focused on precisely one thing.

How exactly did one catch a traitor?

Ko-Rel supposed the easiest way would be to catch them in the act. When the act was passing information that didn't lead to a direct result until many hours or rotations later, though, making that connection was difficult. If not that, then finding an overwhelming amount of damning evidence would certainly do the trick. She didn't have that either, though. And she didn't have the time to wait.

All she had was suspicion. Intuition.

Some facts certainly pointed one way, but not enough to

make a robust case. Barring that, Ko-Rel did what Tar-Gold had always encouraged her to do: she trusted her gut. And her gut was pointing her solidly in one particular direction. Some latent pattern in the data her subconscious mind recognized but her conscious mind couldn't connect. Maybe something Suki had said, or something Ko-Rel had observed that had lodged itself in the back of her mind. Either way, her field of candidates had whittled down to three names. And of those three, one rose to the top.

Waiting for the suspect to slip up wasn't an option. Every rotation that went by was another opportunity for an attack. Every operation they conducted was potentially compromised. Ko-Rel decided on the direct approach.

She'd just... ask.

She opened the door to her quarters and nearly closed it in Peter's face, though he threw out a hand to stop it just in time.

"Wait, Ko-Rel, how can I—"

"How can you *help*? Is that what you're about to ask me right now?" Ko-Rel spat. "My second-in-command is dead. There's a traitor trying to make sure the rest of us follow him. If you know who it is, then by all means, say so. Otherwise, stay *out of my way*, Quill."

She whirled around, set down Lar-Ka's effects on the desk, ripped the nightshirt over her head, and stripped out of her shorts. She'd thrown both on in her haste to get to the scene of the attack, but pajamas wouldn't do for what she had in mind next.

Ko-Rel donned her uniform pants and undershirt with

quick, efficient motions. She strapped on her sidearm, stuck a knife in her ankle holster, shrugged on her uniform jacket, and stared at herself in the mirror for a brief moment. The woman who stared back was every inch a perfect military officer. Once upon a time she'd had a many-layered, colorful, vibrant life. A military officer, yes, but also an artist. A wife and mother. An appreciator of good music. A well-rounded person.

Those parts of her were gone. The officer remained. And the officer *would* deal with this problem.

Time to oust a traitor.

Ko-Rel burst into the hallway, walking straight past Peter with precise, measured steps. People jumped out of her way, wove around her, tossed her salutes that she returned without conscious thought. Her quarry would most likely be in the command hub this time of the day cycle, which wouldn't make for the most private of confrontations, but it would have to do. In fact, she tapped her comm and rallied together all her suspects.

"Officers Yumiko, Adomox, and Tasver to the command hub."

A chorus of, "Yes, ma'am," returned. Good. With any luck, this would be over soon.

At a junction of two hallways, she hung a sharp right, and Peter ducked around in front of her, hands held out as if to say *slow down*. "Hey, can we talk about this? What's the plan here?"

She turned, momentarily pulled from her focus by the only person who seemed able to successfully distract her of late. At the moment, though, that wasn't a good thing. At the moment, she wanted Peter Quill out of her face.

"There's no plan you need to be part of, Quill. This is a military matter, and you are not military. I am the commander of this base, and I have a personnel issue that needs addressing. Go back to the *Milano*."

She stopped in the middle of the hallway and looked Peter over head to toe, pursed her lips, and nodded.

"In fact, go back to the *Milano*, get in, and fly away. You're a distraction I don't need right now. This place is falling apart, and you're the only one who isn't obligated to be here. So go, Peter. Save your own life. At least one person should live to remember us all."

Peter blinked and let his hands fall to his sides.

"Wow, that got dark."

There was a beat of silence.

Ko-Rel burst out laughing. And then, all of a sudden, she was crying.

"Hey, no, I—oh man, I'm the worst at this," Peter said, ushering her into the bathroom across the hall and locking the door behind them. He pulled Ko-Rel into his arms and held her as she laughed and cried, and she knew she was making a mess of his precious jacket, but she didn't care. He'd probably grow out of it eventually anyway.

When she pulled back to wipe her dripping nose, she caught a bit of shine in Peter's eyes, too. She backed against the far wall and slid down it into a crouch, shaking her head at herself.

"I can't send you away. You're the only person I trust right now."

Peter smiled, though it was a little wobbly, and sat down against the wall opposite her. "And I'm not ready to leave yet, either."

Some tiny knot of fear under her breastbone unraveled at that. On some level, she'd thought Peter was moments from abandoning them all to their fate. She really had come to rely on him, especially since she felt like she couldn't much rely on herself at the moment.

"I've got to stop falling apart like this," she said. "I'm the d'ast commander of this base. I can't keep crying in closets."

"Okay, first of all," Peter said, holding up one finger, "crying is a completely acceptable reaction to all this, in closets or bathrooms or otherwise. There is some heavy scut happening here and I don't think it would exactly be helpful if you were an emotionless robot."

He hesitated, as if debating whether to continue, then held up a second finger. "And two... Ko-Rel, I think you have a lot of stuff you haven't really dealt with. I don't know what it is about that white football thing you took from Lar-Ka's room, but I know he was married. This is about your husband, right?"

It should have been awkward, the man currently warming her bed bringing up her late husband. It wasn't, though. They weren't romantic rivals or anything, and they both knew that. Their "relationship," if you could call it that, wasn't about commitment or love or anything like that. It was comfort, and tension release. It was staying alive.

That didn't make it any more comfortable to discuss, though.

"Even if you're right, what does that have to do with anything right now?" she asked. "We have a job to do."

"Yeessss," Peter said, drawing the word out. "But that job is gonna be a whole lot harder with you breathing fire and making like you're going to eat the face off the next person who looks at you wrong. We're going to catch this traitor. But to do that, we're going to have to play it a little more cool, right?"

Ko-Rel leaned her head back against the wall and let herself be overwhelmed by it all: grief over losing Lar-Ka, the hopelessness of their situation... and the still raw, oozing, infected wound that was the loss of her family. She let herself feel the phantom weight of Zam's head resting on her chest as she prepared to put him down for bed. Tar-Gold would stand next to her with his hand at the small of her back and sing Zam to sleep, always a lullaby of his own creation.

His voice was sweet and confident, the melody gentle and the words comforting nonsense. Zam loved it every time— couldn't sleep without it, in fact, which had caused problems on more than one evening. Ko-Rel smiled at the memory of one disastrous evening when Tar-Gold had been out for a late evening performance, leaving Ko-Rel to attempt to recreate the lullaby. She was an absolutely terrible singer, and Zam had protested with all his tiny toddler might.

She laughed at the memory, letting it fill her up. When she blinked her eyes open, they were wet at the corners.

"It feels like the Chitauri are killing them all over again," she said finally.

Peter nudged her boot with his and gave her a sympathetic smile. "Yeah. I can see that."

Ko-Rel sniffled hard and stared at Peter for a long moment, then held out her hand for him to take. He did, and they hauled each other up to standing. The silence that followed felt heavy, expectant. Ko-Rel knew this was the part where she was supposed to pull herself together, declare herself fine, and go forth to catch the traitor. She just... wasn't sure she could do it. Fine felt as far away as the Shi'ar Empire.

"Did your mom's death ever stop hurting?" she blurted out.

Peter fell back a step. He clearly wasn't expecting that line of questioning. A thoughtful expression crossed his face, and he hooked his thumbs through his belt loops.

"It'll never not suck," he said. "But in a way... the person I am now and the life I have are so different. The thirteen-year-old kid that watched the Chitauri kill her feels like a whole different person. And the more I do to build this whole other life that she never knew about, the more that... *gap* widens. You know?"

Losing a parent and losing a spouse and child were two very different things, and Ko-Rel wasn't sure she'd ever get to the point where she could think of Tar-Gold and Zam without feeling her soul break in two. But rebuilding herself into a whole new person with a whole new life... that sounded like exactly the kind of project she could throw herself into, once this was all over. Maybe Rider would rebuild the Nova Corps eventually, after the war. Maybe she could be a Centurion like him, find some little corner of the galaxy to protect and work on widening that gap.

It felt impossible in the moment. But it always would be, unless they survived this forsaken mission. If she'd been there when the Chitauri attacked Hala, she would have fought them with her bare hands to save Zam and Tar-Gold. But she hadn't been there. She'd been crash-landed on a planet, struggling to keep her crew alive, also thanks to the Chitauri.

This time, she had a chance to fight back. This time, justice was within reach.

"Come on," Ko-Rel said, wiping her eyes. "Let's go see if we can scare a traitor."

22

PRESENT DAY

MERCURY BASE – 7801

GAMORA Zen Whoberi Ben Titan was the deadliest woman in the galaxy. That she didn't kill Suki Yumiko instantly said a great deal about how much she had evolved over the years. Granted, Peter had only her reputation and a very few stories to go on, but if you'd asked him back during the war, or even a few cycles ago, what would happen in this exact situation, he'd be calling for a clean-up crew.

As it was, Gamora merely held her blade out to her side and allowed Suki to press the knife she'd drawn against her throat.

Suki's eyes shone with the perceived victory.

"Yooooou," she whispered. "Daughter of Thanos. Assassin. Murderer. So many others looked to the side when you joined the Resistance. They even say you won the war for us. Maybe it's true. But choosing to murder for the other side doesn't erase your past sins. The Chitauri who invaded this base were the same ones *you* fought alongside. If you hadn't lent them your power, perhaps they would not have been so strong and bold and daring. Perhaps they would not have killed here."

Gamora stayed silent, which Peter honestly thought was the smarter choice. He couldn't think of what to say that might get through to Suki, though. The wrong word could set her off again, and while Peter was pretty sure Gamora could get out of this situation and take Suki out without any issue, it wasn't exactly a risk he wanted to take with a knife at her throat.

Surprisingly, it was Drax who reached out.

"You have lost someone," he said to Suki. Not a question, but she answered anyway.

"I have."

"May I know their name?" Drax asked.

Suki's lips went pale as they pressed together, hard, holding back twelve years of pain.

"Many friends. But mostly..." She took a breath, bracing. "Hal-Zan. She was here, Peter, and you *saw* her but you never *knew* her, because she *died*. You never even got to meet the best person here. Because she was gone."

Rocket's gun drifted down a few inches. "What happened?"

Suki's eyes drifted to Rocket and took him in for a long moment.

"I'm sorry for you," she said, then looked away, back on the situation at hand. "You know what happened already. The

Chitauri came. Sneaky snuck inside the front door wearing someone else's skin. Killed them all. Peter and his dad paid them back for it."

"Whoa, Yondu is *not* my dad," Peter said, but a glare from Drax cut off any further protest.

Suki continued as if he hadn't even spoken. "And we thought that was it, but then they came again. Snuck right up on us. The Chitauri knew things. Had friends. *Here* friends. Someone to tell secrets and answer the door. You know, Peterrrr."

Peter shook his head, looking around at the others. "I really *don't* know. Ko-Rel thought she knew who it was, but she could never prove anything. There was definitely someone doing dirty work, though. From the time I arrived, weird stuff kept happening. Supplies went missing, people died, and missions that should have been total cake walks blew up in our faces."

"Cake walk?" Drax asked, puzzled. "Is that related to the teapot dance?"

"I will cut out your tongue," Gamora hissed.

Peter ignored them and kept his attention on Suki. "It was awful, but we didn't have enough proof to figure out who it was. Actually…"

Peter trailed off, then pointed at Suki.

"*You* were one of her suspects. It was you three intelligence officers."

"It was *one* intelligence officer," Suki shouted with sudden ferocity. "You were exactly right, but you gave up too easily!

You gave up, but I *never* did. I'm here, and I have it, the proof, the evidence. It's here, and I am so close so close so close to having everything. She was just too *good*."

"Who, the traitor?" Rocket asked.

"No!" Suki spat. "Hal-Zan. She was our systems security specialist, and *she* was more talented than any nasty lizard people or nasty traitor people."

Suki readjusted her grip on the knife at Gamora's throat and blinked rapidly.

"She was so good that I can't get past her encryption. The evidence is here. And I can't get it. It's so close. So close, so close, so close, sooooo…"

The Guardians looked at each other in silence. No jokes. No words at all, really. They'd all lost, and they'd all sought revenge in their own ways. The quest for it had nearly destroyed them all, too.

Drax finally broke the silence, taking one slow step toward Suki.

"I know what it's like to lose someone you care for very much, and to be willing to do anything to avenge them. I lost my wife and my daughter in the war, and countless comrades." He paused, then took one more step. "I also lost myself. I killed a great many innocent people in my madness. It wasn't until I turned myself in and asked them to lock me up that I could make myself stop. Grief… it can twist us until we are barely recognizable."

Suki stared straight into Drax's eyes. Gamora could easily have moved away, or taken the knife, or killed the girl, honestly. But she stayed stock still, letting the moment play out. Suki's eyes went far off for a moment.

"I tried to turn myself in." Suki blinked and returned her gaze to Drax. "Not to jail. I have not done anything worthy of jail until now. I tried a church. I begged them to save me. They said they could remove my grief."

"That sounds a little too good to be true," Rocket said. Groot rumbled his agreement.

"It was," Suki said. "They couldn't do it. Nothing could do it."

She shook her head, and said so quietly it was barely a whisper, "Nothing can do it but this."

Gamora took a slow, deep breath, closed her eyes, then opened them again to meet Suki's gaze.

"I am so sorry for your loss, and for my part in the war," she said. "I am no longer that person, but that does not excuse what I've done. I am so sorry for what the Chitauri did to Hal-Zan."

Suki lifted her chin and looked down her nose at Gamora, her eyes intense. "Am I to believe that the war changed you so much?"

Gamora shook her head as much as she dared, considering the knife. "Not the war alone. That started me down a new path, but it took me many years to walk any appreciable distance. I am still walking. I will be walking for the rest of my life, trying to put distance between myself and my father's influence. I know that remorse won't bring your friend back, but I want you to know anyway."

Peter cut his gaze to Drax, to make sure he wasn't about

to start in on Gamora yet again. Now was *very much* not the time. Drax frowned and looked away, but didn't comment. Gamora continued.

"We will help you get the proof you need. And once you have it, we will take you wherever you need to go. If you aren't sure where to go, then I have friends who would take you in, friends who can help heal your mind and feed your body. We will get this proof, and you will have your vengeance. And then you can have rest."

Suki's mouth quivered, her eyes going shiny and damp.

"I'm tired," she said, barely a whisper. Gamora's face crumpled, and she nodded, knife be damned.

"I know," she replied.

A beat later, the knife fell away. Groot's tendrils unwound, releasing Suki, who collapsed in on herself without the support Groot had clearly been providing. Groot rumbled gently and held out a hand toward her.

"Thank you, Mr. Tree," she said, taking his hand to steady herself. He hummed a quiet reply.

And with that, Peter finally allowed himself a quiet sigh of relief. Immediate crisis averted. No dead bodies in the room. That was not as common an occurrence as he'd like.

"So, then. Suki," Peter said, serving up his most disarming smile. "You said you had evidence, but you couldn't get to it. How can we help?"

"Yes. Proof. We had the proof then, too, but we didn't even know it. They killed my Hal-Zan. And we found who did it, you *know* we did, you were there, Ko-Rel was there, we were all *there there there* but noooooo. They were tricky and hidden and played so innocent. No justice. Not then." She smiled, her whole face brightening. "But *now*. There is proof, right in here, in *this*."

Suki lovingly patted the display in front of her. Several windows of data popped closed or slid across the screen with the motion.

"Yeah, no offense, lady, but I'm thinking you're never gonna find that data in your current, uh… *mental state*," Rocket said, as delicately as Rocket ever said anything. Gamora shot him a dirty look, then approached Suki slowly with one hand outstretched.

"You've been working on this for a while, haven't you?"

Suki nodded solemnly. "Rotations. A lot of them. I know I can do it. I used to do it. I used to be the master of allllll these. All of them. I just… need time. To remember."

She turned back to the display and swiped a few windows around, cycling through them without appearing to take in any of it.

"Remember, remember, remember, remember, re…"

She turned to face Peter, then sighed.

"I told you to look back. You never did."

Peter frowned, wrinkling his brow. "Uh… no, looking back's not really my style."

Suki rolled her eyes and heaved a second sigh, really laying on the theatrics to get her point across.

"No, Peter. You always miss the obvious. Literally… Look. Behind. You."

Peter's mouth snapped shut, and he turned slowly to look at the door they'd come through.

Mox was standing there, palm outstretched in a gesture Peter was unfortunately all too familiar with. It was the stance of a Nova Corps Denarian ready to draw on a bit of that Nova Force to blast some faces off.

"Whoa," Peter said, drawing both his guns and pointing them at her. Gamora followed suit and pointed her blade at Mox, edging over to stand protectively in front of Suki. Drax and Rocket glanced at each other, shrugged, then brought their weapons to bear as well.

"What are you doing?" Mox said incredulously. "I'm the one that hired you! She's the one you're here to deal with, so deal with her."

Ah, okay, so the threatening palmistry was for *Suki* not the Guardians. Still not great, but an important clarification.

"Sorry, sorry," Peter said, waving for the others to lower their weapons. "Thought the *talk to the hand* was for us. Nice of you to join."

Mox shrugged and took a few steps forward. "I'm glad I wasn't too late. The paperwork for that last investigation took ages."

She looked Suki up and down, taking in the scar, the hair, the ragged clothing. "I've been so curious to know who it was that decided to walk all over the memory of our people to bring this base back online. I shouldn't be surprised. You were always up in the hub late at night doing who knows what. I don't think the commander ever really suspected you, but I knew better. You played up the grief, but it was you passing information to the Chitauri all along."

Suki blinked once, then threw her head back and laughed. And laughed. And laughed, until it got awkward.

"Oh, Peter's not going to fall for that," she said finally, pulling herself as together as she ever was.

"Oh, uhhh," Peter stammered. "Right, yeah, but... she really did hire us to come here."

"Peter, don't be swayed by her ramblings like you were during the war," Mox said. "She's clearly gone mad. More importantly, though, she's trying to erase the evidence of what *she* did. You have to get her away from that station."

Suki laughed again, edging toward mania. "It... is so wrong! Wroooong, wrong, wrong! I am here, yes, I have the evidence, yes, but not to erase. Nevernevernever, noooo. Peter, you *know*. Look back."

"Look, Star-Lord, if you want the hundred thousand units, you have to do the job," Mox said.

"Units, units, there are no units. Peter, Peter, Peter Quillll, I have the proof—"

"She has *nothing*, Star-Lord, but you need this job. Your team is a mess. You—"

Peter put his hands over his ears and shouted.

"I need everyone to just *shut up* so I can think!"

INTERLUDE: 12 YEARS AGO

MERCURY BASE – 7789

A wildly bad idea was forming in Ko-Rel's mind. Of course, options were extremely limited, and "wildly bad" might be just the thing they needed. For now, she pored over words in her head, trying to find the precise ones that might get the traitor to out themselves and make a run for it.

Until the leak in their organization was patched up, until the traitor was caught, it wouldn't be safe to run another operation. It was breeding suspicion among the troops… but also fear.

Her people were afraid. Fearful soldiers made mistakes. They didn't stand up for each other.

And maybe fear could be the answer.

"Oh, scaring a traitor. That sounds like a party," Peter said. His face grew serious. "You know who it is, then?"

Ko-Rel's mouth pressed into a thin line. "I can't prove it. I *know* it's one of our intelligence officers, though. Now I just need to get them to slip up. And to do that, I need you. We're going to scare them, Peter."

Peter grinned. "Okay, I'm down. How do we do that?"

"Just follow my lead. You know how to improvise. Just try to look serious and tough." Ko-Rel paused. "Actually, maybe this is a bad idea."

"Hey!" Peter protested. "I can look serious and tough!"

"Well, then do it," Ko-Rel hissed. "And don't let anyone hear you say that, because it *really* doesn't help."

Peter grumbled something unintelligible, but squared his shoulders and kept his mouth shut. A moment later, they rounded the corner into the command hub and Ko-Rel came to an abrupt halt, her eyes raking over the intelligence officers at their stations. Only two of them.

Adomox was not present. Interesting. Suspicious.

"Yumiko. Tasver," Ko-Rel said, nodding to each. "Where is Adomox?"

They looked at each other and shrugged, shaking their heads. Okay then. A tiny smile began to form at the corner of Ko-Rel's mouth. Maybe this would be easier than she'd thought. Maybe their traitor had already done a runner.

Then the door to the hub zipped open, and Adomox rushed through, jogging to stand beside Tasver.

"I'm here," she said, coming to attention. "Apologies, ma'am. I was in the shower."

Her blond hair was dripping wet and hastily tied back, and

her pale cheeks were flushed red from the heat, corroborating her story. Ko-Rel controlled her disappointment externally, but wanted to growl with frustration. Of course it wouldn't be that easy.

"Peter," she snapped, never taking her eyes off the assembled officers. "Cross reference everything you're about to hear against this."

She drew a portable display from a nearby station and pulled out the screen, bringing up a random document. To Peter, it would look like an outdated inventory report. To everyone else in the room who couldn't see the screen, it could be any text-heavy document, whatever their wildest imaginations (or fears) could conjure.

Peter, to his credit, answered right away in an appropriately stern voice. "Yes, ma'am."

Ko-Rel folded her hands together behind her back and paced back and forth in front of her people, studying their faces intently.

"So, let's get to it. I know one of you three is the traitor."

Both Suki and Adomox took tiny sharp inhales. Tasver just rolled his eyes. Okay. Interesting.

"I don't suppose you want to save us all some time and just confess? Anyone?"

Tasver barked a laugh and stepped forward, holding his arms out to the sides as if to say, "Here I am."

"You got me. I'm the traitor. It's me."

Peter lowered the screen, his mouth hanging open. "Wait, really?"

Tasver rolled his eyes again with maximum drama and dropped his arms back to his sides. "No, pirate, of course not. Did you really think that was going to work?"

"No," Ko-Rel said honestly. "But on the off chance it did, I figured it would save us all an awful lot of hassle. Yumiko? Adomox?"

Suki's expression flipped from blank to furious in a heartbeat.

"Oh, *flark* you," she snapped, her olive-skinned cheeks darkening with the flush of rage. "Are you accusing *me* of working with the people who killed Hal-Zan? She was the most important person in the world to me, and you think *I*—"

She cut off, glaring back and forth between Peter and Ko-Rel, her breath coming faster and faster.

"How *dare* you so much as *suggest* that—"

"Okay, okay," Adomox said, laying a hand on Suki's arm. "I don't think anyone really suspects you, Suki. They're just being thorough. We all know you would never have hurt Hal-Zan."

Adomox arched an eyebrow significantly at Ko-Rel, who looked at Peter and sighed.

"So, we'll move on to reports instead, then," Ko-Rel said. "It occurs to me that I've been receiving all your reports filtered through each other, compiled into single documents. I'd like to hear a summary of everything you know about our enemy on this planet verbally, right now, in the presence of your fellow officers. We'll start with communications. Tasver?"

Ko-Rel looked to Tasver expectantly.

"O-kaaaay," he said. "Everything has been in my reports, but the short version is that we haven't had luck cracking their comm encryption. We know there are Chitauri communications coming from the two forward outposts they still hold, but that's it. And to be completely upfront, so you don't think I'm a traitor or anything, I feel like I have to clarify that even though there are incoming and outgoing comms from the listening posts, that doesn't mean the Chitauri are physically *there*. They could be using them as relay stations."

He stepped back to his station and flipped through open documents until he found the one he was looking for. With a quick gesture, he slid it from his display over to the main display, where it took up the whole area.

"These are the detailed logs of all communications we've managed to intercept. But again, there aren't any transcripts of what was said, just dates, times, length of calls, and so on."

He scrolled through to show them all the long list of communications, then turned back to face Ko-Rel, his face stony. "All due respect, ma'am, I'm not going to read the logs to you. You can see for yourself."

Ko-Rel had half a mind to reprimand Tasver for his tone and attitude, but she didn't have time to get into it with him. Let him be angry. *If* he wasn't the traitor, maybe he'd take it upon himself to investigate his fellows. Instead, Ko-Rel turned to Suki and gestured for her to give the next report.

"So? What have you been working on, Yumiko? You've been up all hours, putting in a lot of time on something."

Suki kept up the glaring as she pulled up her own work

on her display, then transferred it to the main screen as Tasver had. It was a collage of images, each featuring a single Chitauri with a white number label.

"I took over Adomox's project of counting all the Chitauri here on the planet. I haven't reported this yet because I'm not one hundred percent sure, but I…"

She trailed off, then looked to Ko-Rel with a solemn gaze.

"I really think there may only be ten individuals left on the planet with us. The original reconnaissance force that got spotted sniffing around out here, the whole thing that prompted us getting sent out here… if we're correct in our thinking that they're the ones who have been launching these attacks, that *they* didn't receive any reinforcements either, then look for yourself."

She tapped at her display a few times, then transferred a second document, this time with somewhat gruesome images of dead Chitauri from around the base, also numbered, and tagged with corroborating evidence from the medic reports following the counterattack cleanup. All totaled, between the two groups of images there were about thirty individuals.

Ko-Rel hummed thoughtfully. "And the maximum complement for the ship we think they came in on—"

"—is about thirty, yes," Suki said.

Peter's eyes went wide, and he looked to Ko-Rel, but she dodged his gaze and gave the barest of head shakes. Keep your cool, Quill.

"Okay, good work, Yumiko," Ko-Rel said. "And Adomox, what have you been working on?"

Adomox sighed and turned to her own console. "I don't have much to show you, but it's not because I'm a traitor or anything. I worked on the counting project before Suki took it over, and since then I've been trying to triangulate potential locations where the Chitauri might be hiding. And Tasver was right, I actually don't think they're using the forward bases. They might be holding them with just one or two people per outpost, or they might have no one there at all and be automatically routing communications."

Adomox moved a large-scale map of the base and surrounding area to the main display.

"I've been replaying battle footage and trying to determine the direction each attack came from. The shuttle that dropped off the Chitauri troops for the counterattack came in from the east," she said, double checking her coordinates and then drawing her finger through the air above an area east of the base. A glowing arrow appeared. "And the bomber flew in from that direction, too. Slightly different trajectory, a bit more southeast, but considering they were targeting the southern part of the base, we can likely account for that."

Ko-Rel nodded thoughtfully. "So, we think they're somewhere to the east of us."

Adomox drew two more circles on the map, this time far out to the west and north. "These are the locations of the two forward outposts, so I think this data reinforces the idea that the Chitauri are not using those stations as their primary bases."

"It certainly doesn't seem like the attacks are launching

from there, at any rate," Ko-Rel agreed. "Good work, people. Dismissed."

Tasver barked a harsh laugh and looked back and forth between Ko-Rel and his colleagues.

"Wait, so, you call us here, accuse us of being traitors, and now you just… let us go? If you think one of us is betraying the Resistance, why aren't you just throwing us all in the brig?"

Ko-Rel gave him a wry smile. "Two reasons, Officer Tasver. One, because we have so few people that I can't afford to lock up two innocent officers of any sort, much less my *entire intelligence division*. And two, because you're all going to watch each other, now. You know it's one of the three of you. Who better to ferret out the traitor than you three? Consider it your number one mission from now on. Questions?"

Many glares, but no questions, apparently.

"Great. Minimum two people on watch at a time from now on. No one is on watch alone. Rework the schedule, starting now. Peter, with me," Ko-Rel said, and walked out without another word. Much grumbling followed in her wake, but Ko-Rel just smiled to herself. Let them grumble. She didn't need them anymore.

"Well, that ought to keep them occupied for a little while," she said to Peter as he came alongside her.

"Uh, yeah, no offense, but that completely flopped," Peter said, trotting to keep up with her, purpose driving her steps.

"Not entirely," she said, turning to Peter with a sly smile. She sped up her pace and took the next left, leading Peter toward her brand new idea.

"But we didn't find the traitor." Peter shot her a quizzical look. "Are we heading to the landing bay?"

"Yes we are," she said. "I think it's high time you had me on board the *Milano* again."

PRESENT DAY

MERCURY BASE – 7801

PETER opened his eyes and took in Mox and Suki, standing almost where they had been back then, when he and Ko-Rel had confronted all three intelligence officers. In hindsight, only one of them had given new information in that moment, though she'd disguised it well.

"Adomox," Peter said. "You knew the Chitauri were in the caves to the east. You never said anything until you were forced, and even then you gave us just the basics."

Peter shook his head. "Dang, you played it so cool. Ko-Rel never did manage to prove anything. You said Tasver was dead in prison—that was you, wasn't it?"

Mox—*Adomox*—sighed, her shoulders falling slightly, the act slipping away from her in an instant.

"Yeah, I don't have time for this," she said.

ZZZZAP!

A beam of golden energy lanced out from Adomox's palm, striking Suki square in the chest.

"No!" Gamora shouted, leaping toward Suki's blackened form, too slow to keep her head from cracking against the floor. A smear of bright red human blood stained Gamora's fingers when she pulled her hand away. Peter drew his guns and fired in one motion, but Adomox leapt into the air, hovering near the ceiling as the bolts passed harmlessly beneath.

Most of Adomox's face was hidden by her Denarian helmet, but her mouth was perfectly framed by the gold metal as she smiled. Drax and Groot both charged at her, blades and fists at the ready, but Adomox produced an energy barrier with a quick swipe of her hand. The shimmer of gold light was faint, but clearly strong enough; Groot and Drax both bounced off as if they'd plowed into a wall. Mox's smile only grew.

"Oh, you're in for it now, lady," Rocket said, his ridiculously large gun unfolding in preparation for his first Denarian slaying. Adomox rudely chose to interrupt, dashing in for a vicious punch to Rocket's stomach. He folded in on himself with a wheeze and flew backward, slamming into the wall behind him. Adomox dove for Rocket, palm out and charging for a blast to finish the job, but Drax cut her off, rushing forward like a mac truck. He barreled straight into her, knocking her off course and into a grappling scuffle too close for Peter to shoot into. A flash of golden light, and Drax flew backward and smashed into the wall next to Rocket. He roared in protest and charged right back in.

"That gun is too big, Rocket," Peter said, firing off another round at Adomox while Drax was clear.

Rocket laid down some crossfire with his smaller, yet still quite substantial, gun. "There's no such thing!"

"There *is* such a thing," Gamora agreed. "If it takes so long to draw it leaves you vulnerable to your enemy, then it's *too big*."

"Oh, so Miss Stabby Stab is suddenly an expert on guns, now, is that it?" Rocket sneered.

Gamora spared Rocket a quick glare. "Don't forget Miss Slicey Slice, or Miss Cut Off Your—"

Drax cried out in pain as he took a blast to the shoulder, and Peter took the distraction as an opportunity to pepper the air with autofire.

"Can we please focus?" he shouted, as they all seemed to take turns doing. The fight was going extremely poorly, even by their standards. Before they could regroup, though, Adomox turned to smile at Peter.

"Thanks for taking care of all those obnoxious security systems. Never would have made it in here on my own," she said, taking a transmitter from her pocket. "Unfortunately, you're useless to me now."

She hit a button, and the whole central hub system went haywire.

The lights flickered, then went off, quickly replaced

with red emergency lighting. The formerly soothing voice of the hub system's computer network talked over itself in a cacophony of overlapping "things are going badly now" messages:

"*Data wipe initiated.*"

"*Base security disabled.*"

"*Venting oxygen.*"

"*Mechanical failure.*"

"*S-s-s-self-destruct has been set. Self-d-d-destruct will occur in twenty min-in-in-inutes.*"

"Oh, twenty minutes," Peter said. "That's not that bad. Actually pretty generous."

"That's not the best part," Adomox said with a wicked smile. "Farewell, Star-Lord."

Then the other guardians disappeared in a flash of harsh golden light, and Peter's vision went blank.

For a weightless moment, there was nothing—no sight, no sound, no sense of any kind.

Everything came rushing back far too quickly. His stomach twisted in a way that reminded him far too specifically of a terrible childhood afternoon filled with Jell-O salads and hot dog casseroles. It was the last time he ever let himself be talked into eating something to be polite to church ladies, and also the last time he went to church. When his vision cleared, he immediately fell to his knees and vomited, the phantom taste of Jell-O in the back of his throat.

"Oh, gross, Peter," Gamora's voice said from somewhere

behind him. She sounded strained from more than just annoyance, though.

"Are you hurt?" Peter asked.

"Hurting, but not injured. My head feels like Rocket's been tinkering inside it," she said, walking into his field of view with one hand pressed to her forehead.

Peter got slowly to his feet, propping one hand against the wall to steady himself. "Yeah, well, I'm pretty sure Rocket hasn't taken up brain surgery yet, though we will absolutely all die painfully if he does. Speaking of—where is the furry little sociopath?"

"And Groot? And Drax? What the hell just happened?" Gamora tapped her comm. "Hey, is everyone alive?"

A long pause, then a very faint reply:

"I… am Groot?"

"Yeah," Rocket said, sounding out of breath. "You got that right, buddy. I feel like a week-old orloni carcass. I'm in some hallway with a bunch of doors."

"So you two are together, then? Where's Drax?" Gamora asked.

"I am here," Drax said.

Everyone waited.

"Oh, was that it?" Peter asked. "Because I thought you were going to tell us something about your location, maybe, some useful fact that would help us all locate each other…"

"I am standing next to a walking, talking tree creature."

"So you're with Groot," Peter clarified.

"Is that not what I just said?"

"And Rocket is there, too?" Gamora asked.

"I do not see any raccoons."

"I'm not a flarkin' raccoon," Rocket shouted. Peter and Gamora both winced at the volume. "Don't be listening to Peter's garbage Earth animal talk."

"Okay, so Groot and Drax are together… somewhere," Gamora said. "Peter and I are here together, and Rocket is alone in a hallway. What was that, some kind of teleportation security system?"

"I never heard of anything like that being part of the base. Or any base. Have you?" Peter asked.

Gamora shook her head. "No, I haven't. I have a theory, but I don't like it, and I'd much rather be wrong. We need to find Mox."

Peter looked around once his head stopped spinning, taking in his surroundings. They were also in a nondescript hallway lined with unlabeled doors. He wracked his brain, trying to dredge up twelve-year-old memories of the base's layout through his wicked headache. Where had there been hallways like this? They had to either be the labs or the crew quarters. No other place on the base had so many small rooms all in a row. They had passed the labs earlier, though, and Peter didn't see any damage from the scuffle they'd gotten into. Which meant either Rocket was very nearby, or… he was back at the labs. The labs he wanted desperately to blow up.

Flark. He needed to get everyone back together before Rocket got explodey.

"Okay, Drax, can you actually tell us anything about where you are?" Peter asked.

"I am on my way back to Suki," he said. "The tree and I emerged in the cafeteria where we faced Peter's sexual fantasy robots."

"Oh my god, we are *not* calling them that," Gamora said with an eye roll so dramatic Peter was concerned for her eyeballs.

Peter chewed on his thumb and looked around. "Drax, my dude... I'm pretty sure Suki is dead. We only have twenty minutes on this self-destruct. We should probably focus on getting back to the ship."

"We must confirm her death before leaving her behind," Drax said. "We cannot leave her here if she lives."

"I'm with Drax on this one," Gamora said. "I was right next to her before we were separated, and she was still breathing then."

Peter groaned. Okay, that left one other. "Rocket, you good to get back to the ship from where you are?"

"Sure, I'll be there. I gotta handle something first, though," Rocket said ominously. Peter gave it a beat, and when Rocket didn't elaborate, ventured a tiny attempt.

"You know those labs are going to explode right along with the rest of the base when it self-destructs, right?" he said.

"Nope," Rocket replied. "That room is reinforced to withstand the strength of Rak-Mar's monsters, and I know bombs. Unless they took special care to plant something extra big and boomy, this lab area is gonna be missing a wall and a roof and that's it. I want it to be *powder*. I want to blow it up so hard there's nothing but a flarkin' *crater* left behind."

"Damn it, Rocket, Adomox is going to get away," Peter shouted. "Does no one care?"

"She's obviously not planning to pay us, Quill, in case that escaped your notice," Rocket snarled over the comm. "This is yet another flarked-up job where you screwed up and we don't get paid. *Again*, Quill."

"Hey, you all were there when we took the job, too," Peter protested, but Rocket cut him off.

"And do you remember that part where we said *no*? None of *us* wanted in, but you were all, 'I know this place like the back of my hand, it'll be so *easy*!' And look how *that* turned out. So you can take your wannabe heroic team leader scut and shove it up your ass!"

Peter felt it like a punch in the gut. He looked over at Gamora, and she met his gaze steadily, giving him no quarter. There was no deflecting or denying. The Guardians of the Galaxy was a failing marketing scheme, a team that couldn't hold together. And it was largely due to him. His lack of leadership. His lack of impulse control. He had no idea what he was doing.

Gamora reached up and tapped her comm to turn it off, then motioned for Peter to do the same. Once they had privacy, she took a step closer and spoke in a low voice.

"Let them go," she said simply. Peter shook his head, groaning in frustration.

"Adomox is probably halfway to her ship right now. I know it's my fault we're in this at all, but now that we *know* she was a traitor who was responsible for all those deaths during the war, don't we have to deal with her? Isn't that the right thing to do?"

Gamora nodded. "It is. But for Rocket, the right thing is also soothing some of the pain of what was done to *him* because of the war. And for Drax, helping to save someone else who lost their loved one during the war is his version of coping. Groot lost his entire planet and all his people because of the war, so creating more death and destruction is never his first reaction. His instinct is to protect, so of course he's with Drax on this one."

Peter ran a hand through his hair and huffed an impatient sigh. "And what about you?"

"I'm with you. I want to bring Adomox down."

"Okay, so let's—"

"But I want to do it my way."

Peter pressed his lips together and swallowed his protests. "And that is?"

Gamora walked a few steps down the hallway, reached up, and ripped the cover off of an air vent.

"I want to scout ahead, see if I can cut her off or slow her down. She's got a head start, Peter, she'll be off the planet before we ever manage to regroup and go at her. I'll be faster without you."

Peter sighed and put his head between his knees, his hands braced at the back of his neck. He really would rather he and Gamora stuck together. He'd rather they all booked it toward the *Milano* and escaped with their skins. Gamora sighed and folded her arms, looking down at Peter.

"We aren't pieces you can move around on a board. You can't just show off and say some quippy lines and think that makes everyone want to follow you around. Rocket may be a pain in the ass, but he's also *in pain*, all the time. What was done to him was unconscionable. Same with Drax. Same with Groot."

"Same with you," Peter said, meeting her gaze. She lowered her chin in the barest hint of a nod.

For the first time since Yondu got arrested and hauled off to the Kyln, Peter found himself missing the man. He led his portion of the Ravagers with an effortless sort of no-nonsense power. He didn't second guess, didn't wonder what others thought of him, just made the call and moved forward. It was easy to follow Yondu. Trying to lead like him was completely backfiring, though. How could he lead people who didn't want to be there? Who didn't trust each other, or him? He couldn't force them to trust him, or follow his word.

He could trust *them*, though.

Peter gave himself a beat to think it through, then turned his comm back on.

"Rocket, blow that place to hell. Meet us back at my ship once your charges are set."

"My ship," Rocket said. "I'll see you there. Groot, you alright, buddy?"

"I am Groot," Groot replied serenely.

"We are nearing the command hub once again. We will secure Officer Yumiko and the data once we arrive."

Peter felt a protest rise up in his throat, then swallowed it down and nodded. Which, of course, no one could see.

"Okay. Be careful. And fast. All the traps are disabled, so you should be able to make a beeline back to the landing bay once you have her."

"What do flower sex bugs have to do with this, Peter Quill?" Drax asked, baffled. "Honestly, you should focus."

Peter sighed, then looked up at Gamora.

"You want to scout ahead?"

Gamora nodded. "I'm going to, whether you tell me to or not."

Of course she was. Gamora was part of the team, but he wasn't sure she would ever be anything other than utterly alone. Still, he nodded back.

"Okay. I'll catch up as fast as I can. I'm heading straight back to the landing bay, and when I get there, I'm going to try to stop her."

"Don't let her kill you, Peter," Gamora said, already walking backward toward the landing bay.

"Same to you," Peter replied. Then Gamora grabbed onto the open air vent and pulled herself up into the ducts.

And so, Peter was alone. All of the Guardians were off on their own missions. He stood, checked his guns, then set off down the hallway at a jog.

Peter just had to trust they would all make it back in

time. He tapped behind his ear and checked the timer on his display.

Fifteen minutes until explosion time.

Peter double checked that his comm was turned off, then blew out a breath.

"Good luck, everyone," he said.

PRESENT DAY

MERCURY BASE – 7801

THE way out of the base was significantly easier than the way in. Peter dodged easily around security bot corpses, scorched marks on the floor, and found an alternate route around the oil slick hallway. Really, when dozens of things weren't trying to kill you, the base felt quite small. Small enough to make it from one end to the other in about five minutes. Convenient when a self-destruct sequence was active and the whole base was scheduled to go up in—he checked the timer—nine minutes from now.

Unfortunately, unless Gamora managed to slow her down, that meant Adomox was almost certainly long gone by now. Suki was in no shape to be playing her spider-at-the-center-of-the-web role.

"How's it going, Gamora?" Peter asked over the comm. "Any luck?"

A double tap came back, the Guardians' established signal for yes/acknowledged, but there was no elaboration. Peter took that to mean that she was close enough to Adomox that speaking would give her away. He pictured Gamora lurking on the ceiling directly over Adomox's head like something out of a spy movie, waiting to pounce, then pushed the image away before he could laugh. He wanted to check in on the others, too, but held his tongue. That would only be more alienating, probably. Let them do their thing. He needed to concentrate on his own goal. Head for the *Milano*, for Adomox, and stay on target. He probably couldn't take her out on his own, but maybe he'd be able to keep her distracted long enough for the others to get there.

He rounded the last few corners, nearing the infirmary, and hesitated. Which way should he go? There was the infirmary entrance to the landing bay, but the entrance closest to him was a big cargo door funneling from the center of the base, and another entrance from the other side of the base near the living quarters. He decided to go for the gold and make a dramatic entrance through the big double cargo bay doors. Why not? If his goal was to buy time, then there was no point in being subtle about it. He took a breath to steel himself, drew his guns, and hit the door controls with the back of his hand. The double doors creaked and groaned as they slid open, having not been used in many years, and on the other side there was Adomox, just emerging from the door near the crew quarters.

"Hey!" he shouted, then dove to one side as she held up her palm, shooting a blast of golden energy at him without even acknowledging his presence first. Rude.

He didn't want to escalate things into a firefight just yet, though. The longer he could put that off, the better. Instead, he held his guns at his sides and stepped slowly into the landing bay, his eyes briefly cutting over to the *Milano*. Gotta check on his baby, make sure she was safe. Just in case, he activated the ship controls via his visor and turned the force shields on. Couldn't have a stray blast destroying his pride and joy, his longest running companion… and their only way out of here. The shields flickered to life with a hum and a faint silvery blue glow.

Adomox walked deeper into the landing bay and shook her head at Peter, smiling.

"Oh, Peter Quill. Sorry, *Star-Lord*." She rolled her eyes. "Why are you bothering to come after me? What's past is past. I've already gotten what I wanted. You and your crew are all alive and well. What's the point of sending your little assassin after me, to slow me down? Oh, don't think I didn't notice."

"Notice? I highly doubt you ever actually saw her."

Peter casually scanned the loading area, looking for any flash of telltale green skin or red-tipped hair that would indicate Gamora's presence. He couldn't find her anywhere… except oh, *there* she was, clinging to the rafters over Adomox's head. She put a finger silently to her mouth, in a *shhh* gesture. The corner of Peter's mouth ticked up, but he gave no outward indication that he'd seen her. Adomox didn't either.

"I don't need to see her to know she's there," Mox said, keeping her fists held up in a defensive posture, no doubt ready to blast Peter to dust at the first wrong move. "I thought with Suki gone all the security would be taken care of, but *somebody* seemed to be following me, blowing up door locks and triggering droids that wanted to tie me up. Whoever designed the security systems for this place really had a strange sense of humor."

"You know, I think a guy named Hark Taphod may have hired the same contractor. I can put you in touch, if you're curious," Peter said, fishing for something more he could say to stall. "Was it really worth it? Coming back to kill Suki?"

"Oh, come on, Star-Lord, you know that's not why I came back. Not entirely, at least." She came to stand right in the center of the loading zone, her arms folded. "Did you know that most of the people who worked directly with me during the war are dead? A few died in the final offensive in the last cycles and rotations of the war. A few others due to... mysterious circumstances in the intervening years."

"Mysterious circumstances... meaning you killed them. You're covering your tracks."

Adomox shrugged. "*Something* killed them. I guess we'll never know. There have always been a few holdouts, though. I was finally able to get to Tasver. Suki, as you know. Well, knew. Ko-Rel is out and about. She's more difficult, being a Centurion and all. Tougher to kill and always surrounded by guards. And then there was you."

She smiled. "I debated for a while, you know. Whether

it was worth trying to kill you too. You and Ko-Rel were the only other people who knew, or suspected at least, that I had been playing the other side back then. You were nothing more than Ko-Rel's plaything, though. I didn't think there was much point in killing you when you didn't seem to care that much. Not really one for living in the past, are you, Star-Lord? But then this opportunity presented itself. Suki was here. I needed a meat shield for the security systems. You were suddenly so easy to find, being formally registered with the Nova Corps database. The Gardeners—sorry, *Guardians* of the Galaxy, heroes for hire. Comm code right there and everything, so easy to track you down and *hire* you for a 'job.' You certainly didn't make it difficult. I half expected to find a stack of business cards sitting in the lobby of the Nova Corps headquarters back on Xandar."

Ooooh, that's not a bad idea, Peter thought. They did, in fact, have an excess of business cards and a powerful need to distribute them. They'd tried handing them out on Knowhere, but it hadn't brought them very much in the way of jobs. Peter wisely chose not to share the existence of the business cards with her. He didn't think she would respect the effort. Above her head, Gamora rolled her eyes... which made Peter instantly change his mind. You know what? He was proud of the d'ast business cards.

"Here, actually, let me give you this," he said, holding out his one hand in a "don't shoot" gesture while he dug in his pocket for a moment. A few ticks later, he emerged with a business card, on which he had doodled a practice Star-Lord signature. (He may have been imagining signing autographs at the time, but that was completely irrelevant and absolutely did not need to be pointed out in Gamora's presence.) He flicked it to Adomox, who knelt down to pick it up.

"Oh, you *do* have business cards! That is adorable! Thank you for sharing this with me," she said, tucking the card into her pocket. "I'll be sure to tack this up on a board at headquarters with a heartwarming story about how I met you recently. It'll be great cover for when you turn up dead later."

Oh. Well. Maybe not such a good idea, then. Peter sighed internally.

"Okay, look, maybe we should just do this," he said, putting his guns up at the ready. He felt every inch of the echoing launch bay around him. No one at his back. No one at his side. At least Gamora was there, so he wouldn't be one hundred percent alone if he bit the dust. Still, this felt like a moment for the Guardians of the Galaxy to band together and do the heroic thing.

And here he was, alone but for Gamora hanging from the rafters, because he'd chased everyone away.

Ah well. There were still heroics to be done. Star-Lord reached up and activated his red-eyed helm. Ready to go.

Adomox sighed.

"Come on, Star-Lord, don't even bother. Just hang out here for seven more minutes until the base self-destructs. You'll go quick and painless, with all your friends by your side. It's kinda sweet, isn't it? Poetic even. Besides, you can't fight me alone."

"He's not alone, you shiny golden pain in my ass," a voice said from the far side of the landing bay. There, standing in the open infirmary doorway, stood Rocket and his extremely large gun, with the latter pointed straight at Adomox's torso. "He's got me, and *I've* got this amazing gun I designed myself, so I know exactly what it can do."

"Which is?" Adomox said, rolling her eyes.

"Blow your flarkin' head off, you traitorous lump of turd," he spat, cocking the weapon.

"Oh, you boys and your guns. I'm a Denarian. I have access to the Nova Force. You'll never bring me down just the two of you."

"I am Groot," came another very distinctive voice. From the living quarters side of the landing bay, a door had slid open, and Groot and Drax stood there shoulder to shoulder. Groot's back held a bundle wrapped in vines and branches, the tendrils blooming with spring-fresh bright green leaves and golden glowing spores. Suki. Peter's chest swelled with some kind of feeling he didn't want to look at too much. Something adjacent to relief, but having more to do with the fact that all his friends had come back together after all. Everyone was there, in the landing bay, surrounding Adomox, being heroic.

"She alive?" Peter asked.

"She is," Drax replied. "She is a fighter. Her body and mind are strong. She will survive."

Drax's knives appeared in his hands in a flash, and he settled into a fighting stance, his gaze locked on Adomox.

"You, however," he said, lip curling in disgust. "You, I will enjoy destroying."

Adomox threw her head back and laughed. "Oh, please. How exactly are you planning to keep me here? I'll level this base and be gone before you can even put a scratch on me."

"You know what?" Peter said, smiling. "I really, really doubt that. You have no idea who you're dealing with."

Peter brought his guns up to bear and nodded.

"We're the Guardians of the Galaxy. Let's be heroes, kids."

Gamora let go, falling sword-first down onto Mox's head.

PRESENT DAY

MERCURY BASE – 7801

GAMORA'S sword missed slicing through Adomox's head entirely, sadly, but she did draw first blood, and that was an auspicious start.

"Agh!" Adomox cried. She dropped forward, flipping Gamora over her head, sword and all, and leapt backward to put a safe distance between them. She fired twin lances of energy from her palms, which Gamora dove out of the way of easily. The cut at the junction of her shoulder and neck where Gamora's sword had bitten flesh glowed faintly, then began to stitch back together.

"Ugh, healing factor, the worst," Gamora said.

"Not the worst when it's you doing the healing," Peter said.

"My healing factor is nothing like that," Gamora replied, and leapt back into the fray, sword flashing.

"Must be nice," Peter grumbled, but let it go, leaping into the air with a boost from his jet boots. Groot stayed huddled in the doorway, growing extra layers of branches over Suki's unconscious body to protect her from the battle. He needed cover, and a distraction. Peter carved a line of energy bolts around behind Adomox, hemming her in so Gamora and Drax could close in—but Mox leapt into the air, hovering just out of reach of both blade wielders and over the stream of bolts.

"Yo, Quill," Rocket called, then sprinted his way across the loading zone, Peter providing covering fire all the way. "There's something not right with that helmet. She's stronger than she should be."

"What does that have to do with her helmet? It looks like every other Nova Corps helm I've ever seen."

"No, there's something different about it. The helmet is like a valve that regulates a Nova Corps officer's access to the Nova Force. I've fought the Corps' officers before. Trust me. I've only heard of this level of strength from Richard Rider."

"But he had access to the full Nova Force," Gamora said. "She's not that strong."

"No, but she ain't *not* strong either. Have you fought many Denarians in your day, lady?"

"I have."

"Then tell me she ain't more like a Centurion. Tell me she hasn't tampered with that helmet of hers."

Gamora somersaulted out of the way of a trio of energy blasts, then closed the distance, drawing Mox into a close-range sparring match.

"Rocket's right. What's your deal?" Gamora said. "You're a Denarian, but you fight like a Centurion. Like a *strong* Centurion. That weird teleportation thing earlier—that was *you*, wasn't it?"

She ducked under a wicked right hook, throwing her shoulder into Adomox's stomach and tossing her over her shoulder. Mox tried to fly away, but Gamora grabbed her by the ankle and yanked her back, throwing her at the ground.

"I used to fight alongside Richard Rider," Gamora said. "I know a few things about the Nova Force. Enough to know something's not right with you."

Mox landed in a crouch and met Gamora's gaze head on.

"War hero Richard Rider," she sneered. "Richard Rider should have shared the Nova Force when he had a chance, instead of keeping it all for himself. The entire Nova Corps was destroyed at the beginning of the war, but did he rebuild? No."

She launched herself at Gamora, who danced back, making room for Peter and Rocket to fire. Mox raised her forearms, channeling a golden force shield to deflect the blasts.

"He should have figured out a way, should have negotiated with the Worldmind to share the power. Instead, he put us out here on this outpost, normal soldiers with no powers, undergunned, undermanned, just here to die for the cause, for *his* home planet. For *your* planet, Star-Lord. Why should I have gone along with that? Why didn't he share his power so we could fight back for real?"

She shot an energy beam at a barrel of something covered

in warning labels off to Peter's left, and he dove with a little assist from his jet boots. The heat and pressure from the blast sent him tumbling end over end, nearly into the far wall.

"The entire Resistance was doomed," Adomox shouted in the wake of the shockwave. "There was no hope of winning. Only of surviving. If it hadn't been for *you* killing Thanos—" She sent an energy blast at Drax, then at Gamora. "—and *you* with that crazy plan with Richard to kidnap the Chitauri queen, and *you*—"

At this, she didn't bother shooting, only glared at Peter with white-hot intensity.

"Peter Quill dropping in here like some grand savior… if it hadn't been for you three, that's exactly how it would have played out. I would have been the smart one who thought ahead and stayed alive and had a place with the new regime. And you all would have been dead."

Groot reared back and lashed out with both arms, tendrils growing in a flash to form powerful whips.

"But you got what you wanted after the war. You're a Denarian," Peter said, taking advantage of the opening Groot provided, pumping steady fire into her seemingly endless shields while she blocked Groot's lashes. Had to keep her talking and distracted. Maybe she'd slip up, reveal something useful. "You have the power of the Nova Force now. You even have a place in the new regime. It just isn't no people you thought you'd be working for. Why are you still fighting the same old fight?"

Adomox laughed.

"Yes, I got my piece of the Nova Force after all. Once it no longer mattered. But I was more patient this time around. I showed my hand too early during the war. Now?" She smiled. "The war is coming back, Quill. Maybe not the Chitauri, but there'll always be a next war. And when it comes, I'll be ready. I'm gonna take down the whole Nova Corps from the inside. I'll be on the winning side of history *and* destroy Richard Rider's legacy all in one move."

"Like hell, lady," Rocket said, chucking a cluster of grenades at her feet. In the resulting flash of light, Peter caught Rocket shaking his head. "She's lost it. Never thought I'd be defending the Nova Corps. And yet, here we are. Life is strange, isn't it, Quill?"

"Sure is," Peter said, a terrible plan forming in his mind. "You think we'll get premium billing in the Nova Corps database for this? You were right, we're gonna need some better jobs after this."

"I want it noted in the record," Rocket shouted over the sound of his gunfire. "On this rotation, Peter Quill said I was right."

Peter rolled his eyes. "No one needs to note it in any record, because you're never gonna let anyone forget it."

"Accurate," Rocket admitted, then chucked another bomb at Adomox, who kicked it straight back. A brief game of hot potato later, and the bomb exploded far too close to the *Milano* for comfort.

"Hey, watch out for my ship," Peter shouted.

"My ship," Rocket corrected automatically.

Peter glanced at the timer in the corner of his visor—just three minutes until the self-destruct. They needed a plan.

"Okay folks, huddle up, open to suggestions here," he said, using his jet boots to boost near the ceiling and get a full view of the battlefield. Everyone was pulling out all the stops—blades flashing, swords slicing, splinters flying, guns spitting—but Mox took it all in stride.

"She is unhinged," Drax said, throwing himself back at her. His blades glinted in the blood-red emergency lighting as he drove her back with a flurry of blade strikes, finishing with a truly badass kick to the solar plexus. If Drax were Terran, he would make a killer WWE wrestler.

"The Nova Force has driven her mad," Gamora said, blocking a blow with her sword. "Richard used to have problems, too, before he disappeared. The Worldmind helped him manage it, but too much exposure to the Nova Force can break you, body and mind."

Adomox cackled, peppering the entire landing bay with a dozen energy lances. The *Milano*'s shields buckled, and Peter winced.

"Yeah, all things considered, I'd say moderation is not her strong suit. Any ideas?"

Groot planted his feet and clenched his fists, spikes growing from his shoulders as he mustered his strength. "I am Groot. I… am *Groot*."

"He's right," Rocket said. "That helmet has got to go."

"You planning to run up there and rip it off, then?" Peter asked with a sinking feeling.

"Not it," Rocket said, touching his nose. Drax, Gamora, and Groot all managed to do the same while fighting off Adomox's advances. Impressive… and annoying. He wished he'd never told them about the "not it" rules. He'd wasted the opportunity on getting out of cleaning the *Milano*'s single shared bathroom. At the time? Totally worth it! Now, he wished he'd saved that little bit of Earth trivia.

"Fine," he said, activating his body shield and jetting in toward Adomox. "Distract her."

"I am *Groot*!" Groot declared, lashing out with fresh tendrils to wrap Adomox's wrists behind her back. Rocket tossed a stagger bomb that exploded with a bright white flash, momentarily dazing Mox long enough for Peter to put on a burst of speed and leap onto her back, his arms wrapped around the shiny gold helmet. He wrenched backward, throwing all his weight into it, but she tipped forward instead, sending Peter tumbling over her shoulders and crashing to the floor.

Drax leapt in, blades held in stabby fang grip, and managed to sink one blade deep into her shoulder as he feinted with the other, switching to a grab at the last tick. He hauled up on the bottom of the helm, and it came up just high enough for Peter to get a glimpse of her freckled cheek, before she hauled back and headbutted Drax. His nose burst with blood, and he stumbled backward, a hand cradling his face. She thrashed against Groot's hold, kicking Gamora back as she darted in for her own attempt at the helm, a scream building in her throat until it became a roar. A surge of golden energy flooded out from her, knocking everyone back into the nearest wall.

Adomox's eyes were wild, flaring with blue-white light, the power pouring off her in waves.

"Self-destruct in one minute," the base's automated system said. And that, finally, seemed to get through to Adomox.

"Well," she said, tugging her helmet securely back down with her good arm. "This was annoying, but I appreciate your help regardless. The data has been deleted by now, so my mission here is done, I suppose. As much as I'd prefer you dead, you just… aren't that important. Farewell, Star-Lord."

With that, she put her hands together, holding them a few inches apart as a pulsating glow began to form. Golden light flickered and danced around her hands as a glowing sphere grew larger between her palms.

"Duck and cover!" Peter shouted, leaping behind some nearby crates, but he was far too slow. The shockwave hit with a massive *WHUMP*. Peter threw his arms over his head and squeezed his eyes shut—

—as he coasted through the air toward the crates, bonked his head, and floated backward, weightless.

What?

"What the flark happened to the gravity?" Rocket snapped as he went tumbling end over end past Peter. When Peter glanced overhead, he saw Adomox's glinting gold form arrowing into the sky. He set his jaw, glanced back at the others, and made a decision.

"Gamora, get the *Milano* in the air. I'm going after her," he said, firm and sure. "Rocket… I need your help with a very bad idea."

INTERLUDE: 12 YEARS AGO

MERCURY BASE – 7789

SOMETIMES a gamble pays off big.

Sometimes, you have no idea just how big you've *lost* until all the cards are on the table.

Ko-Rel had known her plan to flush out the traitor was risky. If the turncoat felt threatened, their options were essentially lay low, make a run for it, or send word to their Chitauri buddies to create a "distraction." Since none of the three suspects had helpfully outed themself, Ko-Rel had to assume that option three would be in the works as soon as the traitor could disentangle themself from the bureaucratic web she'd just woven with her orders.

By then, it would be too late, she hoped.

"So, don't get me wrong," Peter said as they jogged toward the *Milano*'s unfolding docking ramp. "I'm happy to have you on my ship again. Anytime, really. But… why are we here?"

Ko-Rel took a brief detour to lift a hefty crate marked *DANGER: EXPLOSIVES*, then beat Peter to the *Milano*'s ramp and set it down just inside. Once her arms were free, she went straight for the flight deck, calling back to Peter as she did.

"You and I are going to win back Mercury."

She sat at the front right crew station, looking over the gunnery controls as Peter joined her, blinking in confusion.

"What, just you and me? If two of us could have stopped all this with a crate of explosives before, why didn't we do it then?"

"Because we've been thinking about it all wrong, and we didn't have all the information," she said. "Now we have everything we need."

Peter gave a slight unconscious smile as the *Milano*'s engines thrummed to life.

"So shouldn't we rally some troops or something?" he asked.

Ko-Rel shook her head. "That's the other difference. When we were first planning ops, we didn't know we had a traitor leaking all our plans to the Chitauri. Until the traitor is apprehended and locked down, we still have to assume that every operation is compromised. There are only two people I trust on this base right now—you and me. So we're all we've got. Fortunately, we're all we need. Take us out and northeast. Fly low and slow for now."

Peter's hands danced across the *Milano*'s controls with such comfortable familiarity that he could probably do so blindfolded. He looked up and met her gaze even as he smoothly throttled up and took them out.

"You planning to tell me where we're going, or…"

Ko-Rel glanced quickly over the tactical systems to familiarize herself, then back to Peter as she replied, "You know what's over in that direction?"

Peter shook his head. Ko-Rel grinned.

"The caves. The ones you found us making our last stand in. Pretty decent hiding place, all told. Except for one minor thing."

Ko-Rel called up a map on her display and blew it up larger to show Peter.

"The one thing our scouts did manage to do before the Chitauri made their counterattack was map out the immediate area around the base, including the cave systems. And when I saw the scans I remember thinking to myself, wow, it's a good thing we didn't end up staying there, because there is one big flaw in this location."

She zoomed in on the mountain range and toggled off the top layer to reveal the cave system below, outlined in red.

Including the second exit about a klick and a half to the north.

"Oh, yeah, scut, that would have been bad," Peter said. "It would have been such a shame if someone were to use that second entrance to, you know, sneak in and plant some explosives or something."

"Would have been catastrophic, I think," Ko-Rel said.

"Someone should really show the Chitauri the fatal flaw in their hideout." Peter met her eyes and smirked. "It's only fair, you know?"

"It's the kind thing to do, really," Ko-Rel agreed.

The *Milano*'s engines hummed higher as Peter swung them out wide, looping around far to the north of the cave system. Element of surprise and all that. Once they'd put enough distance between themselves and the base, he kicked the throttle higher and turned on some music, looking up at Ko-Rel for approval. She listened for a moment, nodding along.

"What is this?" she asked.

"Star-Lord!" he shouted over the instruments, then sang along when the chorus came around.

"*No guts, no glory! It's the name of the game, the price for fame, the story! If you wanna succeed, you gotta fight and bleed for your needs! No guts, no glory!*"

Ko-Rel raised an eyebrow and leaned back in her seat, laughing.

"Okay, the translator implant can*not* be getting that right. No *what*, no glory?"

"Guts!" Peter said, bobbing his head along to the music. "Like, courage, bravery, decisiveness, all that."

"And that has what to do with intestines, exactly?"

"I have no idea!" Peter said, and pulled a hard bank into a valley. "Whooooo!"

Peter throttled down a *little* too hard, jerking them both against their restraints, but set them down in a perfectly gentle, flawless landing just a quarter klick from the rear entrance to the cave system. The music kept playing as they unstrapped and began their prep work, cycling through songs such as "Space Riders," "Solar Skies," and "All For One." Peter knew every word by heart and sang them all with gusto, belting out the high notes slightly off key with the unselfconscious confidence of someone who was really feeling it.

They took their time checking their envirosuits and divvying up the explosives, giving a bit of time to see if the Chitauri had noticed their approach.

Nothing, though. No launching ships. No approaching troops. No increase in comm chatter that they could detect with the *Milano*'s limited sensors.

"Let's move," Ko-Rel said. "The quicker we get this done, the less time the traitor has to slip away and warn their Chitauri buddies. The suits won't be able to handle the full sun for more than a few minutes, so we'll need to run."

"You got it, Commander," Peter said with a salute. "Lead the way."

Ko-Rel pulled up the map of the cave system on her HUD and sprinted her way across the dusty Mercurian landscape, keeping her hands wrapped around her pulse rifle. Every step toward the caves rose her heart rate a tick as the force of her inspiration and conviction gave way to the reality of combat operations. This would make or break them and every Resistance fighter on the planet.

"So, what do we do once we're in there?" Peter asked as the mouth of the rear cave entrance came into view. There were no guards posted, confirming Ko-Rel's theory that the Chitauri likely didn't know about it any more than they had when they'd first taken refuge there. Ko-Rel tapped the side of her helmet to zoom in and scan the entire mouth of the cave, but saw nothing.

"We go in, see what we're working with," she said. "And we wing it."

Peter looked at her and blinked. "Oh. That's... actually my kind of plan. Let's do this!"

Ko-Rel winced. "Let's maybe do this... quietly?"

"Oops," Peter said, then lowered his voice to a whisper and repeated himself. "Let's do this!"

If they survived this, it would be a miracle. Ko-Rel rolled her eyes and led the way into the cave.

For the first kilometer, there was absolutely nothing. No sign of Chitauri activity or structure. Rocks, stalagmites, stalactites, and whole lot of dusty regolith. It took them about twenty-five minutes to pick their way slowly through the caves until, finally, they heard a sound. Ko-Rel gave a sharp gesture and ducked behind a small outcropping. Peter crouched immediately behind her, pressed against her back as they listened. Chitauri voices rose and drew closer, and Ko-Rel's finger tightened on her trigger, her breath becoming deep and smooth.

And then the voices faded, moving on past their location. Behind her, Peter let out an audible sigh of relief.

"Can we start planting bombs now?" he asked. "I'm feeling a bit jumpy."

"Best not get too jumpy with a bunch of explosives in your bag," Ko-Rel reminded him. She leaned out from behind their cover and studied their surroundings. There was what at first glance looked like a solid wall of rock, but with a deep crevice near one wall that went all the way through to the other side, artificial light shining through. Definitely where the voices had come from. A natural breaking point between the front caves and the rest of the system. "I'd say we're at a good starting spot. Can you fit through that little passage right there?"

Peter looked out too, then nodded. "I can wiggle my butt through, no problem."

He, of course, had to turn around and wiggle his butt at Ko-Rel to demonstrate. She took a moment to analyze, then slid her bag off her shoulder and withdrew two charges. Two on this side and two on the other side of the wall would likely be enough to cause a cave-in and block the back exit if needed. Good to have options. She set the two charges and synced them to the control on her wrist display, labeling them as Group One.

"We doing timers or triggers?" Peter asked as he squinted through the crevice.

"Triggers," Ko-Rel answered. "Who knows how long we'll be here, or which direction we'll need to leave through."

"Uh, I vote we leave the way we came, personally," Peter said. "If we're leaving out the front, something has gone wrong."

And yet, didn't things always go wrong?

"Move your butt, let's get going."

Ko-Rel nudged past Peter and held her bag by the strap in one hand and her pulse rifle complete with finger on the trigger in the other. She turned sideways and shimmied through the crevice, gun first, of course, scraping along the rocky wall inch by stubborn inch. When she finally neared the end, she stuck her head out and looked both ways. Nothing. No movement, no sound. She squeezed the rest of the way out and knelt with her rifle ready as Peter did his shimmy through.

"Do you remember the layout of these caves? Places where they might stash the good stuff?" Peter whispered over the comm.

Ko-Rel shook her head.

"Voices went that way, so let's go this way," she said, pointing. She led the way down a branching path toward a glowing light. She poked her head into a lit room, rifle leading the way. The room turned out to be a makeshift field kitchen, with crates of rations, heating elements, and their water filtration system. Big score. If nothing else, they could starve them off the planet.

Ko-Rel hurried into the room and motioned for Peter to plant one of his charges behind the crates of foodstuffs. She slung the strap of her rifle over her shoulder and rotated it around her back, out of the way, then knelt behind the water filtration system. It was an older model, one that could only support about a dozen humanoids. Good to have their assumptions about numbers confirmed. She affixed a charge to its power source, low and out of sight of the doorway.

That done, she stood—only to see a Chitauri standing in the doorway with a gun pointed at Peter's forehead.

Peter slowly raised his hands, laughing nervously.

"Relax, brother," Peter said. "These are new shapeshift forms. We're testing them out for another infiltration attack."

Ko-Rel felt a tiny piece of her soul shrivel up and die. That would never work. They were doomed. She shifted her weight, trying to encourage the rifle slung over her back to stay out of sight.

And yet, the Chitauri blinked, cocked his head, and stared hard. "There are so few of those vermin left, though. They'll notice any interlopers. I thought we agreed, infiltration was off the table for any future attacks."

Oh. Well. That was good information to have, at least. And, somehow, this plan wasn't crashing and burning yet. Ko-Rel jumped in.

"That's true, though we got footage of their leader and one of the pirates who stayed behind. We thought replicating those two specifically might bring about some... interesting opportunities."

It sounded good to her, but maybe that was the problem. The Chitauri narrowed his eyes at her, looking her up and down, then did the same to Peter.

"Who's behind that form?" he asked, tone turning suspicious.

Uh-oh.

"What, you don't recognize me?" Peter said with a laugh, holding his arms out.

"Not with that ugly flesh on, I don't. Shift back."

"Hey, who you calling ugly?" Peter protested, and Ko-Rel bit her tongue to keep from groaning aloud.

"We're just about done here," Ko-Rel said instead, holding her arm out in front of the Chitauri soldier. "Give us a minute to wrap up tweaking these forms and—"

"No. Now."

And he grabbed her wrist tight, fingers squeezing the very real, very much not a shapeshifted cosmetic wrist unit. The one with the list of bomb groups still up on the screen.

In the near distance, an echoing *BOOM* thundered through the caves. A moment of silence, then a *CRACK*, and a series of bigger rumbles.

A cave-in.

Oh, *scut*.

"Well, we tried," Ko-Rel said, and lashed out with a powerful kick to the Chitauri's stomach. She used the momentum of the kick to sling her rifle back around to her front, but Peter beat her to the shot. His guns spat double energy blasts in the same spot where Ko-Rel's foot had hit, and the Chitauri went down with a smoking hole in his stomach.

"Guts," Peter said, ducking behind a desk in case anyone came to investigate.

"Guts, yes," Ko-Rel replied. She dragged the Chitauri man by his ankles over behind some storage crates, and huddled there herself, out of sight of any passersby. She looked down at her wrist unit and studied the list of explosives, then closed her eyes in a fleeting moment of despair. "That was the first set of bombs that went off, and the explosion triggered the second set, too. That whole back passageway is probably blocked off."

"So we're going out the front, is what you're saying," Peter said, hoisting his two guns on either side of his glowing, red-eyed helmet.

Ko-Rel checked her rifle and stock of bombs, then nodded. "We're going out the front. But first things first. Let's get some reinforcements, for once."

Ko-Rel tapped her comm.

"This is Commander Ko-Rel. I need every single body that can hold a weapon to the coordinates I'm about to send you. Full enviro gear. We're flushing the Chitauri out."

"Yeah, they're about to come running like their asses are on fire," Peter said, then cackled. "Because they are! They are literally going to be on fire. This is the best rotation of my life. Oh, I can't wait."

Ko-Rel did some quick math in her head. One minute for the troops to muster. Another to get loaded into the shuttle and take off. A quick two-minute flight straight there, no looping paths to obfuscate point of origin. With a bit of wiggle room, they were looking at about five minutes at best. Much more at worst. Once they arrived, they'd have maybe ten minutes max before their suits gave out under the heat of Mercury's daytime.

It was the best shot they were ever going to get.

"Acknowledged? Anyone?" Ko-Rel said.

"Yes, ma'am, already on it," a voice replied, out of breath. Ko-Rel frowned.

"Lieutenant? Are you well enough to be leading this operation?"

A winded "Hah" came in reply, then was swallowed up by the chatter of assembling troops. Okay then.

"Clock's ticking," Ko-Rel said to Peter, smacking his arm with the back of her hand. "Let's move out."

"Let's blow some more stuff up," Peter said, and followed.

They crept through the tunnels, planting charges whenever they came across an interesting target. No more encounters of the lizardy kind, though.

"I thought there'd be more of those scaly bastards wandering around," Peter said.

Ko-Rel shrugged. "Well, it's a big cave system, and there's only, what, ten or twelve of them? Come on, we're getting close to the mouth of the cave. They should have some kind of ops station nearby—"

Ko-Rel cut off and blinked. Around the corner she'd just turned, ten Chitauri stood in a loose circle around a display screen showing an image of the main base.

"Oh, flark," she said.

Peter grinned. "We're testing out some new shapeshift forms for—"

The Chitauri drew their weapons and opened fire, and Peter dove back down the side hallway they'd come from.

"Okay, never mind," he said. "Can you get us out of here?"

Ko-Rel stuck her rifle around the corner and fired wildly as she pulled up the map of the cave system on her HUD.

"Unfortunately, the only way out is through them, thanks to our cave-in," she said.

"Well." Peter grabbed Ko-Rel's bag of charges and added what was left to his own stash, then pulled a charge out of his bag and hefted it. "What do you say we cause some damage on the way out?"

"Sounds beautiful," she said. "Reinforcements should hopefully be here any minute. Let's go meet up with our friends."

Peter counted down—three, two, *one*—and together they dashed out from hiding, laser focused on the dim light in the distance that marked the mouth of the cave, the exit into Mercury's blazing-hot daylight. Ko-Rel kept her finger down on the trigger, spraying fire until her rifle gave a heat warning, then switching to a small sidearm until it cooled. Behind her, Peter cheerfully threw bombs at anything that looked important and triggered the explosions as soon as they were a safe distance away.

"Excuse me!"

BOOM!

"Pardon me!"

BOOM!

"Coming through!"

BOOM!

"Is the commentary necessary?" Ko-Rel asked.

"Don't mess with my creative process!" Peter shot back.

BOOM!

His cheerful chaos created enough roadblocks for them to

get a bit of a lead on their pursuers. As they came to the mouth of the cave, Ko-Rel slowed, then stopped. The Chitauri had erected a force barrier almost identical to the one her forces had set up when they'd taken refuge in these very caves. A line of eight shield projection pylons with heavy metal casings stood between them and the blazing sun that meant freedom and reinforcements. Taking out just one pylon *should* be enough to bring the shields down.

Time to take some notes from the Peter Quill School of Chaos.

Ko-Rel aimed at the nearest pylon and held down the triggers on both of her guns. Energy bolts spat forth, blackening the casing at the base of the pylon. And nothing else. D'ast thing was stronger than it looked, soaking up every blast from both her and Peter without complaint.

"New strategy," Ko-Rel said. "Cover me."

Trusting Peter to guard her back, she dug in her bag for the last of the charges and affixed it to the base of the pylon, then sprinted back toward Peter.

"Come on," she said breathlessly, grabbing hold of his jacket sleeve and hauling him behind a nearby rocky outcropping. No hesitation, no calculating the perfect timing—she sent the detonate order.

BOOM!

The ground just beyond their shelter glittered with bits of metal shrapnel. Most importantly, though, the telltale hum of the force barrier was gone. The way was clear.

"Up we go," Ko-Rel said, yanking Peter by the sleeve

again. She fired a spray of energy bolts back toward their quickly gaining pursuers, then ran at top speed for the mouth of the cave. Her muscles burned and her breath rasped in her throat as she pushed her body to go, go, *go*, until the burning heat of the Mercurian sunlight broke over her.

The sight that greeted Ko-Rel punched a triumphant laugh right out of her.

Some twenty-odd Resistance fighters were leaping from the open shuttle doors before the ship even landed. Trained troopers hit the ground and formed up in a defensive line, rifles and portable force shields at the ready, setting up to defend their less combat-seasoned brethren. Engineers, medics, and all three intelligence officers poured down from the shuttle as soon as it touched down, bearing spare rifles and smaller sidearms.

The traitor was in all likelihood right there on the battlefield with them, but one person couldn't do much in the middle of an armed crowd, and especially not with the writing on the wall for their lizardy masters. They wouldn't dare.

And so, with complete confidence, Ko-Rel turned her back on the traitor and faced the clear and present enemy—the eleven remaining Chitauri who had followed them out of the caves and were currently charging straight for their front line.

"This is all there is!" Ko-Rel called out to her people. "These lizards are all that remain of our enemy on this planet. Let's TAKE THEM DOWN!"

The Resistance fighters roared their approval and opened fire as soon as the enemy was in range. Troops in front warded off incoming fire with portable force shields, protecting the less experienced combatants behind them, who largely focused on filling the air with as many energy bolts as possible.

Peter knocked a fist against Ko-Rel's shoulder in acknowledgment, then leapt into the sky, kicking on the jet boots she'd had *no idea* he wore. He zipped around to flank the Chitauri and harass them from the rear, a pink repeated pattern of autofire causing the lizards to break formation. Behind him, a residual explosion from their planted charges send a last Chitauri rushing out to join the rest of the pack.

"Fire warning!" a voice called out over the comm. "Heavies incoming!"

It was Lieutenant Chan-Dar, the late Captain Lar-Ka's second-in-command… and, Ko-Rel remembered now, his chief heavy weapons specialist. Riding in a hover chair, shattered leg in a brace, with an absolutely ridiculous weapon strapped to her shoulder.

A weapon that was audibly charging up for a very large boom.

"Fall back, and shut your eyes if you love your retinas!" the lieutenant bellowed as the whining reached a steady pitch. Troops scrambled back out of the way, and Chan-Dar fired. The recoil nearly tipped the hover chair backward as an enormous ball of crackling energy shot toward the largest clump of six Chitauri soldiers. The last thing Ko-Rel saw before squeezing her eyes shut was the Chitauri scrambling over each other to get clear.

Then the blast hit with a reverberating *WHOMP*,

accompanied by a flash so bright Ko-Rel could see the shape of it through her eyelids. Dust and rock particles rained down over them all, and the shockwave was powerful enough to knock Ko-Rel to one knee. She staggered back to her feet, blinking furiously against the spots dancing before her eyes.

When Ko-Rel's vision cleared, only three Chitauri remained standing.

Their hands were raised in surrender.

Ko-Rel's breath hitched, and she looked around for Peter, who stared right back. She couldn't see his expression through his red-eyed mask, but somehow… she just knew that giant goofy grin lit up his features.

"Take them," Ko-Rel ordered.

Resistance troops surrounded the remaining Chitauri, forcing them to their knees, binding their hands, and confiscating their weapons. A cheer went up from all the other assembled Resistance fighters as they hoisted weapons into the air and gave each other back-slapping hugs. There were so few of them.

It was over.

It was *over*.

Mercury was theirs once more.

PRESENT DAY

MERCURY – 7801

PETER activated his jet boots and shot into the sky after Adomox, wishing for every scrap of luck in the universe to keep his boots from exploding. They were meant to hover, after all, not *fly*. Rocket, master tinkerer and general chaos agent, had taken a precious few ticks to make a *very* slapdash modification of the power cells, giving him enough extra juice to at least break free of Mercury's weak gravitational pull.

Whether his feet would be blown off in the process remained to be seen.

Peter wanted to look back, wanted to make sure the others had the chance to get back to the ship and clear their heads despite the blast Mox had set off, but there was nothing he could do to help them. He had to trust they could handle themselves. Peter didn't know any fancy martial arts, and he wasn't a powerful tree who could regrow from a splinter, and he had no super strength or super intellect.

He was, however, the only one of the team with some seriously souped-up jet boots.

Triple checking that his shielding was active, Peter arced up and out of the giant hole they'd blasted in the roof of the landing bay, racing after Adomox. Even with the suit and shield's protection, the heat crept through, but he ignored the screaming instinct to turn around. Adomox was still far ahead of him, racing away with so signs of slowing. Peter leveled his guns at her, flicked a switch, and held down the triggers, peppering the air in front of him with a flurry of energy bolts. One managed to hit Adomox despite the distance, not strong enough to do any real damage, but enough to surprise her and send her spinning for a brief tick as she looked back. Peter's visor zoomed in enough for him to see the annoyance visible in the press of her mouth and narrowing of her eyes. Surprisingly, she didn't engage, though, just fired a single blast back at Peter, then turned back skyward with a burst of renewed energy.

Peter groaned in frustration and accelerated after her, wincing at the high-pitched whine his boots made. "How's it going with the self-destruct timer, guys? You on the ship?"

"Forty-five ticks," Gamora said, her voice tight. "We just got on board."

"Ish," Rocket said. "Forty-five ticks... *ish*."

A precious three ticks went by as everyone processed that.

"Okay, but you timed your explosives to go off *after* the self-destruct, right, Rocket?" Peter asked.

Another beat of silence.

"*Right*, Rocket?" Peter asked, a desperate edge to his voice.

"Well, if I did that, Quill, then I wouldn't get the satisfaction of having blown it up entirely myself, would I?" Rocket snapped, the tapping of his furry little paws flying over his station aboard the *Milano* a constant soundtrack under his words. "I didn't think setting it five ticks early would make *that* big a difference."

"Well, *it does*," Peter shouted. "It makes a really big, really *life-altering* difference!"

"Can you control them remotely?" Drax asked.

"Of *course* I can," Rocket said, offended.

If Peter could have smacked himself on the forehead without losing airspeed, he would have.

"Oh my god, so *why aren't you doing that*?" he demanded.

"Because," Rocket said, "it would take more than forty-five ticks to remote in and take control, and by then, it wouldn't matter much, now would it? *I am doing my best*, so just get off my back!"

The comforting and familiar thrum of the *Milano* filled the comm channel as the engines kicked on, and Gamora didn't wait even a breath to hit the throttle and get them in the air. No point in letting the engines warm up. Another few ticks and they'd be plenty warm. Because of the explosion and all.

Good, Peter thought. Should be just enough time to get clear of the blast. They'd all be fine.

Probably.

…Maybe.

Peter took a deep breath and fired off another burst of gunfire. He'd gained on Mox slightly with her earlier stumble, but his hastily modified jet boots were no match for her overclocked access to the Nova Force. He just couldn't close the gap. As they passed through the wispy tendrils of what passed for an atmosphere on Mercury, Peter caught a glint of light off something metallic in orbit around the planet.

A ship. Adomox's ship. No wonder she'd been able to sneak up on them. She'd left her ship in orbit and flown down on her own, a much smaller target. Suki was probably distracted with the approaching Guardians at the time, too.

"Guys, she has her ship up here," Peter said. "If she gets to it, she'll get away, no question."

"Well, don't let her get to it, then," Rocket replied.

"Oh, right, okay, thanks!" Peter said sarcastically. "I had no idea it was that easy!"

Rocket scoffed. "Don't be smart with me, Quill. If you can't hurt her because she's all Nova-ed up, then *go for the ship*."

Oh. That was… actually a pretty good idea.

Peter barrel-rolled to the right to get a clear shot around her, bringing his guns to bear on the ship's engine casing. His visor zoomed in, giving him a view of the damage he was doing… which wasn't much. He was just too far away. Mox reached her ship and climbed inside, the engines firing up a mere tick later… perfectly timed with a massive double explosion from behind Peter, the blasts a perfectly spaced five ticks apart.

Boom-BOOM!

The shockwave reached Peter even as far out as he was, sending him tumbling forward toward Adomox's ship. Mox's engines flared as the ship punched forward, buffeting Peter back in the opposite direction. Peter didn't particularly care for life as a tennis ball, volleying back and forth between things that would kill him. He sent a final flurry of parting shots at the retreating engines as he called out over the comm.

"Hey guys? You make it off the base in time? You okay?"

The silence that followed was brutal.

"We're here," Gamora finally answered, sounding a bit out of breath. Something in Peter's chest unwound a bit at that.

"And how's my ship?" he asked.

"*My* ship is fine," Rocket answered. "A little toasty on the back end, nothing a nice bath won't fix. You coming aboard, or did you want to float around out there for a bit longer?"

Peter looked back to see Adomox's ship racing toward the jump point, engines trailing a faint bit of something bad in their wake. He watched her go, hoping with all his might that the ship would spontaneously explode before she got away. The ship got smaller and smaller as it neared the gate and Peter held his breath.

Adomox's ship broke through the horizon of the jump gate and disappeared.

She was gone.

Peter blew out his breath and closed his eyes. She'd gotten away with it again.

"Come on, Quill," Rocket said.

Peter sighed and looked away from the distant jump gate, back to the ship that had been his home for the last fifteen years. A ship he now shared with a raccoon, a tree, a serial murderer, and the deadliest woman in the galaxy. After an exhausting rotation, he couldn't wait to have the *Milano*'s deck under his boots and some sweet Star-Lord tunes in his ear holes. And, despite it all, his maybe-friends in the bunks right next door, too: meditating, polishing blades, building bombs, tending a garden.

It sounded... nice.

Also, he *really* needed to get his possibly explosive boots off his feet.

"Knock knock," Peter said, firing his jet boots *very* gently, just enough to guide himself to the aft airlock. The seal broke with a hiss, and Groot stood just inside with an arm outstretched to help pull him in.

"I am Groot," he said, smiling.

Peter smiled back.

"Thanks, buddy."

INTERLUDE: 12 YEARS AGO

MERCURY BASE – 7789

THE landing bay was alive with the bustle of packing up an entire military base-worth of gear and personnel. When Ko-Rel had first arrived, once the Ravagers had cleared out the base of Chitauri invaders, the bay had been littered with bodies and streaked with blood and viscera.

Today, the tone was considerably lighter. It was as if the energy Peter had brought with him had caught and multiplied, spreading to every member of the regiment. Well, every surviving member. Though there was plenty to mourn, a new thrum of possibility ran underneath every loaded crate and stowed gear bag. They'd won back Mercury. Every outpost, every forward base. The Chitauri had left the system altogether, partly due to efforts on the ground... but also in part due to war progress elsewhere in the galaxy.

Things were coming to a head. Word had come down that a Katathian warrior named Drax had killed Thanos. Chitauri Prime had a giant target painted on it, and though they were leaving behind a token force to hold the base, most of her people were heading to the new front line. Rumor was, Thanos's daughter Gamora was a big reason behind the shifting tides. Ko-Rel had crossed paths with her briefly while she'd been serving under Richard Rider, and though she'd been wary of the woman at first, she couldn't help but respect her.

People said terrible things about her, spat at her as she walked by, iced her out of the military camaraderie that was one of the few bright spots in this eternal war. And yet, she fought. And yet, she served the Resistance with single-minded focus and not an ounce of visible regret. That was a special kind of strength, far more than the pure physical prowess the woman displayed on the battlefield.

Most of Ko-Rel's people were eager to move on from the dusty gray rock of Mercury, either to fight closer to their own homes or to be part of the final campaign against Chitauri Prime. Others, she was concerned for. Suki Yumiko still wasn't handling Hal-Zan's death very well, and she'd grown hostile toward some of the other intelligence staff. She still wasn't convinced she was wrong, but without proof, there was nothing more she could do.

Suki was the worst off of the team, for certain, though there were many others who suffered as well. Tasver was improving, fortunately. His dark sarcasm was starting to ease, and he'd begun speaking to others again. She'd given all her people resources, referred them to counselors, even recommended discharge for a few of them. They needed every body they could get for the final push of the war, but that didn't mean they could completely overlook the wellbeing of their people.

Another shoulder bumped against Ko-Rel's, drawing her attention momentarily away from her reflection. She glanced over to see Peter grinning at her, eyebrows raised.

"Thinking deep thoughts?" he asked.

She smiled at him, but didn't answer right away. He wouldn't understand the level of care and pride she felt for these people. It wasn't the same as the fierce protectiveness and joy that she'd felt for her sweet boy after he'd been born, but it was related, at least. These people weren't her children, but they *were* hers, and she intended to see that they were taken care of. It was her duty as their commander.

For all Peter's bravery and combat prowess, he was still not a leader. He'd inspired her people, but when it came down to it, he was still young in a way she just *wasn't* anymore. Though the numerical difference in their age was small, the difference in their experience was vast. Her child was gone, but she would always be a mother. She would never lose that sense of greater responsibility.

Peter, on the other hand… well, he still needed someone to tell him what to do. He was those guns he loved to swing around, doing tricks and making "pew pew" noises when he thought no one was watching. He needed someone to aim him and pull the trigger. She wasn't interested in being that person, and he wasn't interested in going where she'd want to aim him anyway. The Resistance could use him, if he were willing.

If he were willing. But she didn't even bother asking, because she already knew. He was heading back to the Ravagers, back to a free life among the stars, raiding supply caravans and enjoying a level of moral flexibility Ko-Rel just didn't have.

And really… it felt fine. She had no illusions about who Peter was, and none about herself, either. She wasn't interested in filling the void of grief left behind by her son and husband with some wartime fling. It had been fun, but she was ready to move on. And Peter? He'd gotten all he needed from her. Bit of fun, bit of *different*, bit of heroics. It had all worked out for everyone involved. And now it was time to go.

"Just thinking about my people," she said. "The war isn't over. There are more hard times ahead for them."

Peter hummed his agreement, though he rocked on his heels with pent-up energy. "They'll win in the end, though."

If only wars could be won on optimism alone. Somehow Peter Quill had rotted in a Chitauri prison for four years and emerged still capable of thinking the best of the universe. Ko-Rel gave a small smile and watched one of the other officers put a hand on a colleague's shoulder and have a quiet word with him. When they parted, both seemed in better spirits, working in tandem to load one of the shuttles. This was how wars were truly won. Not on the battlefield, but in the barracks. Ko-Rel nodded.

"I think you're right, Peter," she said. "We'll win in the end for sure."

The corner of his mouth quirked up in a smile, but he shifted restlessly from foot to foot, gaze drifting to the sky visible through the retracted landing bay roof. Ko-Rel took pity on him.

"You can go, you know. You don't have to wait on the rest of us. You've got the *Milano*," she said.

Peter shrugged. "I know. I am. I just thought I should…"

He trailed off with a vague gesture. Ko-Rel made the vague gesture back at him, and he laughed.

"Yeah, okay, fine. I'm going." He stuck his hands in his pockets and looked away. "You still have Chewie?"

"Still sitting on the desk in my quarters. He watches me sleep. It's a bit creepy, honestly," she said, shooting him a grin. Peter laughed.

"Don't worry, Chewbacca is a married man. He'll respect your privacy. His wife, Malla, might rip his arms off otherwise."

Ko-Rel rolled her eyes and suppressed a chuckle.

"I'll remember that," she said.

There was a brief moment of indecision wherein they both hovered there awkwardly, meeting each other's eyes. Should they kiss one last time? Hug? Shake hands? How exactly did one say goodbye to a wartime hookup that didn't really mean anything, but was also exactly what you needed at the time and helped win a critical battle?

The answer was, apparently: shrugged shoulders, a tiny wave, and a roguish smile she wouldn't forget anytime soon.

"Later," he said.

She smiled. *Maybe*. Someday, when they both were a little older and wiser, and Peter a little less likely to commit crimes, maybe they'd cross paths again.

Peter walked backward a few steps, then spun around and headed for the *Milano*. Ko-Rel watched him go for a moment, his head held high, a bounce in his step, and the wide-open galaxy before him.

Then she turned, strode to the nearest ship, and pitched in with the loading. Her people looked up at her with grateful thanks, then returned to their work, slinging boxes right alongside her. They had a deadline to meet, and there was no time to waste.

They had a war to win.

PRESENT DAY

NOVA CORPS OUTPOST, MILKY WAY GALAXY – 7801

PETER stood shoulder to shoulder with Gamora, looking into the clean, white infirmary that currently held the battered but living body of Suki Yumiko. They'd taken her straight to the nearest Nova Corps outpost and presented her bleeding, passed-out form to their medical staff, though it had taken some coaxing to convince Groot it was safe to let her go. Now, her black hair fanned out over the crisp white sheets, and she slept fitfully, her brow constantly creased.

"She's been in so much pain for so long," Gamora said. She had one arm propped on the glass, her forehead resting against her wrist, expression… not soft, exactly, but lacking the blankness she worked so hard to project most of the time.

Peter hummed his agreement but didn't know what to say

in return. The person he'd been twelve years ago (selfish, impulsive, barely a functioning adult) hadn't given Suki a second thought once Mercury was in his aft exhaust. Hell, he'd barely given her, Adomox, and Tasver much thought while they'd all been under suspicion of treason, and thus actively putting him in danger. He'd just followed Ko-Rel's lead, jumping in where action was required, playing some kind of blockbuster movie version of a hero. He hadn't thought about the people, really. He didn't try to be a leader. He didn't need to—Ko-Rel had been there, and she was ten times the leader he'd ever be.

He would have to do much, much better by his new team.

Gamora pushed back off the glass with a sigh and looked to Peter with that same solemn sort of expression.

"Suki deserved justice," she said. "Hal-Zan, too. It's infuriating, knowing Adomox is still out there with access to all that power. She'll lay low for a while, but Peter, you *know* she's going to do exactly as she promised. The entire Nova Corps is in danger, not to mention the rest of the galaxy if she continues to increase her access to the Nova Force."

Peter shoved his hands in his jacket pockets and shrugged.

"We did all we could, though, right? We told the Centurion in charge here about all of it, and Suki will back up our story when she wakes up."

Gamora opened her mouth to protest, then closed it again and shook her head sadly.

"It doesn't feel like enough."

"No," Peter agreed. "It doesn't."

Inside Suki's room, another door opened and a dark-blue-skinned Kree doctor entered. She ran a scan and checked the readouts on the monitoring equipment, then performed a brief physical examination. When she finished, she looked up and met Peter's eyes through the glass with a small smile.

"One tick," she mouthed silently, holding up a finger, then slipped out the other door to meet them.

"She's going to be fine," the doctor said, approaching them with a portable display in hand. She flipped through some information, then looked up to meet Peter's gaze again. "Physically, at least. You got her here in enough time."

Peter smiled a crooked little grin at the swell of pride those words produced.

Gamora's gaze lingered on Suki for a moment, then she turned to the doctor.

"Do you have mental health services available for her once she's healed? She mentioned searching for help with her grief, and it sounds like she fell in with some bad people. She'll need the tools to keep that from happening again."

The doctor's expression softened, and she nodded.

"Yes. We have a medical officer specializing in trauma recovery. She'll have the treatment she needs. And, I expect, a job waiting for her if she can be cleared for duty. The Nova Corps has always made a habit of welcoming former Resistance fighters into its ranks."

Her eyebrows went up as she seemed to remember something, and she held up one finger to signal for patience.

"Also, she woke up briefly at her afternoon check and

asked me to give you this," she said, digging in her pocket for a moment and producing a data chip. Peter smiled and accepted the chip, then held it up for Gamora with a raised eyebrow.

"Justice after all, eh?"

Gamora fought back a smile and turned her gaze toward Suki. "Looks like it."

"What is it?" the doctor asked.

"A data download from the Mercury base," Peter said. "She was searching for hard evidence that would get Adomox locked up. She said she'd found what she needed, so I'm betting that security guy we talked to earlier will want it."

The doctor's eyes narrowed.

"Absolutely. The Nova Corps will find her and bring her to justice. I can't believe we all trusted her with our lives."

Something about those words triggered Peter's brain, and he studied the doctor closer for a moment. Dark blue skin, green eyes, black hair cropped close around her ears.

"Hey, hold on a sec—you look familiar. Do I know you?"

The doctor smiled. "My name is Chan-Dar."

Peter brightened, his memory making the connection almost instantly, for once.

"You were on Mercury, too! From heavy weapons to medical, huh? That's a bit of a leap."

"Yeah, I know," she said, unconsciously rubbing at her right leg. Peter suddenly had a flash back to that awful night, hauling an enormous piece of rubble off her bloody, shattered bones.

Chan-Dar shrugged. "After the end of the war, I'd had

my fill of blowing things up. Decided to try my hand at mending them instead. Set back my advancement timeline, but I'm a captain *and* a doctor now."

"That's… yeah, that's good. I'm happy for you," Peter said.

"Thanks. Me too," she said, then gave a little farewell nod. "Be well, Peter Quill. Thank you for bringing Suki back to us."

"Thank you for taking care of her," Peter said with a farewell wave. He turned to take one last look at Suki, hurt in many ways but recovering. She'd be okay.

And so would the Guardians, if he had anything to do with it. Wherever Ko-Rel was out there, she'd be proud of how he'd cleaned up his act once they got their hero business well and truly off the ground. This whole fiasco may not have gone as planned, but it certainly ended on an auspicious note. Heroic, even, one might say. They'd done something truly worthwhile, and hopefully that would be enough for Drax and Gamora to stick around for a little while.

"Come on," he said to Gamora. "The Guardians of the Galaxy need to have a team meeting."

"To figure out our next destination?" Gamora asked.

"You got it. Any suggestions?"

Gamora laughed. "Anywhere but Contraxia."

PETER stumbled up the *Milano*'s ramp, hair mussed and still slightly buzzed, and was immediately greeted by the smells of breakfast and Gamora's soul-incinerating glare.

"Did it have to be Contraxia?" she asked for the thousandth time as Rocket slid onto the seat across from her with a dramatic sigh, a cup of something hot and foul-smelling in one paw.

"Look, lady, you had your chance to give us a better idea and you had *nothin'*, so shut yer trap about it."

"I am Groot," Groot amended as he came up the ramp from the utility room he'd claimed as his own.

"Yeah, okay, but Knowhere doesn't count as an option, which is *not* our fault."

"I am *Groot*."

Rocket sighed again, with even *more* drama. "Fine. Me and Groot are glad not to be crossing paths with the Collector, yes, we *appreciate* it, I guess. But really, it's Quill's little stunt with his engineer buddy that's the bigger reason for us to stay away for a bit."

"Look, Contraxia is just as good as Knowhere for our purposes," Peter said as he took a seat next to Gamora. "There are jobs to be had and people to sell our stuff to. What more could you want?"

"A planet with fewer traumatic memories that doesn't stink of fornication?" Gamora suggested, sniffing the air in Peter's direction and scooting a few inches away.

"Considering the events of the last few rotations, I'm gonna downgrade the teapot incident from 'traumatic' to 'moderately disturbing,'" Peter said, thinking of Suki.

They'd had to be on their way before she'd woken up again, but Peter had left her a way to get in contact if she needed to. He'd passed along the data, as promised, and confirmed with the Centurion in charge that her status as a veteran of the Resistance guaranteed her a home with the Nova Corps, if she ever felt up to it in the future. Personally, Peter thought she might do better somewhere farther away from combat and constant wartime memories, but what did he know?

It rankled him, knowing Adomox was still out there somewhere after fooling him not once, but twice, past *and* present. The proof was there, somewhere, in that giant pile of wartime data Suki had recovered. Downloaded security footage, comm logs, right down to the granular information about who accessed what files and when. Suki would find it, once she was well again, and this time she'd have a team of Nova Corps analysts to support her. Adomox had gone to ground, but she would pop up again. When she did, she would find that the Corps had been alerted to her past activities and future plans. Conspiracy to take over the entire Nova Force was bound to land her a hefty sentence. Where and when she would turn up again… well, who knew? If the Guardians crossed paths with her again, though, they wouldn't hesitate to take her down.

Or, they wouldn't hesitate to try very, very hard, at least. Sure, Yoda said, "Try not," but Yoda had never fought a Nova Corps officer with a hacked helm drunk on too much golden juice.

"Well," Gamora said in a softer tone. "If we *have* to be here, can we maybe come in with a better plan this time so we don't end up doing our usual special brand of 'winging it,' as Peter says? Where are we going to go to try to pick up a new job?"

Drax rumbled thoughtfully.

"Last night, I had a rousing debate at a bar with a foolish man who thought he could defeat me in battle—"

"In a *drinking* battle, Drax," Peter corrected. "He thought he could *out-drink* you."

Drax paused. "Oh. I suppose I should not have hit him, then."

Peter waved the comment away. "Nah, he was kind of a tool, and he would have ended up on his face anyway if he tried to out-drink you."

"Is there a point to this?" Rocket asked. "You and Peter went to a bar, you got drunk and hit someone, we get it. How is that helpful as comes to moneymaking?"

"Because once this foolish man regained consciousness, his inane blathering eventually yielded useful information," Drax said. "Have you heard of the Monster Queen of Sekarf Nine?"

Peter flinched, banging his knee on the underside of the table and sloshing Rocket's drink. "Ooooh no, no way. I've heard just enough to know that dealing with her is absolute last resort territory."

"Pretty sure we're *in* last resort territory, Quill," Rocket said with a snort. "In fact, I think we *live* here now."

"We do *not*," Peter insisted.

"We could get us a little rundown shack," Rocket continued. "Make friends with the neighbors, buy a plot at the local cemetery, really *settle in* to this last resort lifestyle."

"We aren't *that* bad off, come on," Peter protested.

Rocket scoffed. "Oh yeah? How many units you got, Quill?"

Peter paused.

"Either zero, or nine hundred and eighty-eight thousand, depending."

"Units o*f money*, Star-Butt, I shouldn't even have to—"

"Well, it's not like you thought to ask beforehand either—"

"Can we *please* just— Drax, what kind of jobs does this Queen offer?" Gamora asked, desperately heading off the inevitable shouting match. Peter could swear he caught the edge of a smile before she turned away, though.

Drax narrowed his eyes at Gamora for daring to speak to him but answered her question anyway. "She is the Monster Queen. She buys monsters. It is right there in the name. I've always thought you a vicious, duplicitous traitor, but I did not realize you were so oblivious as well."

Gamora sighed and looked away from Drax. "Okay, queen of monsters, not a monstrous queen, got it."

"She is a respected collector and a powerful leader. You should show deference, traitor," Drax growled.

"So, a monster! There's got to be plenty of those around. Where do we go?" Peter said to break up the brewing fight.

"Not just any monster," Drax said. "To be worthy of Lady Hellbender, it must be a monster of exceptional strength. Clearly we should take this opportunity to travel to Maklu IV and battle the legendary Fin Fang Foom!"

The reaction from the other four Guardians was instantaneous.

"No," Gamora said.

"I am Groot."

"Ha!" Peter laughed before he could stop himself.

"Are you crazy?" Rocket asked. "Never mind, redundant question."

"Okay, I actually know something useful," Peter said. The skeptical glances turned on him. "So, last night I, uh... made a friend. And this friend, she was telling me this wild story about some really rare monster."

"And where was this mythical creature supposedly located?" Rocket asked, arms folded.

Peter sobered. "The Quarantine Zone."

Rocket's eyes lit up. "Ooooooh."

A few rotations ago, Peter's initial reaction would have been exactly the same: to dream of the sweet, sweet looting that awaited anyone who managed to get into the Quarantine Zone. He would have been having visions of dollar signs and fancy flying and the thrill of breaking and entering. Now, though...

"Yeah. Honestly, I'm not *loving* the whole wartime memory lane theme we have going right now. Flying through an old ship graveyard full of junk from the war, right after finishing up a tour of the old Mercury base, doesn't exactly sound like my idea of a good time right now. But..."

Rocket looked over at him, with far more understanding than Peter ever would have expected.

"You have a better idea?" he asked.

"I… do… not." Peter shrugged and looked back out the front viewport.

"I might have a thought as to how to lure this monster," Rocket said, scurrying over to his workbench to dig through his extensive collection of technical bits and bobs. "But there's one big problem with this plan. The whole Quarantine Zone is a no-fly zone, according to the Nova Corps."

"Oh, *well*, in that case, guess we'd better find something else to do, because we *never* break the law," Peter said in an offended Southern lady accent. "Perish the thought!"

Rocket scoffed. "Ha! Please. What I *meant* is that we'll need a way past the giant energy barrier they have blockin' the whole place in."

"Ah, now that's more like the Rocket we all know and don't hate," Peter said.

"I might be able to take care of that," Gamora said thoughtfully, pulling her legs up to cross underneath her. "The energy barrier. I have a contact here who should be able to help. For a price."

"Ooooh, did you make a friend during your little teapot stunt last time?" Rocket said gleefully. "I'm sure he would be *very* happy to hear from you—"

Gamora lunged over the back of the seat and grabbed Rocket by the snout, holding his mouth closed tight. He jerked back and took a snap at her, then scrabbled back on top of his workbench. Gamora snapped right back.

"Don't test me, foul beast," she said, though her tone was teasing.

"Oh, forgive me, murder mistress," Rocket said. "Seriously, though, they ask for an exotic dance demonstration and *that* is what you went with?"

Gamora covered her face with her hands for a brief moment.

"Peter had *just* taught us the ritual that morning, it was fresh in my mind!" she said, letting her hands fall away. "What would *you* all have chosen?"

"That is easy," Drax said. "I would have gone with the Katathian courtship step, of course. I would be happy to demonstrate. I am considered quite adept, and it certainly worked well on my wife. It is an extremely erotic ritual with much emphasis on presentation of the—"

"I'M A LITTLE TEAPOT SHORT AND STOUT," Peter sang at the top of his lungs before Drax could finish that terrible, horrible, no good, very bad sentence.

"Here is my handle," Rocket continued in a sneering tone, straight at Gamora.

"I aaam Groot," Groot finished, perfectly on pitch and making a teapot spout with one arm.

The song continued, Rocket and Groot doing the "dance" in sloppy almost-sync as they paraded around the rec room. A "steamed up" Peter waggled his eyebrows at Gamora, who rolled her eyes.

"You aren't joining in?" she asked. "It's *your* ancestral dance."

"Oh, you all do it so much better than I do." Peter stuck his hands in his pockets and looked down at his boots, then back up at her. "So, sounds like we have another job in the works, if you think you can get that code. Guess that means we're gonna try again? Stick together for at least one more mission?"

Gamora turned to look back at Peter and shrugged, trying and failing to hide her small smile.

"Sure, what's one more? Hey, at least I'm never bored with you guys."

And with that, she went to hide in her quarters, notably *not* performing the teapot dance along with them.

Peter grinned and watched her go, admiring his cobbled together little crew and their dance moves. Might be a weird thing to feel proud about, but he did.

Maybe *this* would be the mission that finally made their reputation. Guardians of the Galaxy: heroes for hire, capturer of monsters, friend of the Monster Queen. Moving up in the universe.

What could go wrong?

ACKNOWLEDGEMENTS

WRITING a Guardians of the Galaxy book is real "dream come true" type stuff for me. Which, of course, means I was utterly terrified to actually start, much less finish, the thing you now have in your hands. These acknowledgements are primarily a litany of weeping, earnest thank yous to all the people who had to listen to me whine, cry, rage, and doubt myself every step of the way. Sorry I was totally insufferable for a while there, friendos. Considering I had to sign an NDA and couldn't even tell you the details of what I was complaining about, you all held up remarkably well and this book wouldn't exist without you. Shout outs to Steph, Jamie, Stephanie, Becky, Kat, and Leigh—y'all are the best. To my wonderful agent, Eric Smith: thanks/sorry/thanks again. What a nerd dream for us both!

Biggest thanks have to go to Mike Rowe, a font of Marvel and Guardians of the Galaxy knowledge with a huge heart, who patiently acted as my Marvel Encyclopedia without ever knowing why I had a sudden passionate need to re-read particular story arcs from years past. You are a hero, my friend, and your support means the world to me. I'm lucky to know you. Your dreams are possible. Additional thanks to friends, fellow writers, and Marvel fans Tom Torre and Sean Easley, who also had to put up with me during the outlining and drafting of this book.

To the whole team at Eidos-Montréal, most especially Mary DeMarle, Jean-François Dugas, and everyone who sat on those zoom calls with me: I appreciate your time and your willingness to share your story with me. I love this version of the Guardians, and all the care and attention to detail you've poured into them really shows. Thanks also to the folks on the Marvel side of things, notably Caitlin O'Connell, Bill Rosemann, and Loni Clark. It's an honor to join the Marvel universe.

The Titan Books team are the ones making this thing book-shaped, and big thanks go to managing editor George Sandison for bringing me on board and editor Craig Leyenaar for shepherding the project along. Thanks also to Davi Lancett for the pinch hit help, Dan Coxon for the copy edits (sorry about the hyphens), and the many designers, artists, typesetters, PR/marketing coordinators, and other folks hard at work behind the scenes who I haven't had the pleasure of meeting.

To my baby bug: Thanks for listening to a non-stop barrage of Marvel audiobooks and movies while you nursed and played and grew from an infant into a whole toddler. And for letting me dress you up as Captain America Deadpool Claus. You probably won't be scarred for life.

And, as always, we end with N: My poor, long-suffering partner who had to live with me through this process. Thanks for not murdering me in my sleep over this book. You would have been well within your rights. I love you.

ABOUT THE AUTHOR

M. K. ENGLAND is the author of *The Disasters* (2018), *Spellhacker* (2020), *The One True Me & You* (2022) and other forthcoming novels. They grew up on the Space Coast of Florida watching shuttle launches from the backyard. These days, they call rural Virginia home, where there are many more cows but a tragic lack of rockets. In between marathon writing sessions, MK can be found drowning in fandom, rolling critical hits at the gaming table, digging in the garden, or feeding their video game addiction. They probably love Star Wars more than you do. Follow them at www.mkengland.com.

For more fantastic fiction, author events,
exclusive excerpts, competitions, limited editions and more

VISIT OUR WEBSITE
titanbooks.com

LIKE US ON FACEBOOK
facebook.com/titanbooks

FOLLOW US ON TWITTER AND INSTAGRAM
@TitanBooks

EMAIL US
readerfeedback@titanemail.com